RAY HUDSON **IVORY AND PAPER**

ADVENTURES IN AND OUT OF TIME

T0164370

RAY HUDSON **IVORY AND PAPER**

ADVENTURES IN AND OUT OF TIME

University of Alaska Press   FAIRBANKS

Text © 2018 University of Alaska Press

Published by
University of Alaska Press
P.O. Box 756240
Fairbanks, AK 99775-6240

Cover artwork: "Mothership" by Carolyn Reed, 1987. Reed has been a resident of Unalaska Island since 1983. Her artwork as an Aleutian artist has been exhibited in over 250 group and solo exhibitions throughout the state of Alaska, nationally, and internationally.

Cover and interior design by UA Press
Author illustration by Cavan Drake
Map drawn by Ray Hudson

"The Sententious Man," copyright © 1956 by Theodore Roethke; from *Collected Poems* by Theodore Roethke. Used by permission of Doubleday, an imprint of the Knopf Doubleday Publishing Group, a division of Penguin Random House LLC. All rights reserved.

Nicholai Galaktionoff, in *Lost Villages of the Eastern Aleutians: Biorka, Kashega, Makushin*, Ray Hudson/Rachel Mason, National Park Service, Alaska Affiliated Areas, 2014, page 13.

Sergie Sovoroff, in *Unugulux Tunusangin: Oldtime Stories*, Ray Hudson, editor, Unalaska City School District, Unalaska, Alaska, 1992, page 163.

Library of Congress Cataloging-in-Publication Data

Names: Hudson, Ray, 1942- author.
Title: Ivory and paper : adventures in and out of time / Ray Hudson.
Description: Fairbanks, Alaska : University of Alaska Press, 2018. | Summary:
   Booker and his new friend Anna, a Unanga girl, use a magic bookmark to
   travel via books and stop a twenty-first century pirate who is taking
   artifacts from the Aleutian Islands . |
Identifiers: LCCN 2017026670 (print) | LCCN 2017039455 (ebook) | ISBN
   9781602233478 (e-book) | ISBN 9781602233461 (pbk.)
Subjects: | CYAC: Time travel--Fiction. | Magic--Fiction. |
   Bookmarks--Fiction. | Books--Fiction. | Aleuts--Fiction. |
   Eskimos--Fiction. | Antiquities--Fiction. | Alaska--Fiction.
Classification: LCC PZ7.1.H792 (ebook) | LCC PZ7.1.H792 Ivo 2018 (print) |
   DDC [Fic]--dc23
LC record available at https://lccn.loc.gov/2017026670

I stay alive, both in and out of time,
By listening to the spirit's smallest cry.

— Theodore Roethke

CONTENTS

Alaska - *The* Aleutian Islands
The Islands of Four Mountains

Russia

Alaska

Canada

Bering Sea

North Pacific Ocean

Pribilof Islands

Aleutian Islands

Alaska Peninsula

Unalaska

Attu

Atka

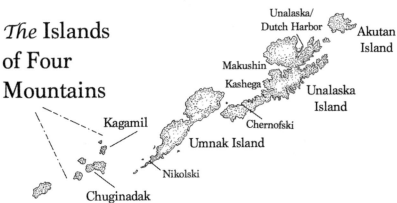

The Islands of Four Mountains

Unalaska/
Dutch Harbor

Akutan Island

Makushin

Kashega

Unalaska Island

Kagamil

Chernofski

Umnak Island

Nikolski

Chuginadak

Nick joked that when people asked him where Aleuts came from, he would tell them, "Tomorrow I come from Makushin!" By "tomorrow" he meant "yesterday" or "that time before."

"I was right," he laughed, "'cause I was born there."

— Nicholai Galaktionoff (1925–2012)
from *Lost Villages of the Eastern Aleutians*
Unalaska, Alaska

I am seventy-four years old now . . . Someone could write . . . the old stories I have told. Even though I am gone, they could mention my name concerning the old stories.

— Sergie Sovoroff (1902–1989)
Nikolski, Alaska

PROLOGUE
IN THAT TIME BEFORE

The boy stepped into the sea. He lifted cold water over his head, and his breath leapt from his chest. Like the men from the village who stood around him, he greeted each morning with a jolt of discomfort. He was called *Lalux̂*—"Yellow Cedar"—the most valuable gift that storms and tides hurled onto these treeless shores. He was crippled, mischievous, and eight. He was smart, and he knew it. He had broken his leg and after it healed, he had limped. His older sister, "Periwinkle"—*Tutuqux̂*—the diminutive shell, called him *Pitch* when he squirmed out of work by complaining that his leg hurt, that he needed rest. He could really limp when he wanted to.

Boys were trained by their uncles more than their fathers in those days. When Lalux̂'s mother visited her brother and complained about her son, he should have listened. But he was poor and grouchy, and he only growled, "Get him away from me. Trouble surrounds him. Before him and after him. He is surrounded by trouble."

Cedar's mother obeyed—her brother, after all, was a shaman—but she left her sister-in-law a gift of red salmon. He would have preferred being a hunter, a builder of skin boats, or a master of crafting bentwood hats. Being a shaman doomed him to poverty. But the spirits had chosen him. From the day his sister visited, he watched his nephew and saw how sparrows and wrens came to him, how he learned what the sky said, how he grew stronger month by month.

Cedar's tenth summer was like all others he had known. He explored the hills and played along the shore. He teased his sister and did his best to annoy her.

"You're not a woman," he said as she picked up her needle and thread. "You should be playing with me."

Her embroidery showed a skill beyond her years. The fine appliqué on the hems and collars of bird-skin parkas was deft, exceptional. But Cedar hid her needles and her sinew thread. And when her latest boyfriend brought fresh salmon to her family, Cedar stood behind him and pretended to fart.

But when he fell, it was Peri who helped; and when his leg ached for real, it was she who split the thick root of bitter celery, heated it, and bound it from his ankle to his knee, protecting his skin with a layer of dried grass.

All summer, while men hunted sea lions and seals on the wide sea and in the pass between islands, women and old men went to fish camp where they lived for the summer. They caught, split, and dried salmon for winter. Cedar scared away the ravens and gulls. He helped old men drag sea lion stomachs, cleaned, cured, and stuffed with two hundred fish, back to the village.

Children were never scolded, but one day his mother said, "Boys are becoming men. They are learning to hunt."

He began to play the games that stretched his muscles. He learned the rules of water, to fit his body to the light skin boat, its swift design arcing the waves. He crafted spears and a throwing board, a beginner's bentwood visor to protect his eyes from the glare of the sun. In the kayak, his crippled leg vanished.

"You are getting skilled with that boat, little brother," Peri said as he brought it to shore. "Soon you will take your first sea lion."

He smiled.

"Come," she said. "I have something for you."

He sprinted to the top of their home, set deep in the ground and constructed from driftwood and sod. He stood at the peak of the roof near the framed entrance hole and waited while his sister descended the notched pole with grace. Then Cedar cascaded into a room that was spacious and warm. A deity carved from white bone hung in one corner.

Peri went behind a grass mat that sectioned off part of the room and returned with a small bundle. Cedar unfolded it and saw a raincoat of sea lion gut, supple, transparent, incredibly strong.

"You made it?" he asked.

"For you," she said.

Drifting like smoke from every spiraling seam were thin white feathers from the heads of double-crested cormorants. Each end of the cord that gathered the hood held a carefully fashioned stone bead.

"Your uncle carved them from amber," she said. "One is for strength; the other is for endurance."

He knew her life as his sister would eventually end. She was indeed becoming a woman. A man would arrive with a stone lamp. He would light it and with as much indifference as she might pretend, she would keep the flame burning and become his wife, a mother, the custodian of her own home. But for now, he was glad when she let those lamps sputter and go out.

Fall storms swept the white-capped bay. Ferns turned yellow and brown. The fireweed raged in full glory, darkened, and went out. Sweet berries lingered on their bare stems. In the evenings, Cedar and his friends listened for hours to stories about wars and marauders. How no warrior ever surrendered. How the skin of a captive was never kept whole. Held down to the ground, he had his forehead slashed open with knives. The stories were even more exciting because rumors had circulated about brief attacks on their neighbors, attacks that had been easily repelled.

The days became the Long Month and then the Month of Young Cormorants, the harsh winter months of early and later famine. Cedar and Peri gazed into the night sky and saw Bundles of Codfish: the Pleiades; Three Men Standing in a Row: Orion; Three Men Standing Apart like Caribou: Ursa Major. Peri extended her hand and traced where the Sister-of-the-Moon had traveled to visit her brother. Across the horizon, at dawn, someone emptied a bowl of blood.

Eventually, pale shoots pierced the crushed winter grass. Light came earlier, the geese returned, and people began digging sweet roots. Cedar and Peri took their cousin's boat to gather seagull eggs. She tucked herself inside while Cedar rowed beyond the village. Their mother would be pleased when they came home, the boat heavy with eggs. The air around the islet was washed with gulls and terns as they pulled the boat above the high-water line on a black sandy beach. Peri had just removed two grass baskets and handed them to Cedar when armed strangers surrounded them.

They were bound, led to an open boat, and ordered into it. The men pulled away from the shore, and before long the islet hovered on the horizon, like a gull in flight, and then it disappeared. Island after island, hour after hour, surrounded by a language filled with unfamiliar words and coarse gestures, Cedar and Peri sat, cramped, afraid, their courage seeping from them. At last they came to Kagamil, among the Islands of Four Mountains, where Little Wren was chief.

Cedar fell on the rocks as he was pushed up the beach, and then he fell again, slicing open his knee. His fine parka was yanked over his head. He was kicked. Wind bit into his flesh.

When they asked him his name, he said, "Lalux̂, Yellow Cedar."

"You're nothing but ashes, boy," they said. "You're nothing but Ash."

He was forced into jobs even old women wouldn't do. He carried filth from the houses into the hills. He scraped decay from damp corners. He lay beside a dying man to keep that bundle of old bones warm. They fed him fish tails. He licked discarded blue mussels for juice and rummaged in the garbage for scraps. He slept without matting, his good leg bound to a post. He was passed from house to house, a worthless cripple nobody wanted to feed.

He did not see Peri for three days, and by then she was married to a slave who made spear points for whaling. There were bruises on her arms and face, shadows around her eyes. She spoke in whispers.

Once she slipped him a sliver of dried fish. Then she, too, went hungry.

All through autumn, the whales stayed away. These people were whalers and needed whales. Not having any, they would starve. Men sat beside a shaman as he entered a trance. "The whales will return," they heard him say, "after two deaths."

First, an old woman who had been ill for weeks died.

From inside another trance, the shaman declared, "The spear-point maker, the whaling slave. He is the one."

They bound him with thongs that tightened when they dried. They opened his throat with an obsidian blade he had fashioned himself. Peri dragged her husband from where he had died. She dragged him above the high water line and buried him without matting or grief.

All winter Ash suffered from the cold until the chief's daughter gave him a coat. The hem was rotted and it blossomed with holes, but it kept off some of the wind.

"It is a disgrace," she said to her father, "to treat anyone this way."

Ash accepted whatever she gave him.

That long winter, there were masked dances and celebrations: drumming, actors, and straw puppets, the dry rattle of festive parkas hung with puffin beaks, and puffin beaks whispering on circular tambourines. Ash watched from the shadows. The best he could hope for was a quick death by strangling if Little Wren or one of his relatives died. He had heard how a chief, after the death of his nephew, had hurled a slave's children over a cliff, hoping to find in his slave's grief some consolation for his own sorrow. Here, on Kagamil Island, Ash was no one's nephew.

Peri's needles kept her alive. She sewed for a woman who had six adult sons. She lived on scraps and handouts. In the hard winter, she grew thinner and began to cough. When spring arrived, she was sent to dig roots. And then, when gulls began laying their eggs on small islands, the sons took her out. Ash saw them depart and come home without her.

Summer came slowly until an avalanche of green overran the hills. Blossoms turned into berries, and one morning a crew of old women went to Chuginadak, the island where the sweetest berries grew. Ash was sent along. As the boats came near the mountainous island, a peak towered above them. He stared up until he was prodded in the ribs and told, "That peak is called *The Beginning of the World*." Further west, the green slopes of the island's great volcano flowed into the sea like a ceremonial robe. They rowed into a cove and carried their boats from the water. The old women, cackling like ravens, sent him after berries.

"Don't you miss any, Ash! You pick them all!" and then they turned to gossip and sleep.

He picked for hours, berry after berry. These were the low-growing moss berries, as dark as night and with a hard-earned sweetness shrouded in seeds and pulp. Raven's berries. He worked his way up the slope, higher and higher, until he looked down into the cove from a high ridge. He saw an old woman rummaging around inside the boats before fog brushed the valley like a shirt of gauze.

He climbed higher and stepped across bare rock into a bank of clouds. The damp air closed around him as solid as water. He stopped and stared. He listened. He tried to see through the murk toward something darker, a shape that smoldered along its edges. He stepped forward as the haze cleared. A woman stood before him holding out a bowl of berries.

"Take this, Lalux̂," she said, using his name.

He saw the glint of iridescence in her eyes. She was a spirit of fire who coated green valleys with ash. She befriended eagles and hawks, kept owls for company. She lived among flames and sulfur. Fire surrounded her with healing.

"Take this," she said.

He extended his hands.

"If you stay here, you will be safe."

That night he slept where the Kagamil men could not find him. He wrapped himself in a blanket of sea otter fur. By the light of a stone lamp, by the light of the moon, he remembered how his sister had looked at him for the last time. And when dawn broke across the sea, the body of a whale rose like a dark tongue.

"This old woman," said Volcano Woman, "is Winterberry's Daughter.

She will teach you what you need to know. She was imperfect until I made her whole."

He had seen the old woman reach inside the skin boats and rummage around. She had been taking the Kagamil charms, the carvings that brought luck and protection. She looked at the boy and then dropped into his hands two amber beads: *One is for strength, the other—endurance.*

Winterberry's Daughter taught him to hunt geese with a bola, how to groove the small round stones and bind them three in a bundle, how to whirl them into a flock with all his strength. He learned to chip obsidian into spear points and how to grind pigments from iron and jasper: red from ochre and a lustrous black from the dried ink bag of the octopus; how to fix colors with heat and the blood of a raven. He became familiar with fire. This and more he understood—not in one year or two, but year after year, until Winterberry's Daughter, bent double and deaf, had gone out digging roots for the last time. No longer a boy, he had become a man.

Living around fire, his hair had turned white and his complexion was as gray as the name he insisted on keeping.

ONE
THE BOOKMARK
AND THE IVORY FOX

1. Anna

I'm not saying this didn't happen or that it couldn't happen again or that I'm sorry it did happen. Only, I should have run when the cupboard door opened and Gram's voice rolled through the air like pebbles into the sea.

"*Ayaqaa!* I thought I had some canned milk."

She stepped off the footstool—she must have gone to the cupboard above the fridge where she stored tidal-wave supplies—and now she stood in the doorway looking into the living room where I was sunk into her couch, my hands immobilized by a snarl of raffia.

"Old Lady," her eyes widened a fraction, "would you go to the Merc for me?"

"Sure, *Tutuqux̂*," I said, using her nickname, a periwinkle, a small snail. I once asked her how she got that name. "I don't know," she said in that musical way she has of speaking, pulling out the second word: "I donnnn't know." But then she added, "It was my aunty's name. We both like stinky oil." That's seal oil that has been sitting around for a long time. Family connections among people in the village can be confusing on their own, but nicknames are even more complicated.

I held out the tangled fibers that fought back even after I had given up trying to wrestle them into the circular bottom of a basket. "This is hopeless."

"I told your dad to come tonight for pumpkin pie." She took the weaving. "Looking good."

"Gram, it's a rat's nest."

She handed it back with a five-dollar bill.

"He'll want more than dessert, Gram." I slipped on my windbreaker.

She nodded toward the Formica table where a happy silver salmon dampened sheets of newspaper.

"He brought it. But I need canned milk for that pumpkin pie."

Dad's not a bad cook, but Gram is better. I have a room at her place and one at home. During the school year, Dad often works late at the cannery and sleeps in long after I should be at school, so I frequently stay with Gram. It was summer now so I slept at home, but I ate most dinners with Gram.

I stepped into what Outsiders call a wind, but, trust me, it was just a breeze. Our real wind is why the Aleutian Islands are blown off so many maps or crimped inside a box like Benjamin Franklin's poor cartoon snake whacked into eight pieces. With the Bering Sea on the north and the North Pacific Ocean on the south, the islands sit in a long wind tunnel where storms can change exhilaration into terror in a second. The islands stretch a thousand miles from Alaska to Asia. In the summer, they are like an emerald necklace; but in the long winter—I've seen photographs taken from space— they glow on the dark water like moonstones. We Unangax̂ are known as "people of the pass or seaside" because we were great kayakers once-upon-a-time, but "people of the wind" would have done just as well. It's pronounced something like "Oo-náng-axh," but Outsiders who don't speak our language call us Aleut. (That has three syllables and rhymes with flute: "Ál-ee-oot.") Gram calls herself an Aleut even though she speaks our language better than almost anybody in town.

"I've always been an Aleut," she says defiantly, "when I talk *Amirkaanchix̂.*"

I'm Unangax̂, but I don't speak much of the language. Go figure. Gram doesn't weave baskets or sew sea lion intestines into decorative containers or make bentwood hats. She watches TV, reads O, and keeps suggesting to Dad that we take a trip to Disneyland.

"I'd like to see one of those movie stars," she says. "Like Bradley or Kate."

My mom had been a real, old-fashioned, genuine Unangax̂. Hadn't Gram always referred to her as *Old Lady*?

"That *Old Lady* never wanted me to perm my hair," Gram told me once after coming back from Eva's with a head full of tight curls.

"That *Old Lady* always wanted to weave baskets. Not me!" And she'd laugh and light up a cigarette.

"Gram, you shouldn't do that," I would scold. "They're poison."

"*Ayaqaa!*" she'd say and stub the cigarette into a saucer, adding affectionately, "Just like that *Old Lady*," and just that easily my mom's nickname passed to me.

When Gram was a girl, her family moved here from Makushin, now an abandoned village on the other side of the island. *Here* is Unalaska, the only town left on the entire island. The island has the same name. I know it's confusing, but don't blame me. She was Margaret Galaktionoff then, before she married Bill Petikoff. I love those Russian names that date from over two hundred years ago. Unangax̂ were given Russian names when they were baptized. There aren't any original Unangax̂ names around anymore, except for maybe nicknames. And my last name? Just my luck to be stuck with *Hansen*. One of Dad's grandfathers came from Norway.

Gram lives in "New Town," two rows of tiny old houses made from cabanas at the eastern end of the town, not far from the lake and just off the creek that flows out and into it. *Out* mostly, but *in* when the tide raises the water level. The U.S. Army had occupied Unalaska during the war, World War II. The Japanese bombed the town and the surrounding military outposts and captured Attu Island, at the very western end of the Chain. All the people in Attu village were taken to Japan where half of them—including my gram's cousin—died. After that, Unangax̂ in all nine villages along the Chain had been ordered off the islands and sent a thousand miles away to southeast Alaska, supposedly for their own safety, where, of course, a lot of them also died. When the people came home, they found their houses looted and destroyed. The military hauled cabanas down from the hills to replace them. That's not this story. This story began when I left Gram's and headed to the store.

The breeze was stirring the lush plants in her yard. Only one family in New Town ever tried to grow a lawn, and it wasn't Gram. She was happy with her old friends: wild geraniums with light-blue petals as soft as butterfly wings, and thick stalks of lupine clumped with five-fingered leaves and dark-blue blossoms. Across the creek, fireweed had ignited the hills with a soft blush. A stunted willow zigzagged upward, competing with the tall grass and the thick brutal stalks of *putchki*, wild celery. I watched an eagle drift overhead, toward cliffs beyond the lake, like a slow-moving cargo plane. Its massive talons gripped a small salmon.

Nobody gets in my way, it seemed to say.

"What a way to travel," I thought.

A raven shot out like a black fist and swiped at the fish. The eagle just banked sideways.

Nobody, not even you.

The raven turned its attack into an aerial somersault and dove toward the creek with a shrieking bark.

"Jeez, I'd like to swear like that," I said to myself. I was about to practice when Moses stepped out of his mother's house. Tall, spindly buttercups beside the porch vibrated when he slammed the door. We called them rain flowers, because if you pick them it rains. Outsiders are always mowing them down with their lawn-mowers and then complaining about the weather.

"Hi, Good-lookin'," he said. He was Dad's friend and drove the road grader and snowplow for the city.

"How's your mother, Moses?"

She had been ill for weeks.

"Crazy woman is sellin' everythin' she owns. She'd sell me if she could."

"Sorry."

"It's her stuff," he said. "The sicker she gets the quicker stuff is gone. But I'd really like the kids to have a thing or two from the family."

"Have you talked to the priest?"

"He walked off with a fox trap an hour ago."

"Jeez."

"A model my granddad made. She gave it to him."

"But still," I knew what he felt.

"He said he'd give it back. That's where I'm headin'."

The young Orthodox priest and his wife had recently moved here from California. Moses turned toward a cluster of small well-kept homes down another street.

"Good luck," I said. I think Gram is a lot like his mother, without a sentimental bone in her body. Whatever Gram keeps around has to be usable or out it goes. The only old things in her house, really old things, are a couple of icons on the corner icon shelf in the living room and a framed photo of my mom. She said the icons came from Makushin.

I walked toward the growling and thumping of a compact bulldozer demolishing the Old Priest's House. It had been empty for decades. If anybody knew who the old priest had been, they weren't saying. The new owner was planning to replace it with a restaurant. A café would be nice, but the house had been around so long, crumbling window-by-window and sill-by-sill, that it was a shame to see it shoved out of the picture with one big push. I was used to that kind of reckless demolition at the school and the canneries, but when it happened in the village—even when villagers did it—I didn't like it. For most of us, this was still a village, a place where everybody that mattered knew everybody else. The town fathers had incorporated as a city during the war to protect their business interests. And now, more than seventy-five years later, we were actually turning into something like a city. Newcomers had to look real close to find the village, but it was still there, getting along just fine.

I love running errands for Gram, but I hate the store. It embodies everything I detest about the commercial fishing industry, its sludge and fury, its arrogance, and the boomtown mentality that covers us like a thick, mechanical fog. The store caters to Outsiders. I don't mind that Mrs. Skagit sells alcohol at bargain prices to fishermen to lure them into the store, but it is just greed when she doubles the cost of food needed by villagers. I once asked Gram about her.

"I want to be nice," she answered, "but, *Ayaqaa!* Anybody close to her gets burned."

There wasn't one local product on the shelves, not smoked fish or berries or even the fine grass baskets that collectors prized. Everything was shipped in from Seattle or flown down from Anchorage, including Alaska souvenirs made in China. I hated those cutesy dolls dressed in rabbit fur and the miniature totem poles in a country without trees! There hadn't been a tree in the Aleutian Islands for ten thousand years.

Every time I entered the store, I had to bite my tongue. Gram had let me know, not directly, but gently, in so many words, that Mrs. Skagit had been asking about me.

"What's up with your granddaughter, Margaret? She's downright unfriendly."

Not as unfriendly as I could be.

Just ask the school shrink. Last January the principal had given me a choice: the shrink or suspension for a week. It seems a couple of teachers had taken offense when I called them round eyes and suggested they go back where they came from. Well, they should. The sooner the better. The shrink was famous among us kids for falling asleep while we talked, but he had stayed awake long enough to hear that I was exactly the way I wanted to be.

"Wait until you're in high school," he had said, stifling a yawn. "We'll talk again."

Well, I'd just finished eighth grade. And the shrink and the teacher who had referred me to him were both gone. Our school was a launching pad a lot of teachers used to blast off to glory. Few of them stayed very long, and none of them needed to know if I had or hadn't changed. It was nobody's business but mine.

The window on the door leading into the Merc had a swath of silver duct tape holding it together. "Why replace it when you can duct-tape it?" was Fred's motto. He was Mrs. Skagit's son and not a bad guy on his own. Mr. Skagit had been pushing up daisies for a long time—if we had daisies at the cemetery, which we don't. Pushing up *putchkis*, maybe. I wove through the herd of three-wheelers Fred had brought in through the delivery door in the back and tethered just inside the entrance. He was behind the checkout counter, and I nodded as I made my way through the aisles. The Merc had grown with a randomness that suggested merchandise had washed ashore, one storm after another, the newer items pushing the older ones deeper into the shelves or further back into the room. I crossed to the ramp that led into the grocery store addition, the part of the store called "New-Store" as in, "Where'd you get that candy?"

"At New-Store."

You could sometimes find the same candy in the old store where it was usually cheaper. I hoped Mrs. Skagit was in the jug store, an annex attached to the Merc but entered through a separate outside door. Full cartons of food, in quantities purchased by fishing boats, were stacked up front, along with racks of candy and white bread, magazines and paperbacks, rain gear and rubber boots. But the food ordinary people needed in the quantities they could afford was kept in the rear, where a few low-watt light bulbs dangled from the ceiling.

I had just stretched my arm to the back of the shelf holding the condensed milk, where cans stamped with last month's prices sometimes lingered, when sibilant hissing swept the room like a snare drum.

"That's twice the price we had fixed on." Mrs. Skagit was built like a bull sea lion. The muscles in her arms had terrified entire fishing crews into submission.

I recognized the growled response.

"The island's damned impossible to anchor off."

Albert Hennig was massive: tall, smelly, and meaner than crabs. He had more hair on his face and paws than the average grizzly bear. The story was that one of his great- or great-great-grandfathers had been in the Aleutians right after the Russians sold Alaska in 1867. But *that* Hennig and all the other Hennigs in-between him and this one had lived elsewhere: Kodiak, Seattle, San Francisco. Once they had filled their pockets here, they had left the "rock," as they called the island, the place where, as the stale joke went, "If it's not the end of the world, you can see it from here."

"Besides, it's worth triple what I'm askin'."

"You send it up," she said. She could match him blow for blow. "I'll let you know if I want it. No promises."

"It's two somethings. I'll bring one of 'em up, but then I'm takin' some birders out to the Baby Islands. That'll give you a couple of days to decide. Where's the pilot bread?"

Hennig's shadow floated into my aisle, so I slipped into the next one. I heard him remove a few boxes of the round, hard crackers that were supposed to be good for seasickness.

"We'll talk after that. You'll be happy to pay whatever I ask."

Hennig's *King Eider* was a sturdy vessel he tied at a corner of the Pac-Pearl cannery dock, just off the town creek. He used it for fishing, running errands, and the occasional charter. I was surprised he could still get customers after the owner of a West Highland terrier reported him for using her dog as halibut bait. The deputy at the cop shop figured Hennig and his mate Torgey were capable of almost anything, but the other crewman, Old Man Sanders, wouldn't have let anything like that happen. The more the woman shouted, the more the deputy found something else to investigate.

Hennig was rumored to loot ancient gravesites and abandoned villages for artifacts—clearly illegal, but remarkably profitable. It was strange how stone and ivory objects made by our ancestors now brought prices few of us could afford. The villages in the Chain are few and far between, and law enforcement officers are fewer and even farther between. We have a cop shop, a couple of old WWII cabanas that had been dragged into town and wedged together. The good-natured cop and his deputy vacate the building on Thursdays when the public assistance officer takes over the desk. The prisoners, when there are any, look forward to the change. It's always nice to have company.

"Anything else, dear?" Mrs. Skagit's voice cascaded back to normal. For a moment I thought she had a thing for Hennig, but then Angelina Resoff placed a couple of jars on the counter.

I didn't hear Angelina's answer. She probably just shook her head. She didn't talk more than once a week except to her TV set.

The bell on the door jingled. That's another thing I hate about New-Store. At least you can come and go from the old store without being announced. I heard a familiar voice, rasped by too many years of smoking, ask, "Afternoon, Mrs. Skagit, any new paperbacks arrive?"

"Over there, Sanders," she said. "You know where to look."

"That I do, ma'am."

I stepped to the end of the aisle and shuffled two cereal boxes together to suggest I'd just walked over from the old store and was looking for something. Hennig was still shopping when I carried the condensed milk to the counter and paid. I didn't once look up even after Mrs. Skagit put my change on the counter and covered a quarter with a broad forefinger. I didn't want her piggy eyes wiggling out from under those heavy eyelids and ogling me.

I picked up the other coins and just waited. I hated looking at that finger. I started seeing all kinds of unpleasant things.

"Say hello to your gram for me, Sophie," she said. I had been named Anna Sophia, and for years I had been Sophie to everyone, but recently, for reasons of my own, I'd switched to Anna.

A sigh slipped between her teeth as she razor-bladed each syllable with her tongue. "*Yes, Miss-es Skaa-jet. And thank you, Miss-es Skaa-jet.*"

She freed the quarter, poor thing.

I swept it into my palm and nodded at the souvenirs behind the counter. "Why are you still selling those fat white women dressed like rabbits?"

Her head jerked toward the shelf as I scooped up the cans and walked out.

Hennig's pickup was parked at the corner of the store. I stood beside it until Sanders lumbered out carrying a cardboard box.

"Hey, Sophie," he asked, "how's it hanging?"

"You are so old-fashioned, Sanders," I answered. "Haven't seen you much. Keeping busy?"

He placed the box in the cluttered bed and adjusted his glasses back onto his nose. I liked the old fisherman. He'd been around the village for years. He'd worked in crab fishing and halibut and salmon up in Bristol Bay, but he was old now and not many boats would hire him. I figured Hennig took him on because he could get him cheap.

"Ah, you know, this and that. Just came in from out west."

"Out to Nikolski?" This was a tiny village at the southern tip of the next island.

"Nikolski and a bit further. Four Mountains."

"The Islands of Four Mountains? What were you doing there?"

"Just lookin' around. I stayed on the ship. The captain and Torgey wanted to check something out on shore a couple of times. It was a good trip. Got a couple of halibut for the freezer."

Clueless, I thought. *The guy's completely clueless.*

"You're getting taller, girl. It's about time."

"I'm almost fifteen, Sanders," I said. "I'm tall enough. And I'm going by Anna now."

"I see you still got that smart mouth! Best keep it. You'll need it one of these days."

I saw Hennig leave New-Store and turn into the jug store. I wondered what he'd dug up this time. The Islands of Four Mountains. Five islands with four towering volcanoes, soft blue against a blue-gray sky. Nobody had lived on them for two hundred years. I remembered Dad's copy of *Aleut Art*, a book that was top-heavy with words but packed full of photos. I had read how the people on those islands had been whalers with all sorts of secret practices.

"My gram has some fresh *alaadikax̂*, Sanders, if you're going to be around."

Maybe if I got him alone long enough I could pump him for more information.

"Your gram's fried bread is the best," he said, "but I'll have to take a rain check."

18

I was surprised at how dusty the roof and the walls of the Old Priest's House were when pushed into heaps. The broken door frames and erupted floors. The guy operating the bulldozer had taken a break, so I stepped up to a pile of debris and picked up a chalky stick that had been part of a wall.

Plaster, I guess.

It crumbled in my fingers. A wide board that must have come from an interior wall had broken in two, and the wound showed a light-reddish interior. Bits of old newspapers adhered where the original builder had glued them for insulation. I peeled off a strip and read where Cheyenne Indians had been raiding farms around northern Kansas in 1880. I wondered what the old-time Unangax̂ had thought about that when they were building their new American-style houses. I started to remove another piece when the man returned and waved at me. I backed out of the wreckage. A few fine drops of rain had started falling.

Gram had just placed a cup of tea in front of a woman when I walked in.

That won't last long in this weather, I said to myself when I saw the back of her stylized hair. Gram was on the school board, and new teachers sometimes came to introduce themselves.

"*Aang, aang,*" Gram greeted me. "Just in time."

I placed the canned milk on the counter before looking at the visitor who lowered her designer sunglasses to better see who had walked in. Sunglasses on a cloudy day?

Definitely an Outsidery thing to do.

Maybe she's the new math teacher, I thought. The last one had run off with the banker. I turned back to the counter, tore off a piece of aluminum foil, and started to wrap up four *alaadikax̂*.

"Sophie?"

"That's me," I said, pocketing the fried bread. "Only I'm Anna now."

A boy, maybe five years old, pivoted out from behind the woman's chair.

"Davie," the woman said as she ruffled his hair, "say hi to your big sister."

What happened next? Maybe she got up. Maybe she hugged me. There was a lavender-like smell. Maybe I hugged her back, but static blared inside my head. Her voice was like wind outside a closed window. There were too many words. Too many colors. Her short hair. Her heavy face. She wasn't the woman in the photograph Gram kept on the dresser.

"Does Dad know you're here?"

"Your dad and me, well, we have an understanding. Yeah, I saw him."

"And?"

"Anna," Gram's voice was real quiet.

But the words kept coming. "He's got his life, Sophie. We move on."

"Anna," I repeated.

"Anna," she said, catching on none-too-quickly. "You look real good."

The woman saw my crumpled weaving on the table. "You weaving another basket?"

Gram shook her head a little.

Gram?

"You always wove real nice baskets," this stranger said as her little turd of a boy reached for it. "I never could. I always wanted to, though."

"Too busy with boys," Gram said.

The woman laughed, and her fingers flashed with gold as she put a hand to her permed hair.

"Don't tell Snyder that," she chuckled. "Although I suspect he already knows."

"You married?" I asked, still amazed. Gram had woven baskets?

"Her husband's manager for North Pacific Fish," Gram said. "She's come up to see him over at Akutan and stopped here to see us, too."

"And then?"

"That was real nice of her."

"We live in Seattle now, Anna," she said.

"Do you think I care?"

Did she really think I cared?

"She's a lot like you, Mom," the woman said. I steadied myself at the sink and looked out the window where the rain fell and the buttercups blossomed and everything was the way it had always been without her.

"It's good to see you."

She was talking to Gram. I needed air.

I yanked the raffia out of five stubby fingers and left.

The silver tape flapped as I pushed the door open to get out of the drizzle and walked straight into a sea of plastic ducks. Tourists off a cruise ship bobbed in every aisle. Every last one of them wore identical yellow rain jackets.

Just who did she think she was?

Gram was real. Dad was real. But she had never been anything more than a photograph. Long straight black hair and a narrow face with something like laughter hovering around her eyes and lips. More beautiful than that gross middle-aged woman in sunglasses. There were no photos of her at Dad's. None on display, that is. Maybe one of his old girlfriends had gotten rid of them. Whatever. But whenever I slept at Gram's I had studied the photograph.

But I had never even dreamed about her. As far as I could remember, I had never even seen her, so how could I dream about her except as a door that never opened? Only now here she was, flinging it wide and barging in.

I slammed it shut as Fred shouted for help. For about twenty minutes I gave him a hand and packaged whatever weird knickknacks the tourists bought. The old store didn't have much in the way of actual souvenirs so people settled for fishhooks and hats. I had just handed a package to a woman when Captain Hennig cruised through the crowd like a dark tanker. He carried a small cardboard box and was headed toward New-Store.

"Gotta go," I said to Fred.

"Thanks!" he said as I ducked out from behind the counter and wedged through the last of the tourists. I crouched behind a row of shelves just inside New-Store. I couldn't see what Hennig showed Mrs. Skagit when he got her away from the cash register, but I heard her whistle.

"The other is like this?" she asked.

"I said you'd like it," he answered. "It's even better."

"Where's it at?"

"Like I said, I'm taking birders over to the Baby Islands for a day or two. You think about it. I'll bring it up when I get back. Your customer will pay whatever you ask."

I exhaled a long breath before I stepped into the aisle as a wave of tourists washed up the ramp. Mrs. Skagit slipped something back into the box.

"Later," she said as she returned to the cash register. Hennig growled his way to the door. I was sure his hands were empty. I backed into a row and waited.

And waited.

Finally, I stepped out.

"You find what you want, Sophie?" Mrs. Skagit asked. "If you do, take it to Fred."

Four men in yellow jackets were still at the counter.

"Follow me, gentlemen," she said and headed to the jug store.

The small cardboard box was below the counter. I fished among the packing pellets and pulled out a two-by-four-inch manila envelope. I tilted out a three-inch spear point, flaked from crystal or glass or the clearest agate in the world, a narrow wedge of light. It was perfectly symmetrical, with fine even ridges on both sides.

It's not his and it's not mine, I told myself as light angled out of it. *But it's more mine than his. It's a lot more mine than his. This belonged to my Unangax̂ ancestors.*

Everything disappeared. Old things got yanked out from under us. The unique things that made us who we were kept vanishing, like the Old Priest's House and the fox trap from Moses's family.

I slipped it into my pocket.

I tucked the empty envelope into the box and returned it to the shelf.

I didn't even nod at Fred as I left the store. I started toward Gram's, pretty sure she'd tell me to take the spear point to Jennifer at the museum. Six steps and that woman and her fart of a kid barged into my head. I headed in the opposite direction to give myself some time.

Torgey was helping a limping Sanders into the passenger's seat of the pickup when I got to the dock.

"He twisted his ankle," Torgey said as I hurried up.

"Didn't see the box," Sanders said. "I'd dropped my glasses."

"He'd just put the box down on the deck," Torgey said. "I'm takin' the old fool to the clinic."

He climbed in on the driver's side.

"That I am," the old man laughed and straightened his glasses. "Up and tripped on it. Captain's gone to the hotel to make arrangements for the birders to get to the boat. Will you tell him we're at the clinic?"

The pocket with the spear point suddenly seemed heavier. They drove off before I shouted that I wouldn't tell the crook anything.

I took the spear point out and saw again how it concentrated the light.

Or maybe I will. I would tell Hennig. I'd look right up at him, innocent and all, and tell him. I remembered the fried bread I had brought for Sanders. I might even offer some of it to him. Then I'd take the point and whatever else I might find on the *King Eider* to Jennifer. She could call the cops. By the time I got back to Gram's, that woman would be gone, off to Akutan. I'd move on, like she said. The sun came out for a bit as I crossed to the gangplank, like it was giving me a green light.

I left the fried bread on the table after a quick inspection of the galley. I flew down a flight of stairs and stuck my head into a small room with compact bunk beds. I closed the door and opened another. This was more like it: a spacious bunk and a built-in desk, a chart of the Islands of Four Mountains pinned to the wall. I flipped on the light and shut the door. Hennig's desk was littered with papers. I pulled open the drawer and ran my hand over nothing more than pens and pencils. There was a cardboard box on the bed with crackers, cookies, and a couple of bottles of alcohol. Two more boxes were on the floor behind a pair of duffle bags. I had just moved one of the duffle bags when Sander's dog started a yapping fit in the hall. I stepped to the door, flipped off the light just as a rockslide of thumps and yelps exploded outside. A kid was at the bottom of the stairs rubbing his butt. He started to stand up when Sander's mutt snapped another pathetic bark from the top of the stairs.

"Shut it, Halibut Bait!" I ordered and jerked the kid to his feet.

2. Booker

For me, the beginning was a lot like the end. I tripped and went flying.

That's not who I am. I like order. I want to know what's going to happen next. I'm like my dad when he outlines the plots for the novels he and Mom write. Most of the time, though, he's a lot more adventurous, and that's when I stay out of his way. My parents, Spike and Tulip, write mysteries. They also love obscure scientific facts, which is probably why I have these odd snippets in my head. Did you know, for example, that thirty-six is both a square and a triangular number? Or that while there are infinite prime numbers, there are only three primary colors? I'm thirteen.

We live at the end of a gravel road west of Montpelier, the capital of Vermont. Our house is almost as old as Vermont. The walls are at weird angles, and the floor boards are super wide. The house is surrounded by apple and pine trees. The yard backs onto a narrow woods. My room is on the second floor, at the top of the stairs. I can look out the window toward the woods and beyond to the cottage where the Elder Cousin and Mrs. Bainbridge live. He's a really distant relative, something like Dad's father's grandfather's sister's son. His name is Allen.

"But always," he once told me, "even when I was a boy, I was called the Elder Cousin."

"You were the oldest?"

"Older than all of them."

Mrs. Bainbridge arrived after Mom found the Elder Cousin unconscious in his yard and called emergency services. When she answered the door, there was Mrs. Bainbridge.

"Like a great swan of a woman," she said, "with a black bag."

Filled with tea towels, it turned out. But Mom didn't know that at the time. The Elder Cousin recovered, and Mrs. Bainbridge stayed. I have never asked, but I think she must have wandered in from the coast. She gives off a slightly salty air. She tells me stories about ships and distant lands where there are bears and wild horses and the wild horses feed on wild apples.

I like her stories, but *Here* is just fine for me.

When I started first grade, Mrs. Bainbridge announced to my parents that they were to start calling me by my real name. Before that Mom had called me *Sparrow*, and Dad had called me *Mouse*. Don't ask me where those nicknames came from. But I think it was *Mouse* because I'm curious about things and *Sparrow* because, well, I don't know. Maybe because I'm a little bit short for my age. Anyway, my parents were startled, but they agreed. I'm almost always Booker now. To tell the truth, sometimes they forget and I automatically answer to *Sparrow* and sometimes to *Mouse*. I don't mind. I'm a pretty happy kid. Don't expect any heroics.

Last Tuesday I was home by myself, pretending to be an orphan. Mom and Dad had driven over the Gap to Middlebury College. Something about Irish poets. She's part Irish. The Elder Cousin and Mrs. Bainbridge had gone into Montpelier to shop and then have lunch at Sarducci's. I've eaten there twice. Just thinking about their food makes me hungry. Being without parents has advantages when you're on the edge of starvation and close to the kitchen.

I made a peanut butter and pickle sandwich and went into the living room.

Hopeless, I thought as I looked around. Books and jackets covered the living room chairs. The desk by the window had a shoe holding down what I figured was a pile of bills. I put the plate with my sandwich on an empty corner of the coffee table and shifted a pile of Sunday supplements on the couch. Then I squeezed in between them and a half-dozen copies of my parents' latest mystery. The photograph on the back of *Death and the Uphill Gardener* looked nothing like Spike or Tulip, but everything about their books was a bit far-fetched.

If I were the king of the world, I said to myself as I looked around, *I'd get things in order.*

Orphan king or not, I had soon devoured the sandwich.

I remembered the candy bar in my backpack. My parents discourage candy unless it comes from the co-op and tastes like paste. I had traded this one for helping Robbie mow his lawn. I usually keep my backpack under an old school desk that Mom found at a yard sale and installed in a corner of the kitchen. But it wasn't there. It wasn't beside the fridge or on the washer in the pantry. I stepped into Dad's study where a cork board mounted on the wall had three-by-five cards pinned on it as he worked out the plot for their next book. But no backpack. I went upstairs. It wasn't on or under my bed. Something flashed outside the window. I looked out. The backpack wasn't on the roof.

Of course, it wasn't on the roof.

There was a raven on the roof reading a letter.

Back downstairs, I fished the remote out from behind a couch pillow where I'd put it for safekeeping. I sat down and turned on the TV.

Reading a letter?

I was outside in a flash. And straight into a cyclone of flying paper. It was like every letter and envelope, every piece of graph paper and colored paper, every sheet of anything was flying through the air. I latched onto a couple sheets and saw they were addressed to the Elder Cousin. He needed to know. I ran for the path into the woods, plowing through a snowstorm of paper. Then I remembered he wasn't home. Then I remembered why I had rushed out in the first place. I looked back. The raven on the roof was only a crow with a coupon in its beak.

I ran like crazy toward the old shed just where the woods ended and their lawn began. It was really ancient, with square nails and everything. The shed door had blown open, and papers were gushing out, just swirling into the air in all directions. I stepped onto the lawn and everything froze, like a gigantic screenshot with paper just hanging in the air. The shed door slowly closed. I heard the latch click, and the old building quivered and stomped and exploded.

I pried open my eyes. The tops of the trees bellowed overhead, weaving in and out of swirling paper. *Like a tent made of cauliflowers*, I thought. I pushed a few sheets away and tried to sit up as Mrs. Bainbridge stuck out her hand.

"They're gone, Booker," she said and gave me a tug to my feet.

"Gone?"

"Back. I mean they've gone back. Allen is driving. He'll be back soon. Come inside."

I stumbled after her, but I glanced behind. Sheets of paper were evaporating like fireflies into the darkness.

I sat at the kitchen table. Mrs. Bainbridge fished inside a cookie jar. I half expected her to bring out a fistful of paper. She kept looking at me. Like maybe I'd float away, too.

"Did you see what happened?" I asked.

She set a plate of chocolate-chip cookies on the table.

"Have a cookie."

It was like my arms were paralyzed.

Cookies? I had just seen part of the world break into pieces.

"Good for you," she insisted and inched the plate closer.

Okay. I had taken a bite when the Elder Cousin arrived. His eyes went to Mrs. Bainbridge, who was shaking her head. "We'll tell him later," she said in a whispered rumble.

Later. I liked that word. Much *later.*

"Thanks," I said and licked a chocolate chip off my finger.

"Don't forget what I told you," Mrs. Bainbridge said as I stood up.

I walked past a rectangle of earth where the shed had stood. Every slip of paper was gone. What had she meant? She hadn't told me anything. The path back home was paper-free. The crow was sitting on the roof. Sunlight turned some of its black feathers silver and some of them chalk. The coupon was in its beak. It bounced to the edge and tilted its head as I stood directly beneath and looked up. The narrow slip of paper twirled down, down, down, and right into my hand. The bird launched itself into the air and twisted toward the woods with a sharp *graw-caw*. I looked at the paper in my hand. It wasn't a coupon at all. It was heavy, like if the paper were made out of oatmeal. It was covered with Russian letters. I knew that because that's the sort of thing I know. I also knew it was a bookmark. Around our house, bookmarks are as common as books.

I went inside. I turned off the TV.

I sat on the couch and tried to think.

We'll tell him later, she had said.

I picked up *Death and the Uphill Gardener*. I put it down and laid the bookmark on it.

I needed to pee.

I went into the bathroom and shut the door. Finished, I turned around and there was my backpack, minding its own business in a corner. I carried it back to the couch and tried to put my thoughts in order.

She had said for me to remember something. But she hadn't told me anything.

I studied the Russian letters on the bookmark. I flipped it over. There was a photo of a bookstore with a bench in front of it. When I started to turn it back over, the photo turned into one of bleachers above a football field.

Like a fancy holograph, I thought. But while I held it still, the football field gave way to somebody's living room. A porch with a wooden swing on it was pushed away by a bus filled with people reading or staring out windows. I felt sucked into the changing scenes.

A few colorful beach chairs at the edge of a lake were replaced by the crowded seats of an airplane.

I yanked myself back to attention.

I needed an explanation. About everything.

It wasn't much later, but it *was* later. I put the bookmark and the paperback into my pack and started back.

"She's sleeping," the Elder Cousin said when he opened the door.

"Did you call the police?"

"It's all been reported."

"I have something to show you." I dug into my pack.

"Come back in an hour. She'll be up then." He started to shut the door, reopened it, and said, "Thanks, Booker."

I sat down on the steps. The bookmark was in my hand. It was a little bent. The scenes kept playing. A jogging trail dipped into a crowded subway car that lurched into a hammock hanging between two trees.

I was about to drop it into the pack when I realized it could get really bent. I took out *Death and the Uphill Gardener*. On the bookmark, a waiting room dissolved into an office filled with cubicles. A modest brick hotel had just appeared when I slipped it between two pages and was—well, I guess this is where the story begins.

I was hurled into a blur—except that a blur takes at least a second and in less than that I was flying through a brass revolving door. It whispered behind me as I skidded into a room, tripped on a frayed carpet, and catapulted into the back of a chair upholstered in brocade and dust.

A shriek curled into the air, followed by a paperback, one sailing—or so it seemed to me—slightly higher than the other.

"Sorry!" I said to the woman in the chair as I bent down to retrieve the book. I gawked at the cover: *Death and the Uphill Gardener*.

She relaxed her grip on the padded arms and shook blood back into her fingers.

"You gave me a start, young man," she said as she tugged the paperback from my fingers.

"But that book," I began. I looked around. I was in a hotel lobby.

She adjusted her rhinestone-studded glasses. I stammered another apology, but she had already started reading and raised her hand to quiet me.

"Sorry," I said again.

She turned a page. I looked around. Definitely a hotel lobby.

She uttered a sigh of contentment.

My parents' books always end with good winning over evil.

"Excellent," she said. "Excellent." She closed the cover. I heard an explosion, let out a yelp, and felt a backfiring suck of air.

Something damp was soaking through the seat of my jeans.

I arched my back for leverage off the wet grass as the Elder Cousin extended a hand.

"Come," he said.

I stumbled after him on the second weird trip of the morning. Or the third. Or the fourth. I was too confused to count. I followed him through the kitchen and into the living room where all the chairs were upholstered except for a single wooden one. He pointed toward it with his cane.

"Until your pants dry a bit," he said.

I looked around the familiar room. Knickknacks and souvenirs crowded each other on every flat surface: the coffee table, two glass-fronted display stands, three ornate corner shelves, and a two-drawer filing cabinet draped with an Indian paisley shawl. I relaxed a little as I realized that everything was the way it always had been. *A place for everything*, I said to myself. A tin drum balanced beside two porcelain teapots shaped like cottages. Had they always had puffs of smoke coming out of their chimneys? There were artificial ferns with real blossoms.

Ferns have spores, not blossoms, I said to myself.

I sensed the Elder Cousin studying me. His normally blue eyes were sharkskin gray.

"I feel fine," I said. "Honest."

Fine, but a little wilted.

"You're certain, Booker?"

I nodded.

"Let me make you a cup of hot chocolate," he said. "Just in case."

A bowl of buttons sat beside a bowl of polished stones. *There's nothing unusual about buttons*, I thought, and then they shifted as a current rumbled through them.

He returned in a few minutes and handed me a mug. "You may be wondering," he said, and, of course, I was, as he slipped his cane over the arm of his chair and sat down, "just what happened to you."

I held the mug with two hands and sent a cloud of ordinary steam across the surface.

"Books are pretty much just books," he began.

"Of course they are," I said. Who had said anything about books?

"And bookmarks are bookmarks," he continued. "Books take you places."

He was starting to sound like the school librarian. "I know," I said. I was feeling a little wobbly. "We had a display at school."

"And so can bookmarks. Let me put it this way." He leaned forward. "Once when you asked to accompany your parents when they were researching one of their novels—"

"*Death and the Delicate Arch*," I interrupted. "I wanted to visit a desert."

"What an absurd title!" Mrs. Bainbridge had strolled in like a piece of furniture too large for the room. "Sounds like a bad pair of shoes."

"Maud, please," he said. "I'm trying to explain."

She wedged herself into a chair.

And then he started over, but I was so confused by what had been happening that I didn't hear half of it until the words "the bookmark" and I looked at my pocket.

"But I left it in the book."

"Where it did its job," he said, "and came back."

I removed it and felt again how thick the paper was.

"It's very old," Mrs. Bainbridge said when she saw me turning it this way and that. "Made from a most unusual paper. We think it was cut from the page of a book."

The Elder Cousin put out his hand. "May I see it?"

I watched how intently he studied it.

"Any change, Allen?"

"None," he said to her. "None that I can see."

"Have you told him where it came from?"

"Not yet, Maud," he said.

"Or how you got it?"

He shook his head. "Now is not the time."

"It came from Siberia," she said.

"Years ago," he sighed, "when I was in the used book business, I took a consignment from a woman whose aunt and uncle had been in the Russian Far East. This particular collection came from Petropavlovsk in Kamchatka. It's not really Siberia."

Mrs. Bainbridge shrugged. "But close enough."

"Anyway," he continued, "the bookmark was among a few papers tucked into one of the books. I had a dickens of a time getting them translated. They were part of a travel log. A voyage into the North Pacific Ocean. They provided clues about using the bookmark."

"And the Russian words on the bookmark itself?" I asked.

"That I don't know," he said. "Nobody has been able to translate them."

"Old, old language," she said.

"All of which I can explain later," he said, "but the important thing now is that you understand what the bookmark does."

I was beginning to suspect.

"It starts with a book. The scenes on the bookmark show places where the book that you're holding is being read."

He tilted the bookmark so I saw a series of images drift across its surface.

"When the bookmark is slipped into the book, that's where you go."

"Where?" It seemed a little arbitrary.

"Where the book is being read."

"And does the book go, too?"

"No. Readers have their own copies."

"It doesn't work for everybody," Mrs. Bainbridge said. "For most people, it's just a bookmark."

"How do you know all of this?"

Instead of answering me, the Elder Cousin said, "Not everyone who can use it wants to." He looked at Mrs. Bainbridge. "Maud, for example," and he smiled at her, "is quite content to remain here."

Mrs. Bainbridge didn't look like somebody who avoided adventure. With her cropped hair and sturdy body, she reminded me of a painting by Picasso that Mrs. Sweets in art showed us of a famous woman author glowering in a chair. "It is not a matter of bravado," he continued as though reading my mind although I had to think twice about what "bravado" meant.

"Not that I haven't traveled! Not that I won't travel again!" she said and laughed.

"Do you recall where you placed the bookmark?" she asked.

I shook my head.

"Near the end, I think," she said softly.

"At almost the last page, if I'm not mistaken," the Elder Cousin said. "Once the reader finishes the book and closes the cover, home we go, like it or not."

"The first trips can be a bit disorienting," Mrs. Bainbridge said.

Smokestacks and rumbling buttons, I thought.

"And if I want to get back before the book is finished?"

What I really wanted to ask was, "*Why me?*"

"You've a number of things to learn," the Elder Cousin said. He took a wooden box off a shelf, removed the lid, and placed the bookmark inside.

"And it's important that you do. But first—" and his eyes blinked rapidly as he stared into the distance and sat perfectly still. I thought he had heard something outside the window. A moment later he shook himself and asked, "Would you like more hot chocolate?"

"Some for me and more for him, Allen," said Mrs. Bainbridge.

The Elder Cousin took my mug and said, "We suspected you were like us."

Crap, crap, crap, I thought.

"What Allen means," Mrs. Bainbridge said, "is that we think you might be in danger."

She leaned a little closer.

"Lots to learn, Booker. Lots and lots. Tables of Continuance, Ratchet-backed Endnotes, the Silk Road, and, my favorite, Disambiguation."

Then she raised her hand in half a salute and half a toast.

"To new and startling days!" she boomed.

I didn't like the sound of that at all.

There's something to be said about a place for everything and everything in its place. For order and predictability. For staying away from bears. Every afternoon of the next week, I got bookmark lessons from the Elder Cousin. How to freeze the image of the place where we wanted to go. (He simply covered the image with his thumb.) How to travel together. (I merely held onto his arm or sleeve.) How to get back. (I just put the bookmark upside down back into the book. If I didn't have the book, I put it upside down in my pocket.) It was simple, but it all took practice. He kept the bookmark in the box when we weren't using it. One afternoon he went into the kitchen for a glass of water. I knew where he kept the box. I wasn't going to actually use the bookmark. I just wanted to hold it. It felt, well, it felt *right*. The speed with which he gripped my wrist amazed me.

"The bookmark is yours, Booker," he said and let go of my wrist. "You'll find it's yours maybe more than you expect."

I just looked at him.

"You won't be able to get rid of it," he said

"Why would I want to?"

"No reason," he said. "No real reason. You'll grow into using it gradually."

My parents. I should explain that I didn't tell them anything. Mrs. Bainbridge said we should keep this among the three of us. At least for now.

"Things would just get complicated," she said.

I had never kept a secret of this size from them. It felt good.

The Elder Cousin and I spent a night in Bulgaria. We were in the mountains where there were bears. I was certain there were bears. Something brushed against the tent, and I wondered if my parents would work my disappearance into a book. *Eaten by Bears in Bulgaria.*

"Will my parents notice that I'm missing?"

"I would hope so, Booker."

"I mean," I said, "how does time work?"

"No," he answered. "In that sense, you won't be missed. Good books never age, and even these"—he nodded at *Death and the Uphill Gardener*—"age slowly."

I was not eaten by bears, obviously. I soon knew the bookmark basics. Coming and going. Nothing complicated about it.

Back from Bulgaria, I sat at the kitchen table waiting for the Elder Cousin while Mrs. Bainbridge attacked a carrot with a vegetable peeler. After supper I was going to get introduced to what he called A Little Bit Onward. We were still using *Death and the UHG.*

I was sitting at the table. "You said I might be in danger."

"I suppose I did," she said and started on another carrot.

"Well?" I asked when it seemed like she wasn't going to explain.

"I get carried away, Booker. The truth is, we thought we were done with it. That we'd put the bookmark away for good, buried it in a shed full of papers."

"Why didn't you just destroy it—burn it or tear it up?"

"Can't. We tried. So we did the next best thing."

"And then I found it after the shed exploded."

"Yes." It was clear she wasn't going to explain how or why that had happened.

"Only I didn't exactly find it. I caught it when the crow dropped it."

"So the crow must have found it," she said. "That seems right."

She began slicing the carrots into thin disks.

"Allen had the bookmark for years before he fully discovered its traveling capabilities," she said. "By accident. Like you. After that, my personal opinion is that he used it too frequently. He'll say otherwise. But things started to happen."

"I'm not surprised," I said.

She gave me a look. Like she was humoring me.

"One day he used the bookmark in that original volume where he had found it, the book from Siberia. For two and a half days he couldn't get back."

I was puzzled. "I thought he said that time doesn't pass when you're using the bookmark."

"It doesn't. Usually." She scooped the carrot chunks into a bowl and covered them with water. "But he had slipped out of time. When he got back, well, that's when your mother found him and when I came along."

"Where had he been?"

She didn't answer right away. She started peeling a short crooked ginger root. Sweetness, like a toy sword, jabbed at the air.

"I don't think he actually knew. That old book probably hadn't been read for centuries, not really read. Wherever he ended up, it wasn't Kansas."

I knew what she meant. Sort of.

"Had he traveled back in time?"

"Maybe into it. Or through it." She had a habit of not answering my questions. She said, "He insisted it was nothing."

She grated the ginger into a small bowl.

"For a couple of years after that, Booker, we traveled together." She put the ginger aside, slipped a dollop of butter into a saucepan and put it on the stove over a low burner. As it melted, she drizzled a tablespoon of honey into it.

"The danger isn't," she said, "that something is after you. It's that you might do something dangerous yourself."

"Unlikely," I said. "Very slim chance of that."

She again looked at me like she knew something I didn't. She stirred the ginger into the honey and butter mixture. An invisible cloud of fragrance filled the kitchen. She drained the carrots, added them to the saucepan, and put on a lid.

"The bookmark will sometimes find the book," she said. "Sort of like the way it found you."

I went into the living room and picked up the wooden box. The Elder Cousin wasn't so touchy about me handling the bookmark after I'd taken two short solo trips. I'd proved myself able to handle it. Even though they kept it and understood it more than I did, it belonged to me, like the Elder Cousin had said. When I held it, it was like I was in serious control. It felt good. It also felt goofy. The giant lions of the New York Public Library drifted past, followed by a blue heron lifting off a gray lake. The gold and glass interior of an elevator sped upward. People seemed to be reading the book everywhere.

My parents must be rich, I thought. *I should ask for a bigger allowance.*

A fishing boat was tied to a dock. At least I thought it was a fishing boat. There was a cabin near the front. At the back—the aft? the stern?—anyway, behind the cabin there was a mast without a sail. I saw a covered hatch and a tangle of cables and nets. Behind the ship, on the land, there were hills as bright green as emeralds. They glowed in the sun. They rose up, higher and higher, until a rocky peak jutted out at the top. It towered above everything.

"Ireland," I said and froze the image.

The Irish had been the first to measure wind with the Beaufort scale. They had invented shorthand and tattoos. Or, at least, a tattoo machine. I didn't have a tattoo. *And shamrocks,* I thought. Lucky shamrocks. One for me and one to surprise Mom with. How long would it take? By the time I get back, I'll still be waiting—if I understood what the Elder Cousin had said about time.

I slipped the bookmark into the first chapter. The floor lurched sideways. I braced my feet against what felt like hard rubber on the deck. I gulped some sharp salty air.

"Whoa," I said as the ship rocked gently and another boat glided past. My knees started to detach themselves from my legs, but I steadied myself by touching the side of the cabin.

The bright sky grew a little fuzzy as the sun went behind a cloud. Actually, the whole sky was overcast with just a little gap that allowed the sunlight to turn the hills so green. They were still green, but not that electric green. A breeze spread the pungent odor of fish, salt, chemicals, and work being done. I walked along the side of the cabin until I looked out over the back deck. Clumps of machinery of one kind or another had been pushed to one side. I stepped around the corner and looked into a room. There was a table covered with green rubber netting and bordered with a narrow raised lip. *Death and the Uphill Gardener* was sitting on it. I stepped inside. Next to the book was an open tinfoil wrapper with a few wrinkled pastries that looked like maple bars without the maple frosting. The room was really just a small kitchen. Nice and compact. And orderly. The way I liked things. I think I said that before. Varnished wood glowed on the walls. Even though I had put the bookmark at the front of the book, I didn't want somebody coming and reading the last page and sending me back before I had picked a couple of shamrocks, so I dropped it into my backpack and went onto the deck to see how to get off the boat.

A kind of walkway angled up to the dock from the back of the boat. It was just a couple of two-by-twelves fastened together with slats. *Gangway?* Or was that what you shouted to get people out of the way? Anyway, the closer I got to it, the steeper and narrower it grew, like the drawing Mrs. Sweets showed us of a staircase that goes both up and down. Under and behind it, dark pilings crusted with barnacles supported the dock like a forest of massive burned trunks. I don't like heights and my balance has never been great, so I used my hands like an orangutan, took a deep breath and rushed up.

The dock was bigger than a basketball court. It had to be super-thick, but it hummed like it was purring.

Left or right?

Right, I said, just as a siren blasted a hole in the air. A flood of men and women in jackets and blue jeans poured out of a tall building, all corrugated tin and slick metal. I joined the crowd that flowed past more doors and steam vents until the dock abruptly changed to blacktop. Everybody seemed to go off toward other buildings. I jumped aside as a yellow forklift twirled its massive jaws toward me.

I followed the blacktop until it changed into a dirt road along a small stream. The plants growing at the edge of the river were heavy and dense. There was grass with blades as wide as iris leaves and longer than my arms when I stretched them out. There were feathery plants like undernourished ferns. I crushed a few leaves between my fingers and smelled a strong medicinal odor. There were bright-yellow buttercups on spindly stems and a tall plant with a thick stalk and leaves like elephant ears. I spied a clump of what looked like clover. Shamrocks? But when I took a handful they smelled like parsley. I settled for a few buttercups.

I figured I should return the book before getting back to the lesson with the Elder Cousin. It took some balancing, but I got down the ramp. The kitchen was still empty, fortunately. Like I said, my dad is the one good at plots, and I hadn't invented a story to explain why I was on the boat if somebody showed up. I slipped off my backpack to get out the paperback when the light at the end of the hallway flickered. I don't mean a light bulb. It was just a quick shadow that nagged at the corner of my eye. The hall was about fifteen feet of narrow emptiness.

I listened real hard. I walked to where there was a handrail curling down a short flight of stairs. I held on and leaned over. An engine growled complacently from somewhere below. I felt the vibrations softly rubbing the metal handrail.

Nothing, I said to myself and started to straighten up.

"Err-roof!"

My arms turned into jelly. I knew it was a dog, but it was like my arms just evaporated and I fell, twisting and hitting the handrails until the stairs met my rear, one bump of my rump at a time.

"Err-roof! Err-roof!"

I looked up from the bottom of the stairs. A white, wiry dog like a bad hairdo on legs snarled down as it delivered a ferocious spit.

I rearranged my legs.

That's when this tall girl extended her hand.

Did I say I was short for my age?

3. Anna

I hauled the runt into the stateroom. He straightened his gray sweatshirt, adjusted his blue jeans, and unsuccessfully pushed back the mop of brownish hair that fluffed out like a cloud of chicken feathers. Typical cannery brat. I didn't recognize him from school, so he had probably just arrived with parents who let him run wild. I shushed him when he tried to speak and shushed him again when he started to object.

"What are you doing here?"

He held out a few wilted buttercups and mumbled something about Ireland. I more or less anchored him on the bunk when he started to leave. He took a narrow piece of paper from his pocket and toyed with it. Turning it this way and that. His feet were twitching and hitting the bed frame. That's when the crate under the bunk caught my eye. I got to my hands and knees and pulled it out. I tilted back the lid. It was filled with crumbling ancient basketry, fragments of wood that was bent—probably from bowls—stone points, and pieces of sewed bird skin and gut. This had to be it.

He leaned over the crate.

I shoved my face up into his. "Who are you?"

"Booker," he answered, jerking back. "Booker John."

I handed him a stone lamp. It had a circumference about the size of a cereal bowl, but shallow and flat inside. He turned it over.

"Neat," he said, without explaining his odd name.

"There's got to be more than old basketry and stone lamps." I shifted some of the grass matting.

"Stone lamps?"

"You're holding one."

He looked at it again. The cavity of the bowl was blackened from burned oil. He handed it back and reached across my arm to lift out a shiny spear point, perfect and exquisitely carved.

"That's sharp," I warned.

"Looks like obsidian," he said. "Obsidian is really volcanic glass."

"Duh," I said.

"Who are you?" he asked. "What are you looking for?"

"Anna Hansen," I said, not sure I wanted to tell him what I was doing.

"Are you from here?"

What a dolt.

Then I blurted out, "It's illegal to deal in looted artifacts."

"Looted from where?"

"The Four Mountain Islands, I think." I nodded at the chart pinned to the wall. "They're famous for volcanoes and mummies."

"I've heard of Irish mummies," he blathered. "Discovered in peat bogs, but volcanoes? I don't think so. Maybe in Iceland. Who does this junk belong to?"

I figured that if he didn't know, he didn't need to know.

"I don't have time to argue," I said. "Captain Hennig digs stuff up and sells it Outside."

"In a yard sale?"

"*Outside*. Stateside. The lower '48. Where you're from."

Time was running out.

I held up a hard piece of hide, maybe a fragment of a parka made from bird skins. I'd never seen one except in photographs. I returned it to the box next to fragments of stiff cordage, finely braided from thin leather, some round and some square. The more I saw, the madder I got.

"Sinew," I said when he picked up one of the braided strands.

"From what?"

"Maybe whale or caribou muscle. Maybe gut."

I have to give him credit: he didn't flinch, but instead he studied it more carefully. I decided to give him a break. "All this has been taken from burial caves further out in the Chain," I said, leaning back and looking at him, "on one of the Islands of Four Mountains. Hennig broke a boat-load of Alaska laws getting it."

"Alaska?"

I took the cordage back and put it in the crate.

"What happened to Ireland?"

He studied me like I was some kind of specimen.

"You're an Eskimo?"

He knew he'd made a serious mistake even before I said, "I'm Unangax̂. I'm not Eskimo, cannery-boy, Inuit or Iñupiaq. I'm Unangax̂. When did you get here anyway?"

"Oo-nung-uh?" he repeated.

"Close enough. You've heard of Aleuts?" Dumb cannery brat.

He nodded, or maybe he just twitched.

"Unangax̂ is our own name."

I lifted a small piece of wood from the crate. On one side was a graceful incised curve with a faint reddish color. I wondered if it was part of a mask.

He was quiet and just staring at me.

Then he said, with something like triumph, "You're one of those disappearing peoples! I read about you in school."

A couple of choice words let him know I wasn't about to disappear anytime soon.

He shut up for a second, and then he asked, "What are you looking for?"

"Something," I said. "I don't know. Something valuable."

He reached into the crate just as Hennig's voice boomed from the galley.

"TORGEY! SANDERS!"

I slammed down the lid just as the kid jerked his hand out. I shoved the crate under the bed and snapped off the light.

"TORGEY!"

The ship hammered like a drum under a cascade of boots as Hennig launched himself down the stairs.

I flattened myself against the wall as the door cracked open.

"They're here, Captain! The bird people!" Torgey's squeaky crackle froze everything.

"Damn it!" Hennig growled and pulled the door shut.

The kid got to his feet from where he had dropped to the floor. I don't know, maybe he was going to pretend to be a rug. I listened until I heard Hennig climb the stairs before I pulled out the crate again. I selected the sturdiest fragment of grass weaving I could find and carefully folded it into my pocket, being careful to not put it in the one that had my own pathetic start of a basket. It wasn't much, but maybe with the spear point it was enough for Jennifer to call the cops.

When I stepped out of the room, I could hear the birders grumbling up above. They were not happy campers.

"We'll be two nights," Hennig bellowed from somewhere. "And sleeping on deck will add to the experience."

I knew that was a joke, but it produced a universal groan.

The kid followed me up the stairs. There were about a dozen birders packing the galley and flowing into the hall.

"We've got one stateroom with bunk beds," Hennig said. "And another with a single."

I wedged myself behind the birders as I inched into the galley. There was no way out except to go through the crowd. A couple frowned when I bumped into their massive cameras and dangling lens cases, but their indignation was focused on the captain. They had obviously been expecting a bit more from a vessel pompously named the *King Eider*.

The kid apologized to everybody he squeezed past. I kept my head and body turned away from the captain and Torgey, who chirped in with, "And Sanders's bunk. We got that, too." I slithered past the last birder and out the door onto the deck. Now if Hennig saw me, he wouldn't know where I had come from. I could tell him about Sanders, although I suspected Torgey already had.

"And mine," Hennig added. "Hell, you can use mine, too."

I heard the kid apologize again. *Enough of that*, I said to myself. *He's on his own.*

I was almost at the gangplank when Mrs. Skagit started down. She flushed as livid as her red bandana when she saw me. I guess I looked guilty. Her piggy eyes almost exploded.

"THIEF!" she screamed, and I plunged back into the crowd of birders, knocking Booker aside.

A berserk kid hurling through them convinced a few that this was a convenient time to abandon ship.

"Stop her, Hennig! She's got the spear point!"

Not only berserk, but armed.

That sent the rest of them toward the ramp. Except for one big guy who hauled me up by the armpits.

"She's here!" He probably had the best of intentions.

"You can let her go," Hennig said. He was dripping sweat right beside me. I stopped struggling.

"If you're sure she'll be all right."

Hennig placed a heavy hand on my shoulder.

"She's my niece," he lied, his voice dripping sympathy. "I'm afraid she's gone off her meds."

I think the guy was happy enough to escape.

"She'll be fine," Mrs. Skagit assured him as she and Torgey blocked the doorway.

4. Booker

The *what's-it* girl who wasn't an Eskimo went limp against the wall.

I had ducked under the table after she barreled back into the room. Ireland or Alaska, I had no business being here. I took out the bookmark.

"You slimy spoiled thief."

A woman with a voice like a gravel truck was between me and Anna. This sounded too good to miss. I put the bookmark away.

"You ungrateful, ill-mannered brat," she resumed, "You pile of—"

"Err-roof! Err-roof!"

My head slammed into the underside of the table as that doggy hairball snarled in complete delight.

"Err-roof!"

I sprinted out as Anna slipped under the woman's arms in time for us to collide with one of the laws of physics. Like a couple of clowns. A creepy guy hauled me backward, but that gorilla woman started pummeling Anna who thrashed with every appendage available.

"Got it!" the woman said and held up a piece of glass. She tossed it to the captain as Anna took a swing at her. The woman ducked and scooped her up like she was a sack of carrots. Anna kicked, but the woman held her tight until she just sort of collapsed. The guy called Torgey grabbed me, as the captain barked out an order. We were hustled back down the ladder, pushed past the room we'd been in, and shoved into another. I heard the lock click behind us. I stood there in the dark.

Well, it wasn't entirely dark. There was daylight dribbling down through a high round window. Anna went to a wall and turned on a light.

Bunk beds. A desk. A shelf with a few books. The floor was covered with a thin carpet. I reached into my pocket for a Kleenex and brought out something else.

"Anna?"

She ignored me.

"Anna Hansen, look," I said. I extended a finely braided cord. A small leather pouch dangled from the end. It was larger than a tea bag and smaller than a deck of cards. The cord seemed remarkably supple considering how stiff the other leather in the box had been. It was long enough to slip over my head.

"I forgot I had this. I jerked it out of the crate when you slammed down the lid," I said. "You almost crushed my fingers. You want it?"

I had crammed the little pouch into my pocket during our escape. Well, I guess we hadn't really escaped. Speaking of which, it was high time I got home. I lowered the pouch onto her hand. The leather was dark and soft. There was fine stitching at the sides. A faded reddish-brown triangle had been sewed onto the center. She turned it over. She removed a minute ivory peg that secured the flap. She tilted it over her palm, and a carved animal rolled out.

"A fox," she said.

"Or a collie," I suggested.

"A fox," she repeated. "Ivory."

It was not snow white but heavier in color, like cream. Its two alert ears pointed upward. The back legs were tucked under and the wide tail curved to one side. The carver had created black pinpoints for the eyes and a black button at the end of the snout. Tiny circles were on its back. Was it asleep or just waking up?

"May I?" I asked.

The moment she placed it in my hand, I felt the carving radiate a weight greater than its size. An unfamiliar boldness flowed out from it and into me like an incoming tide.

"Do you want help?" I couldn't believe I had asked that. I blinked rapidly and handed it back.

She looked at the carving. "You do whatever you want."

"Fine," I said. "Forget it. I'm expected home."

She slipped it into the pouch.

"What I'd really like to do," she said, "is return it. Whatever that means."

"It means," I said, "the obvious. You find somebody from that place and hand it over."

"Nobody has lived on the Islands of Four Mountains for at least two hundred years."

"Where'd they go?"

She looked me in the eyes and said, "Where most of my ancestors went."

5. Anna

Face it. I didn't really know what to say. The *Amirkaanchix̂* had found what I was after. A little bit late, as a matter of fact. But he had found it. And what had I really meant about returning it? More than just getting it to Jennifer and the cops? I hung the pouch around my neck and tucked it under my sweatshirt. I looked around the room that must have been prepared for two of the birders. A bookshelf held mostly birding manuals, along with one or two novels of the thick variety. I removed a tall, thin volume, bound in brown leather. Even the cover seemed heavy when I opened it and read the inscription—"To Rev. Father Shaiashnikoff, With Compliments of the Author, W. H. Dall, 1880."

I sat down.

"The title's as long as the book!" Booker said when he looked over my shoulder.

On the
Remains of Later Pre-Historic Man
Obtained from
Caves in the Catherina Archipelago, Alaska Territory,
and Especially from the
Caves of the Aleutian Islands
by
W. H. Dall
1878

I angled a page of brownish photographs toward him. "That's like the obsidian point you found in the box. And here's a seal."

"No fox," he said as I flipped to another set of photos.

"But this," and I touched a photo of a folded container at the top of the page, "is like the one you found. Only mine's a lot smaller."

"Yours?"

"Listen," I said, ignoring what he had asked. It *was* mine, or in any case it was a lot more mine than it was Hennig's. Anyway, I turned to the text. *"The most celebrated of these burial caves was situated of the island of Kaga'mil, one of the group known as the Islands of Four Mountains, or Four Craters."*

I turned the page.

"With regard to the age of these mummies—"

"Mummies!" he said. "Cool!"

I tilted a page toward him. A startled corpse gaped over one shoulder while its body balanced in a crouched position. I continued reading.

"With regard to the age of these mummies . . ." There was a really dense paragraph full of names and dates, and then this sentence: *"The earliest date therefore which we can assign to these remains would be 1756, making the oldest of them about one hundred and twenty years old."*

"Let me see the title page again," he said. "Wow!" He made a quick estimate. "They'd be about 250 years old now."

I ignored him—although I was impressed. *"On the island of Kagámil lived a distinguished toyon—"*

"A what?"

"A chief," I said and went on without explaining that this was a Russian word and not ours. *"—a rich man, by name Kat-háya-Koochák."*

"Bless you," he said, and I gave him a punch.

"He was a very small man, but very active and enterprising, and hence much respected, and even feared by the natives of the adjacent region. He had a son 13 or 14 years old, whom he fondly loved. He built him a little bidarka (or skin canoe) and painted it handsomely."

"Have you seen one of those?"

"In the museum. But I've done some kayaking, only mostly on the lake."

"When the bidarka was done the son begged earnestly to be allowed to try the boat on the sea. After much urging the father permitted him to go with the injunction not to go far from the shore."

"Look," he interrupted. "I think I know how we can get out of here."

He didn't even let me go on reading. He took a paperback out of his backpack.

"It's not a boat, but I've got this bookmark."

I started to ask if the mental facility knew he was missing. Suddenly, the door flew open.

"We have a problem," Hennig said as his bulk filled the doorway. "A little problem, more or less." He talked as though kidnapping was just a mild rash. "One that can be solved pretty easily."

"You, to be more precise," Mrs. Skagit pushed past him, "are the problem."

Now it sounded like an outbreak of scabies.

"You probably know more than you should," Hennig said. He went to the shelf of books and smothered each spine as he ran his thick fingers across the titles. "It might be good for you in the long run."

"You and the girlie here," Mrs. Skagit nodded at Booker. He glared out from under his curly canopy.

"I see you like history." He nodded at the old book I had jammed between Booker and me. "Too much history disappears. Especially out here. People forget what the past was like."

Like the bulldozer at the Old Priest's House, I thought.

"That's even more true of Aleuts," he said. "They were amazing artists."

I had to agree.

He kept on about how archaeologists just took stuff away, and if they wrote reports, nobody could read them. And how to them everything was just about the same to them: a chipped arrowhead or a carved sea otter. He wanted to get things into the hands of people who would appreciate them for the beautiful objects they were. I don't know how much the kid understood what he eventually offered. A partnership, of sorts. If I kept quiet, if I didn't make a fuss, from whatever they sold they'd share the profits with me.

"You'd be helping preserve your own history," he said.

"You could buy yourself a three-wheeler," Mrs. Skagit added.

"Buy yourself a nose job, lady," I said.

Hennig restrained Mrs. Skagit by touching her elbow. "You put the kibosh on my birding charter," he said to me. "So we're headed out to the Four Mountains. And you two are coming along."

"Hennig's going," Mrs. Skagit contradicted him. "I have business here."

Hennig looked a little too satisfied with himself. "How does it sound?" he asked. "It seems like a fair offer."

"Your family is good at keeping secrets, Sophie."

I glared at her.

"We're just asking you to keep a few more."

"I don't keep secrets," I said.

"Maybe not," Mrs. Skagit said, "But your gram has kept a few. There are things she wouldn't like getting out around town."

I wasn't about to dignify her pathetic attempt at blackmail with an answer.

"She's a respectable elder, Sophie. At least to those who matter, those who don't know her. She's on the school board and everything."

Mrs. Skagit pursed her lips like she was expecting a kiss. Repugnant.

Hennig could tell things were not going his way.

"Coming back depends on you," he said.

Mrs. Skagit was like a dog with a bone.

"It might be news to you, Sophie, but when your mom was pregnant with you, your gram gave her a horrible time."

"Liar," I said under my breath.

"Drunk or in the slammer. Mostly drunk."

"Fat-assed liar," I said. Louder now and looking at her.

"I was there. You ever ask your mom why she left? Why she won't have nothin' to do with your gram?"

"Lot of deep water out there," Hennig steered the conversation back to himself.

Of course I had never asked her. Until a short time ago I had never even seen her. I didn't know her. I don't want to know her.

"Accidents are happening out there all the time."

That less-than-subtle threat finally did it for Booker. He jolted off the bunk.

I grabbed the old book and whacked the captain across the forehead as Booker lunged for the door and threw it open.

And there was Torgey, right outside, holding a length of steel rebar in his hands.

We sat back down.

"Better tie 'em up a bit, Torgey." The captain rubbed his head. "Not too tight. They're just kids."

The mate took a length of soft rope out of his back pocket.

"We'll see what they have to say when we get to Kagamil."

Torgey pulled Booker up, twirled him around, and had him put his arms behind his back.

"Take the bookmark," Booker whispered. He glanced down at his shirt pocket. "Turn it upside down and put it back in and hold on to my arm."

Why not join him in the loony bin? I asked myself and reached out.

Mrs. Skagit's eyes bulged with suspicion, and the moment I took it, she snatched it away. Booker threw himself out of the rope and onto her like a certified maniac. Hennig swore. Mrs. Skagit jumped to the side as Booker pulled the bookmark from her hand, and Torgey grabbed him by the waist. I lifted the old book and started swinging. I accidentally walloped Booker's hand and the bookmark sailed into the air. Mrs. Skagit lunged after it, shoving him and Torgey aside. She collided into me, sending the old book flying—its pages flapping every which way. I caught the book the same time I caught the bookmark. Mrs. Skagit was quick and latched onto the other end of the narrow paper. Booker charged into her midriff as I tore it out of her fingers. I had both the book and the bookmark. The bookmark seared my palm as I shoved it between two pages.

And then three things happened simultaneously: Booker grabbed my arm and shouted, Mrs. Skagit screamed, and we vanished.

Maybe that was four things.

TWO
BLUEBERRIES AND
THE PAGAN RAVEN

6. Anna

Mrs. Skagit's scream echoed through my ears and disappeared in the dark room. My voice flickered like a candle in a draft.

"Where are we?"

My eyes adjusted to the dim light filtering through a porthole high on the wall. I looked at my wrists. They were sticking out from frayed cuffs embroidered with yellow flowers. My sweatshirt and jeans had become a brown cotton dress over which I had on a dark-blue sweater. There were more disgusting yellow flowers along the hem of the dress.

"Booker!" I felt like the floor was slipping out from under me. "What's happened?"

"We escaped," he said in a mousy whisper. "It's the bookmark."

"And where have my pockets gone?" I asked indignantly as I jammed a fist into what was little more than a decoration. Booker examined his jacket and pants. The lucky stiff had pockets everywhere. We were dressed like a couple of refugees from the History Channel.

"It's the bookmark," he repeated and pulled it from his shirt pocket. He handed it to me.

"I thought it was in the book."

"It has a habit of coming back to me," he said. "It's complicated." Then he grabbed it out of my hand.

"It's ripped! You tore the bottom off!"

"I didn't tear anything."

"You did! You and that maniac gorilla!"

"Don't blame me," I hurled back. "You're the one who tackled her." I gestured around the cabin. "Where are we? And what about this?" I shoved my arms covered in that ridiculous dress at him. That's when I saw the discoloration on my right palm. It didn't hurt, but it was like I'd been scorched by something.

He collapsed onto a nearby bunk. "I was told it could happen," he said. "I'm trying to remember what it's called."

"What what is called?"

"When you travel back in time."

I sprinted for the door.

I flung it open and saw an old-fashioned iron staircase at the end of the hall, I turned back inside. No light bulb hung from the ceiling. No carpet covered the floor. No bookshelf was on the wall. There was an absolute absence of engine noise.

He looked up from the bunk. "Do you have that book about the mummies?"

I shrugged, closed the door, and turned up my empty hands.

"Okay. Try this."

"What?"

He walked over, hesitantly took my hand, upended the book-mark, and slipped it back into his pocket.

I don't know what he expected. We just stood there. Holding hands. Yuck.

"It worked before," he insisted as I shook myself loose. He sat down and took it out again.

"What language is that?" I pointed at it.

"Russian," he said.

"I thought so. It looks like something from church."

Then he told me how he had found it, and how he had used it.

"But nothing like this ever happened to me before," he said.

"Your parents don't work for a cannery?"

"They write books," he said, "murder mysteries."

He said something about a trip to Bulgaria. He was a total nut case.

"Do you have anything in there?" I nodded at his backpack, hoping to get the conversation returned to something like normal.

"Nothing but a pocketknife, a compass, and a candy bar, I think." He put the bookmark between his teeth, rummaged around inside the pack, and took out the candy bar. He broke it in two. Instead of taking the half he held out, I gave myself a good slap on the chest. He jumped, but I wiggled a finger under the collar and pulled out the small pouch.

"This is still here," I said. I slipped it off and tilted the carved fox onto my palm. I took my half of the candy bar. He took the bookmark out of his mouth. So there we were. He held the torn bookmark and I held the carved fox. Ivory and paper. Totally weird.

I looked around again. Wooden crates and boxes were stacked against one wall. A couple of wooden barrels stood in the middle of the floor. There was a second bunk with wooden crates stacked on it.

"Anyway," he said, "I used the bookmark to get to Ireland, only it wasn't Ireland. It was here, on that other boat. And when you put it in that book of mummies, it got us here."

He gave me a startled look.

"What's the matter?" I asked.

"The bookmark is just a bookmark for most people."

"That should tell you a thing or two," I said.

He was about to object, but somebody knocked. It was faint, and it came from outside. I was off the bunk and through the door and climbing that old iron staircase to the deck before Booker followed. What I had thought was darkness was simply fog as thick as milk. It suffused a soft yellow glow around an open door.

We heard somebody ask, "My father wonders if you have finished with the book he loaned you and if he could have its use for a short time?"

"Absolutely, Vasilii," a deeper voice answered. "It's not the sort of volume I'm likely to read straight through."

I stuck out my arm when Booker tried to slip past.

"Tell your father I thank him. I may ask to borrow it again if he would be so kind. My copy is in San Francisco."

"Of course, Captain. Father sends his regards."

"And I send mine to him, Vasilii, and to your mother."

The light shifted around the door as somebody stepped out of the room. I flattened Booker against the wall with another swing of my arm.

"Have you given any thought to what we talked about?" It was the deeper voice again.

"I have, Captain," the figure in the doorway said. "It's a generous offer. I would enjoy the trip, but my parents are discussing it."

He turned from the door. He was about my age. We both saw what he held in his hand.

"It's the book," I whispered as he walked up the ramp to the wharf.

I led the way past the now closed door. Booker hesitated. The water below us was gray and cold, and the dock pushed in and out against the hull.

I extended a hand and pulled him up the gangplank.

We followed the boy with the book along a narrow boardwalk through the thick fog. We passed two single-storied, steep-roofed buildings. A third clearly held valuables because the door was padlocked and the whole windowless structure was sheathed in metal. Up ahead, a gray mass darkened before becoming two and a half stories of white clapboard crowned with a steep roof. It was like a ghost ship riding at its ghostly anchor. A few windows glowed with candles behind their curtains. The next building was single-storied with a wide overhanging porch. In front of it, a half-dozen cannons brooded around a tall flagpole. Something wasn't right. I pressed my face and cupped my hands to the wavy glass on the door. The shelves inside were stocked with cans and small boxes. Fur pelts hung from pegs along one wall. A woman lifted a samovar from a shelf that held two or three of those egg-shaped Russian containers used for heating water and making tea. I'd seen one in the museum. She turned, placed it on a counter, and glanced up. With a shot of recognition I shoved away and rushed into the fog.

It isn't possible, I said to myself. But I knew those piggy eyes. I knew that hatchet face.

The boardwalk ended, and we started down a well-packed trail. On my left, I heard the gentle push and pull as the sea scraped against a rocky beach. We passed three or four small houses on the right before I saw a large church at the top of a gentle rise. Through the fog I saw the outline of a familiar onion dome on the roof.

"Anna," Booker said, but I had taken root.

"Move it," he said and gave me a push. A wave of dense fog had drifted in. "We're liable to lose him."

I just stood there. Fog drained the color out of everything and left the world washed-out.

"It's like we're in an old photograph. A really old photo."

"He's gone," Booker said.

"We're right where we started."

"What's the matter with you?" He actually kicked a few rocks on the path.

As if to show him, the fog did what fog sometimes does. It slowly evaporated into the air. We were on a wide trail above a familiar beach. I saw the shrouded silhouette of a familiar mountain straight ahead. I looked back at the cannons clustered around the flag pole. The limp flag was definitely an American flag.

"He's not likely to leave the island," I said.

"What island?"

"Here," I said. "Right where we started from." Then I took in a deep breath and said, "Okay." Usually when I say that, something follows. Like whatever comes next. The next thing to do. Or not do. Only this time, it didn't.

"Okay," I repeated. "Vasilii is a pretty common name."

I saw a house past the church and just beyond that there was a row of small red cottages and then three or four more wooden houses in the distance. I started for the first red cottage.

"You mean," Booker asked as he caught up, "you want to knock on every door?"

7. Anna

The first cottage was a small place, and after I had rapped loud enough and nobody had answered, I stepped away from the door. Booker pulled my sleeve and pointed toward the larger house that sat back a bit from the church. A man had just stepped out. We hurried toward him. He turned to an older man dressed in simple black clerical robes and standing in the doorway.

"Thank you, Reverend. It has been a pleasure as always."

I surprised myself by making the sign of the cross. I mean, I did that in church and older Unangax̂ sometimes did it when they came to visit Gram and saw the icons in the corner.

"Come again," said the priest.

"You can be assured that I will," the younger man said. He smiled at us. "You have guests. Probably here to see the young deacon."

The priest nodded and gestured for us to come inside.

"Please," he said.

We entered a small sitting room as the priest went to a doorway and raised his voice, "Vasilii, *haqada!* You have visitors."

He picked up a small leather valise. "He should be here in a minute. I'll leave you, if you don't mind."

And he stepped outside, closing the door behind him.

"That was easy," Booker said.

We had the beautiful room to ourselves. My eyes were taken by a graceful couch, upholstered in blue silk and placed at the edge of a dark blue carpet. Booker walked over to a bookcase stocked with books. Books also competed for space on a corner table that held a vase filled with familiar deep-blue violets. On the wall above the couch was a framed colored engraving of the peaks of Yosemite.

"Abraham Lincoln gave Yosemite to the people of California," he said, turning away from the table. "Yellowstone was the first national park, but Yosemite paved the way."

"You know the oddest things," I said. "So, who's this?"

I pointed to an ornately framed image of a thin man sporting a mustache that flowed across his cheeks into robust sideburns. His military uniform was festooned with medals and ribbons.

"It's the czar," said a voice behind us. "Alexander II. Who are you?"

I turned around and met the eyes of the kid we'd seen on the boat. I realized he was older than me, perhaps sixteen or seventeen, but he was not much taller. He smiled and gestured at two chairs as he seated himself on the couch. And waited.

Booker looked at me.

"We saw you with a book," I jumped right in, "coming off a ship at the dock."

"At the dock," Booker repeated.

"It belongs to my father," the boy said. "He has more books than anyone, and he's always looking for more. As you can see." He nodded at the table. He didn't seem to be in any hurry to show us the one we wanted.

"Am I supposed to know you?" he asked.

We introduced ourselves.

"I'm Vasilii," he said, "Vasilii Shaiashnikoff. Call me Bill."

"Bill," Booker said.

"Vasilii is Russian for William," I explained to Booker who asked, "You're a Russian?"

Vasilii smiled. "I'm Aleut," he said. He looked it. We have tons of Shaiashnikoffs in town. He looked like any of them and like none of them. I mean, his dark hair was just a little curly and his dark eyes—I'm getting carried away. His dark eyes weren't any darker than mine. He was just a normal guy.

"I know a Hansen," he said. "Maybe you're related."

"My gram's family came from Makushin Village," I said.

Booker gave me a look.

"Booker here is from King Cove," I said, trying to remember if King Cove even existed back whenever. Exactly what year was it? "Where all those white folks are moving to," I continued. "He was on the ship with me."

"I was on the ship." The kid was turning into a parrot.

Vasilii walked to the table and brought back a book. "This is it. Are you interested in antiquities?"

Booker walked over. I could tell he was thinking about slipping his bookmark in and bringing the visit to an abrupt end. I shook my head. He returned to his seat.

"I found something," I said, keeping the book firmly closed, "that I think is important."

I poured the small fox onto my palm. Vasilii knelt down to examine it.

When he took it in his hand, I expected him to feel what Booker and I had felt when we first touched it. Maybe he did, but all he said was, "It's certainly beautifully made." He turned it from side to side. "And heavy for its size! Those old-time people had amazing skill. Where did you get it?"

I couldn't very well say that I'd looted it from a twenty-first-century pirate.

"It's been in her family for a long time." Booker finally said something original.

"And you think it might be in there?" He handed back the fox and pointed at the book. "It's by William Healy Dall, by the way. I call him Vasilii Healy, and he calls me 'deacon.'"

"Are you a deacon?" I asked opening it up.

"It's only a nickname. Maybe later," he said. "Dall was just here. You'll notice that he inscribed it to my father."

We had seen the inscription on Hennig's boat.

I thumbed through the first pages. "We were reading this story when we, ah . . ."

Booker cut in, "When we got interrupted."

My fingers froze when I saw a small torn fragment of Booker's weird bookmark wedged between the next two pages. I quickly turned the page.

"We got as far as the boy and his boat."

Had Vasilii seen the slip of paper? He wouldn't have known what it was, where it had come from, what it had done.

I started reading aloud where I had left off. *"The boy saw on the sea a diving bird (diver), followed it, and shot at it with his arrow. The diver retreated further and further from the shore. The father saw him (the boy) getting farther away, and shouted to him."*

"That's a really sad story," interrupted Vasilii. "Old Man Rostokovich told my father that story. He's told my father a lot of those old-time stories. I sometimes think this one must be about his own family."

"His own family?" Booker echoed again. What was going on with him?

"Well, you know," Vasilii said. "Unlucky. They're all unlucky, those Rostokoviches. They get lost. They are not good hunters. They have accidents. Sometimes, they have even caught on fire for no reason whatsoever. And in that story, if you don't mind me giving away the ending . . ." —and both of us nodded *okay*— ". . . the boy's *baidarka* overturned and he drowned. Then his sister fell during the funeral and died, and consequently, her unborn baby died."

"Jeez," I interjected.

"*Baidarka?*" Booker asked.

"Kayak," I said.

"*Iqyax̂*," added Vasilii.

"Finally, the chief himself died of a broken heart," he concluded. "My father got that story for Captain Hennig when he came back from Kagamil—"

"Captain Hennig?" Booker and I interrupted him at the same moment.

"—on the *Eider*," Vasilii continued. "He brought back the mummies Dall has written about in here."

Then I started to understand. "His grandfather," I said to Booker, "or his great-grandfather. The Hennigs have been in the islands for a long time."

Vasilii looked puzzled. "Whose grandfather?" he asked.

Instead of answering, I asked, "Have you been to the Islands of Four Mountains?"

"No, but I'd like to," he answered. "Tough water out there. There are just one or two good anchorages, but in a *baidarka* it wouldn't be that dangerous. It took Hennig a dozen tries before he got his mummies. He said there were all kinds of old-time stuff in the burial caves."

Ivory and Paper

"Didn't anybody object?" I asked.

"To what? Taking the mummies? Not that I know of." Vasilii continued, "Anyway, those people weren't Christians, so what does it matter?"

I was about to tell him why it mattered when he added, "He's offered to take me out west on his next trip, but I'm not sure I want to because, like I said, those long-ago people weren't Christians, and some people, well, they treat those mummies like they still have power over us."

Now Booker seemed really interested.

"Do you believe that?"

"I shouldn't," he said. "Not if I'm going to be a priest."

"Are you?" I asked.

"It's what my father wants," he said, "but who knows?"

He stood up. "Old Man Rostokovich might be able to tell you about that carving."

"He's still around?" I asked. I imagined he must have been really ancient to know all that stuff.

"He's very much around," Vasilii said. "Peter's pretty amazing. How about tomorrow morning," he said. I handed him the book as an answer. I knew Booker wanted me to keep it, but learning about the fox seemed more important than us getting back immediately. The moment I gave him the book, I remembered the torn end of the bookmark was still inside. *Oh, well*, I thought, *it's safe there. I can get it if we need it.*

"Anything else?" Vasilii asked.

"It turns out we're orphans," Booker said.

Total schizo.

"Not exactly orphans," he stumbled along. "We're waiting."

"For your parents to die?" Vasilii seemed interested.

"I mean, we got here ahead of them. Of our parents."

Now I knew where he was headed.

"He means that we're stranded. Until they arrive. Their ship was expected to get here before ours."

"So why did you travel on different ships?"

62

This was getting ridiculous. I wondered if Vasilii believed any of it. "I was staying with my aunt."

"In San Francisco," Booker added. He lied like an expert.

"So, anyway," I continued, but Booker cut in with, "We need a place to stay."

And that's how Vasilii came to introduce us to Ivan Zhen. He was a young Asian—I guessed Chinese—who worked for the company that owned the large white building that turned out to be the office and hotel of the Alaska Commercial Company. It was clear that Vasilii and Ivan were good friends.

"You Aleut?" he asked after Vasilii had made the introductions and explained that we needed a place for a night or two.

"*Aang! Aang!*" I answered.

"Orthodox," he said proudly and touched his forehead, chest, and shoulders from right to left. His eyes twinkled. "I am Huang Zhen. My baptized name is Ivan."

He was dressed in Western clothing except for a dark-blue skullcap with a red circle at the crown.

"I'll see you tomorrow morning," Vasilii said. "Thanks, Ivan."

We were standing just inside the door. A hall extended into the back of the building where laughter and the clatter of silverware and dishes reminded me I was hungry. A carpeted staircase rose on the right.

"This way," Ivan said and took hold of the graceful handrail.

We followed him up to the second floor landing where there were doors on each side of a wide hall and a window looking out at the end. He turned a corner, opened a door behind the stairwell, and started up a flight of uncarpeted stairs. These were steeper and made a faint rocking squeak as we climbed.

Ivan tapped on the nearest door and said, "Where I stay."

He skipped the next door and opened the third. Inside there were two beds, separated from each other by an assortment of crates and boxes.

"This room is used for storage," he said. "But I think it will do."

I went to the window that looked down and out toward the flagpole surrounded by cannons.

"This is perfect, Ivan," I said. "Are you sure people won't mind?" I remembered the woman in the store. Maybe I hadn't seen her at all.

"The general manager is visiting the villages," he said, "to collect furs and to check their books. If anybody asks, just tell them Mr. Neumann arranged for you to stay."

"Thanks," I said.

"Which he would have if he had been here," he added. "He is a very nice man. If you need anything, you ask me."

"What day is it?"

"Saturday," he said. "August 15."

"Eighteen—?" I started.

"Eighty. Of course. All year!"

"Unreal," I muttered and sank onto one of the beds. I half expected the room to fold up on itself like a fan and shoot us into some other weird time and place. Vasilii left and before Booker and I had explored the room, he returned with a tray with two bowls of delicious stew and several thick slices of bread.

We found a couple of patched down comforters, and, before long, wondering if the world would float back to normal by morning, I fell asleep.

8. Anna

I knew it was morning, but I kept my eyes shut, hoping for any sounds that might suggest I was back home. I sniffed the air for any familiar scents. I inched my fingers to the edge of the mattress. Finally, I opened my eyes to a metal-embossed ceiling straight out of an old western.

Rats.

I threw off the comforter and sat on the side of the bed. I had to see if I really was where I thought I was. I got up, straightened the wrinkles in the cotton dress as best I could, and went out the door. I closed it quietly so as not to wake Booker, and tiptoed down the hall. The heavy front door opened easily, and there I was: looking out on the same beach, the same hills. I was home. But everything had changed. The road that followed the beach had shrunk into a trail. The scarf of grass above the beach was thicker than I'd ever seen it. I pushed my way through and found a wide rock. I just sat there, totally confused and more than a little curious. I picked up a small stone and half expected it to dissolve in my hand.

Further down the beach, a woman was poking the water with a stick. Every now and then she bent over, lifted something from the sea, and dropped it into a basket that hung from her shoulder. As she worked her way closer, I saw she was a girl not much older than myself. I sat real still, not wanting to interrupt, but also not wanting her to walk away. Her dress was worn and mended and had obviously once belonged to a larger woman. She was barefooted and stepped from stones to sand and back again with practiced balance.

When she got closer, I said, "*Aang, aang.*" Good morning, good morning. This was a very handy word. How it was pronounced changed the meaning from *hello* to *yes* to *absolutely!* But it also could mean, *How are you doing? I hope things are good with you.*

She looked up. I dropped the stone and touched the wide rock. She sat down beside me. For a few minutes all we did was watch the sea. I asked if I could hold her basket.

"It's not much," she said as she handed it over. "Maybe tomorrow." Inside were some half-dozen chitons, their black leathery backs curled down. The underneath foot of the *bidarki* was sliced and eaten raw. My science teacher had said chitons were a good source for calcium and vitamin A. I should tell Booker that. If he's still around when I get back. But I was interested in the container itself. I knew we had made workbaskets from woven grass, but these had long been abandoned for tin and plastic. This was the real thing: a grass fish basket. I turned it in my hands. Woven from the blades of strong wild rye or beach grass—the very stuff that was all around me—it was golden brown. The straight open weave allowed any water to drop away. The rim was topped with a tightly braided cord that rode the circumference on braided posts about a half-inch tall.

Had Gram actually woven baskets? Why had she stopped? What else had she done? Was she really keeping secrets, like Mrs. Skagit had said? What secrets?

I handed it back, smiled, and the girl got up. "See you," she said and returned to the water's edge and her search for food.

I realized I would never be what she was. More than a century of deep changes had made me something else. I picked up another smooth stone. People talked about subsistence and practiced living off the sea because there was nothing tastier than real Unangax̂ food. But most of the food we ate came from the store. Nobody, not even the oldest woman at home, could weave a basket like that one.

Then I saw a circle of women and girls holding hands—me, Gram, this girl, some others, any others—would any one of us see anything of ourselves in the others? I looked at her and she looked at Gram and both of them looked back at me and at each other. And then before I could stop it, that woman from Gram's kitchen stepped into the circle and stared across at me.

Your dad and me, we have an understanding.

I looked away.

Straight into the puckering mug of Mrs. Skagit. *Secrets. Lots of secrets.*

I hurled the stone at the water.

Think about something positive, I told myself, and pictured her fury in the *King Eider* just before we vanished.

Ataqan, aalax, qaankun. I tried counting on my fingers. *Siching, chaang.*

All the Unangax̂ kids I know speak English. Very few can say much of anything in Aleut, *Unangam tunuu.* Over a hundred years of English clear-cutting every language within sight or hearing in schools and businesses, kids getting their mouths washed out with soap if they used our language, parents and grandparents "doing us a favor" by trying to use only English. But it wasn't very good English. Gram had struggled to make sense of the world with strange words. With her own language marginalized all around her and her English substandard, she had been a linguistic pauper and this poverty had spread to every corner of her life.

English had even embedded itself into my fingers. I could type and text without thinking. I felt like a fraud. I was just another slightly brown-skinned *Amirkaanchix̂*.

Gloria Nguyen still spoke Vietnamese to her parents.

Damned wind. I wiped my eyes. I needed to get back to Booker before he did something stupid.

It would do me more good if I learned Filipino or Yup'ik or Vietnamese. The most the native corporation did was to decorate a column or two in their annual reports with *Unangam tunuu*. Nothing substantial. Nothing that made learning the language a real benefit over those who didn't bother. They should pay me to learn Aleut. A buck for every two words. Five bucks a sentence.

I looked at my hands. They were incredibly dirty, grimy and discolored with blueberries. That dark irregular patch I had noticed on my right palm still lingered there. It disappeared a little when I rubbed it with my thumb. I hadn't looked in a mirror. My face was probably a mess.

When I stepped inside the hotel, the smell of bacon drew me down the hall. What did Ivan say? *"Tell them a Mr. Neumann had let us stay?"*

I walked into a room where two men were sitting at a long table reading newspapers and drinking coffee. One of them looked up and nodded as I went to a sideboard where I poured two cups of tea. I found a serving tray, added two soft rolls on a plate, and carried it all upstairs.

Booker was on his bed looking at that bookmark. I almost felt sorry for the kid.

"How'd you sleep?"

"Good," he said. "Until the storm."

I tried not to smile. I'd heard the wind, but it wasn't much more than a healthy breeze. I gave him the tea and a roll. He took both, but he looked at the tea like it was vinegar.

"Try it," I said.

"You should have let me try the bookmark with that old book about mummies."

"From what you told me," I said, "it's not a revolving door."

He mumbled something with his mouth full, swallowed, and started over. "What do you mean?"

"If we left, how would we get back? I think the reason we ended up here has to do with this as much as with your bookmark."

I picked up the leather pouch from the nightstand, removed the carving and handed it to him. I could tell he was again surprised at how heavy it felt.

"I mean, it didn't disappear," I went on. "It stayed with me. Besides, I was going to turn it over to the cops before your crazy bookmark did a time flip. Now, well, I think we need to do more. If we can find out what it really is, we'll know what to do with it."

What was all that *we* stuff? This was my business, not his.

"I said I would help, Anna," Booker said. "So count me in."

He handed the fox back, jerked a little, and looked like he'd changed his mind.

"After you tell me where you got this roll."

I led the way. The men were gone and the long table had been cleared. We helped ourselves to scrambled eggs and bacon from covered serving dishes and sat down just as Ivan came in with a pot of tea.

"Good," he said. "You found breakfast."

Voices in the hall sent him slipping from the room just before a tall woman strode in. Our eyes met. Different eyes. She wasn't Mrs. Skagit or Mrs. Skagit's ghost or ancestor or whatever. She was somebody else. She was followed by a man who deferred to her with practiced grace. A small girl in a frilly white dress stayed at the door, stuck out her tongue, and ducked down the hall.

"Of course, Mrs. Otis," he said with a slight Russian accent. "They do their best against insurmountable difficulties. Remember that the United States has been here for only about a dozen years."

"Nonsense!" she declared like a descending meat cleaver. "It is a matter of old-fashioned gumption. Mr. Gray, you are educated. You must see that."

Her maroon dress rose to a collar buttoned so tightly around her neck that I marveled she could squawk out a syllable. She seated herself at the opposite end of the table without so much as a nod. That was fine with me.

"Is there tea?" she asked. "But of course there is. This is, after all, the outskirts of Russia. The tea is superb. Where is that boy? A cup, please, Mr. Gray, if you would be so kind. And perhaps one of those rolls. Not croissants, but they will do."

She unfolded a white cloth napkin and spread it on her lap. "Despite the tea, Mr. Gray, this is a dismal country."

He nodded slightly and began pouring.

"You need to return to civilization," she said as she added a spoonful of sugar to the tea he brought her. "You have lived too long among the savages."

My jolt must have been pretty high on the Richter scale because Booker's tea sloshed over the rim. I hadn't noticed that he'd poured himself a cup.

"Even the birds in California are happier than they are here," she tinkled the teaspoon against the rim of her cup and charged on. "At home they have a sweeter song. And who could blame them? Am I not correct, Julianna?"

She glanced beside her, saw no one, and bolted upright, sending her chair toppling over.

"Julianna!" she shouted and disappeared through the door.

I saw the slightest smile lift his face as Mr. Gray carried a plate with a roll to the woman's place. He straightened the fallen chair and only then walked to the door where a small girl, her right hand held straight above her head, was being propelled into the room. "My dear, you must never," The woman was out of breath, "never, disappear like that! Sit. Mr. Gray will bring you some milk." She straightened the ruffles of her daughter's dress.

"Here you are, Julie," Mr. Gray said, adding with a twinkle, "fresh from Daisy." Then he turned to Booker and me. "Good morning," he said. "I am Nicholas Gray, the company bookkeeper."

"How do you do, Mr. Gray," I said. I could tell Booker was a bit suspicious at my manners. "I'm Anna Hansen. We, . . . I mean, Mr. Neumann—"

But before I could continue, the woman purred, "Ah," without introducing herself. "Your father must be Scandinavian. They are a very resourceful people."

"Both my parents are Unangax̂."

"Aleut," explained Mr. Gray.

She looked at him over the rim of her teacup and then at me. "I suppose it is possible."

"And this," I raised my voice a bit, "is the orphan Booker Johnskii."

Booker choked.

"His father was a Russian sailor."

The woman's eyes did a quick dissection of the kid as she rotated her cup on its saucer.

"He doesn't talk much," I continued. "Spent most of his life in a cave. Living on rats." His hair looked like rats could have had a nest somewhere in there.

"My dear!" Her teacup rattled as she lifted it from the saucer.

Her daughter, however, carried her glass of milk and took the seat next to mine. The woman addressed Mr. Gray.

"The Otises are nothing," she said, "if not egalitarian."

"Of course," Mr. Gray replied and winked slightly at me. I spread a thick coat of blueberry jam on a piece of toast. "Mrs. Otis and her daughter are en route to the Islands where her husband is the superintendent of the sealing operations."

"Islands?" Booker asked. "I thought we were in the islands!"

I shook my head at what diet had done to brains and continued slathering the toast with jam. "They're talking about the Pribilof Islands, B-Johnskii, about two hundred miles north of here."

"We shall be almost beneath the North Pole," exclaimed Mrs. Otis with triumph.

"A thousand miles beneath," I muttered under my breath. I cut the toast in half and left it on the plate. "I think we should be going," I said. "Nice meeting you."

I prodded Booker in the arm and stood up. He slipped a couple of rolls and two apples into his backpack as we passed the serving counter. Just outside the door, I pulled him to the side and put a finger over my lips.

"They seem like nice children," Mr. Gray was saying. "She mentioned Mr. Neumann. I wonder what they're doing here?"

"Nice, but, alas, my dear Mr. Gray," Mrs. Otis explained, "half-breeds, you know. Half-breeds." And then, as though on my cue, she screeched again.

"Julianna! Your dress!"

I grabbed Booker and made for the outside door. "I figured her brat would want more to eat," I said. "Good thing I loaded the toast with jam!"

We took the path along the front beach, the path that would eventually become a road. I stared at the church and tried to place it in the old photographs I had seen. Some time at the end of the nineteenth century, this church had been replaced with the one we had now. The colors surprised me. The sides were light yellow and the onion dome of the cupola was blue. It was topped with a white cross. And there, perched on the cross, was an eagle. One thing that hadn't changed.

"Tiĝlax̂," I said as the great bird shifted its massive shoulders and lifted into the air. I was surprised at how many Unangax̂ words I was remembering.

"This must be a healthy place," Booker said and pointed at the churchyard.

"Why's that?"

"Not many graves." He nodded at the few crosses.

"Only priests, deacons, and bigwigs get buried there," I said. "The rest of us—" and I pointed toward a slight rise at the far end of the bay. "We should go have a look. I'd like to see who's arrived."

I stared at the mountain rising above the cemetery. "I wonder what they call it?"

"Call what, Anna?"

"Mount Newhall."

"Well, they probably call it Mount Newhall."

"The Newhalls won't be arriving here for about twenty years," I said and waved at Vasilii who was walking toward us.

Creepy, I thought when a woman opened the rough door and stared out with a clouded and frozen eye. Then she shifted the dark layered clothing that had swallowed her face, and with her good eye recognized the priest's son.

"Marva," Vasilii said as he handed her a package, "Mother sends you this bread."

She stepped aside for us to enter.

I was embarrassed at how quickly unkindness had elbowed itself to the front of my thinking.

The three of us had wound through the village, past several homes that looked like elevated caves or large grassy mounds lashed with rope. I knew from photographs that they were *barabaras*, our original homes. I was anxious to go inside one. Odd bits of wood and tin protruded at random places. They had deep-set windows and metal smokestacks and only a few were larger than cabins. We had arrived at a particularly desolate one, and Vasilii had stepped down into the narrow recess that framed the door. He hadn't knocked but had cracked it slightly and called out, "Peter! You home, Old Man?"

But it was Marva who opened the door and nodded for us to come inside.

Booker and I followed into a space that was little more than a wide closet. Uneven planks formed the rough floor. I smiled at the woman who reacted with a hesitant nod, and then I concentrated on breathing. The air was studded with odors that I thought it best not to try identifying. A cold diminutive iron stove crowded one side of the space that was both kitchen and storeroom. Two open wooden crates held dishes and pots. At Marva's nod, Vasilii opened a second door.

"He's resting," she said. "He needs to get up."

This room was even darker, and the air was even denser. My eyes gradually adjusted, nudged by dim light from a window with six panes of clouded wavy glass. I couldn't believe I was actually inside a *barabara*. A small table cowered below the window, ashamed to show its chipped and scarred face. The walls and ceiling were lined with irregular boards from which most of the whitewash had worn off, revealing the raised grain. In one corner, near the ceiling, a triangular shelf held an unframed solitary image of a saint. Vasilii crossed himself in its direction as he stepped forward. I followed his example. Booker gave a courteous nod. Better than nothing, I guess.

The plank flooring in this room had been laid with greater care so as to create a smoother surface. As Vasilii approached a narrow bed built into the wall, congested breathing erupted into broken snoring. And then the room drifted back into silence. Marva wedged herself between Booker and me, walked to the bed, and slammed her hand down on the wooden frame.

"Old Man! Wake up! You've got company."

She left the room as the snoring catapulted into choking snorts and a pile of bedding gathered itself upright. A thin gray blanket fell away, and there was Peter Rostokovich, rubbing his eyes and coughing.

"Agh! Who's there now?"

"Vasilii, Old Man. It's Vasilii. I brought people to see you." Then he asked, somewhat after the fact it seemed to me, "Can we come in?"

"Make yourselves at home," Peter replied as he groped the edge of the bed and swung his legs over the wooden platform. Humpty Dumpty came to mind as the old man rocked back and forth. I braced myself to leap out of the way if he started to topple toward the floor. But Peter Rostokovich slowed his rocking and sat still. I could see his chest vibrating as he took a series of shallow breaths. He must have stored air inside his lungs because in a moment he burst out with, "CHAI! MOTHER, CHAI!"

But Marva was already coming back through the door with two metal cups overflowing with steam under which was presumably a brew of tea. *How had she heated the water?* I wondered, recalling the cold stove and the cold room we had walked through. She placed them on the table and went out. She returned with two more cups of tea, this time in heavy, chipped white mugs. Booker found a wooden bench against the wall. I think he was trying to disappear. He did his best to ignore the scalding liquid she placed beside him.

"This girl," and Vasilii paused to allow Peter to focus his eyes, "she has something to show you."

I withdrew the small leather pouch, poured the fox onto my palm, and closed my fingers over it. I wondered if Peter could see even my hand through eyes that were little more than crusted slits. I stepped forward, extended my arm, and opened my fingers.

"*Guuspudax̂!*" the old man cried as he made the sign of the cross and scooted back, drawing his covers around him. "Lord!"

"You recognize it?" Vasilii asked.

"It's from those long-ago people," he said, inching forward. His eyes widened as he extended his hands toward the carving. He hesitated before forming a broken dome above it. "Four Mountains. Before my time even. They could turn themselves into foxes, those people. It's strong, that thing," and he separated his hands. "Where'd you get it?"

"Ah," and I was glad I remembered the story Booker had made up. "It's from my family."

"Four Mountain family?" The old man eyed me suspiciously.

"No," I said, retreating from the lie. "I don't know where they got it."

"I am Four Mountain people," he said and tapped his chest with the fingers of his right hand. And then he asked as though the question followed logically from everything that had been said, "When you gonna take it back?"

"Back?"

"That boy needs it," the old man said. "My sister can tell you. She knows all about that thing. It has lucky powers."

"Who is your sister?" asked Vasilii.

"She's Fevronia. At Nikolski. Everybody knows that woman, they do," he said. "I think she was the last one who knew how."

74

"Knew how what?" I asked.

"I told you," he said as he lay back down. "Those people could turn themselves into foxes." He covered himself with the ragged blanket. I saw him keep one unobstructed eye on me as I slipped the ivory fox into its pouch, hung it back around my neck, and tucked it out of sight. The fingers of his right hand opened and closed as though they were groping for something, until he stilled them at the edge of his bed. Vasilii and I moved to the table where we sat on the two chairs. We looked at each other in the dim light.

How much did Peter Rostokovich suspect? I wondered and stared at the bundle on the bed.

"Your tea will get cold, Old Man," Vasilii said gently. "She's put it away."

Marva returned with a plate on which there were four generous slices of the bread she had been given. She placed this on the table and took a jar of crushed berries or jam from somewhere out of the folds of her clothing. A spoon appeared next. She studied it, wiped it on her dress, and set it beside the jar. As she turned to leave, she delivered a terrific wallop to her husband's backside.

"UP!" she shouted. "Where's your manners?"

Peter growled, but knew better than to object. Once he was upright again, Marva left the room. Vasilii handed him a cup of tea and a slice of bread. He studied me. He ignored Booker entirely.

"How you treat it is how you will be," he said.

Looking at Vasilii, he continued, "The people of the Four Mountains were starving because they had no good-luck charms. They came here, to *Ounalashka*, in three skin boats. They could turn themselves into foxes, those people, and they stole the charms from the chief and his second chief."

"That made things better for them," Vasilii said. He smiled when he saw Booker enjoying both tea and bread.

"Those Unalaska people, long time ago, they could turn themselves into eagles, and they got those Four Mountain people when they were sleeping." Peter paused and nodded at the jar of jam. I handed him a spoonful that he spread over what remained of his bread. "They cut the skins off the *baidarkas* of the Four Mountain people, their skin boats, you know, and broke the frames and took back the charms. That's what they did. Those old-time people said that."

"Do you believe it, Old Man?" I was surprised Vasilii would be so blunt. "I mean, turning into eagles and changing into animals is a little bit strange."

Peter shrugged. "Before they were Christians," he said and looked at me, "those old-time people could do a lot of things." A smile untangled itself from his wrinkled features. "A lot of things." His eyes ebbed back into silence. "Not anymore."

"The Russians brought Christianity here," Vasilii said, looking over at Booker, "maybe a hundred years ago. All the Aleuts became Christians except a few Outside men. That's when we got Russian names. My father is the first Unangax̂ priest from this area. His teacher from Atka village out west was the very first. That's partly why he wants me to become a priest."

"But the people on those islands—" I started to ask.

"Gone," Vasilii replied.

Peter had not taken his eyes off me.

"You talk to my sister," he repeated. "She can tell you how to do it, where to find that boy." He nodded toward my chest and tapped his own. "She knows all about that stuff."

9. Anna

The old man had been petrified of the carved fox. *Well,* I thought, *he had seemed totally unhinged if the truth were told.* He had said, "That boy needs it," as though the boy was still alive. But hadn't Vasilii told us that the story said he had drowned? The carved fox had come from a burial cave. You don't bury people unless they're dead.

When the old man mentioned turning into foxes and eagles, Vasilii had started fidgeting. I wanted to ask him why he'd been so nervous, but he was anxious to leave. On the way back to his house, he invited us to go blueberry picking with him and his mother that afternoon.

"I could use the help," he said. "Mother will probably just read and boss me around if it's just she and I!"

"Her and me," Booker said in a voice soft enough that Vasilii didn't hear and soft enough that I didn't have to slug him. What a creep.

Vasilii told us where they were going after berries. It wasn't far, and Booker and I could hike there. We returned to our room and gulped down the rolls and apples he had brilliantly taken at breakfast, and then we headed to the creek.

Scarred and muscled salmon whipped themselves up the shallow stream as ravens and seagulls dove at them, croaking and squeaking in rapture. A photographer had positioned a very old-fashioned wooden camera on a tripod and aimed it toward the church.

"Hold still, Christopher!" he shouted at a man who stood next to a deep-throated skiff and was throwing his broad-brimmed hat into the air and catching it. "You'll be nothing but a damned blur."

"That's Pyramid," I said, pointing to a high triangular peak in the distance.

"Reminds me of Ireland," he said.

"You've been to Ireland?"

"No."

"That low hill," I gestured immediately across the creek, "is another place you've never been. Haystack."

"Big haystack," he said.

"It's covered with roads and houses now," I said.

"I like it this way," he said. I had to agree.

There were things that hadn't changed: the wild geraniums and lupine, the fireweed, and the only things that passed for trees, the shrubby low-growing willows. The stunted trunks of old ones were twisted after decades of wrestling the wind.

A little further up the creek, Vasilii was helping a woman I took to be his mother into a skiff. She stepped with familiar ease and seated herself at the bow where she adjusted her black-laced bonnet and arranged a blanket across her lap. He saw us and waved.

We went over and I untied their skiff. Mrs. Shaiashnikoff was about to say something when the man who was being photographed bounded up. Vasilii slipped in past his mother and seated himself at the oars. The man directed the boat into the current, and Vasilii rowed his mother and himself into the center of the creek.

"*Spasibo*, Mr. Hansen," Mrs. Shaiashnikoff called back and raised a gloved hand in greeting.

I turned to the man, but he had already sprinted up the bank.

"Chris," he shouted down, and then he was gone.

"That guy," I said as Booker and I started toward a shallow part of the creek, "I think he's one of my relatives."

"Him?"

"One of my dad's grandfathers, or he could be."

Booker followed me from rock to rock across a shallow stretch of water. I led the way through a low pass on the left side of Haystack, wading into the lush vegetation that swelled across the gentle slopes. After a mild climb, we looked over a deep inlet surrounded by peaked mountains.

"This is Captains Bay," I explained. "There's a road now that runs all along this side out to a couple of processing plants and several fish camps. It's amazing to see it so empty and untouched."

"How do you get used to no trees?" Booker asked. "At home, we're surrounded by beech, sugar maples, pine—"

I interrupted before he turned into a forest ranger. "Can't miss what you never had."

I knew that wasn't true. I missed all sorts of things I had never had.

"Where'd you come up with making us orphans?"

"It worked, didn't it," he said. Jeez, he was getting touchy.

"For now," I said.

Blueberry bushes rose to our waists. Blue-green leaves and reddish-brown stems and berries the size and weight of marbles. I saw Booker sample one and then another and finally he just stood there picking berries.

"Good?" I asked. "Let's keep going."

"Amazing," he said as he pulled off a closely clustered handful.

"There's a bridge now, about over there." I pointed toward a narrow stretch of water. "It goes across to Dutch. This is so totally unbelievable."

"Dutch?"

"That island," and I nodded to my right. "Amaknak Island. There's a deep harbor on it called Dutch Harbor, so the whole of Amaknak"—I drew a circle in the air that encompassed a good part of what we could see—"is sometimes called Dutch."

Booker reached for a heavy stalk to pull himself up.

"Watch it!"

He stopped in mid-reach.

"It's *putchki*. You'll get a good welt on your hands from the juice."

"This place is more dangerous than it looks," he said. "Anything else I should know?"

"Keep an eye out for bears," I said, and for the next half hour I could tell that he did little else. He followed me down to the shore. When I came to where the bank hung over the water, I used long green stalks of grass to swing across. There were no waves, no incoming or outgoing tide, just a gentle lapping and a slow pulse that suggested the great heart of the sea was elsewhere. I saw Vasilii wave toward a narrow stream rippling into the bay as he directed the skiff toward shore. I had no sooner helped secure it than his mother stepped out and extended her hand.

"Mr. Hansen didn't give me time to greet you properly," she said. "He's always in such a rush."

Vasilii introduced us, and then he gave Booker three metal berry buckets while he hefted a lunch basket and led the way up a narrow trail until we had a view of the bay. Here, on a plush carpet of moss berries, like soft dry miniature pine boughs with perfectly round blackberries, Vasilii spread out a blanket. His mother lifted her skirt slightly and seated herself. She took a small volume out of her pocket. It was titled in Cyrillic letters. She caught Booker's glance and asked, "Do you know the poems of Pushkin?"

"Don't let Mama terrorize you, Booker," Vasilii said. But her question had apparently given him an idea. He held the bookmark out to her.

"Can you read this, ma'am?" he asked. "I think it's Russian."

She took the narrow piece of paper and studied it. I was about to start picking berries from the closest bush when she said, "It isn't Russian."

She frowned at him. "Where did you get it?"

She studied his reaction, but didn't give him time to answer. "It is in my language," she said, "*Unangam tunuu,* but it's that very old language, the first language we wrote."

"Can you read it, Mother?" Vasilii asked.

"The language has changed, but it's a passage from a song," she said. "You didn't tell me where it came from."

"It was an older relative's," Booker said. "He found it among some ancient papers in a book."

"It is about that pagan Raven, the Real Raven," she said. "It's a song from way out west. You shouldn't have it. It's dangerous."

"It's just paper, Mama," Vasilii said.

"It's trouble," she said as she tucked it into her book and slammed the cover shut. I jumped, half expecting her to vaporize. But there she sat. She waved a hand toward a blueberry bush and then folded both her hands over the volume of poems. As Booker picked up a bucket, she touched his sleeve. "Come to vespers tonight," she said and her voice was really a command. "That will help a little."

We picked from tall bushes while Mrs. Shaiashnikoff read and occasionally checked that our buckets were not too crowded with leaves.

"This is super," Booker said. His fingers and lips were blue.

"Better picking than at King Cove?" Vasilii asked. "I'm glad we don't have to worry about bears."

Booker looked at me.

I raised my eyebrows.

"No bears here?" Booker asked Vasilii.

Before he could answer I started laughing. I laughed until Booker scored a large blueberry into my open mouth.

By the time we had filled every container to the brim, loaded them into the skiff, and seen Vasilii's mother seated, clouds had gathered over the western ridge at the end of the bay. Vasilii studied them and said, "I think we should hurry in order to get back before the storm."

"Storm?" Booker looked where Vasilii indicated clouds massed and drooping as though they, too, were loaded with blueberries.

Church confirmed that there was something ancient and unsettling about the carved fox.

I insisted we should at least wash up before vespers, even if we didn't have other clothes to change into. Both our hands were stained with blueberries, and Booker's lips looked like he had been bruised in a fight. We appeared a tad better when we finished. My fingers were hardly blue at all, but I still had that ragged stain across my palm. If anything, I thought, it was a little bigger and darker after all the surface dirt had been washed away.

The cupola and cross were silhouetted as we walked through a misty rain up to the church. On each side of the portico there were two ruby-colored glass lanterns with flickering candles inside of them. I hesitated before going inside the building. It was like walking into an old photograph. A warm glow filled the interior of the church from a massive three-tiered silver chandelier ablaze with candles. From all sides, light ricocheted off silver-faced icons and banners embroidered with metallic thread. This wasn't the church I knew at home, but some of the icons and the chandelier were old friends, and the wonderful pungent scent from wax and incense was the same. Orthodox churches have a wall separating the area where the people stand from a smaller area where the altar is located. This wall is filled with icons. In fact, it's called an iconostasis. That's a long word, but it's one everybody in the village knows. The icon screen in this church had white pillars with scrolled crowns highlighted in gold. They rose between taller paintings of Christ, the Virgin Mary, and assorted saints. Through the central door I glimpsed the altar standing in solitary glory.

I could tell Booker was surprised by the absence of pews, but I liked standing in church. It wasn't done to make us feel like we were suffering or anything. We had a few chairs in the back for folks who needed to sit. Standing made me feel closer to the people around me. Booker glanced nervously at the icons. I wouldn't have been surprised if a few had frowned down at him for all the lies he'd been telling. He followed me to the left side, but I gave him a slight shove to the right where the men and boys were standing. I took my place among the women and girls. I didn't see the woman from the store, but even if she had been there, she wouldn't dare make a ruckus. The older women wore somber shawls and black head-scarves, while younger women, not unlike today, used church to show off anything new. The men wore simple dark suits. The liturgy began as Father Shaiashnikoff stepped from behind the icon screen and the choir broke into a solemn and joyous melody. It was some time into the service before I recognized Vasilii among the boys who helped the priest.

I could see him as a priest, I thought.

Then he caught my eye and winked.

Two very serious old men threaded among the worshippers, stopping before icons and at the floor stands to replace candles that had burned low. I knew what to do, when to stand, and when to kneel. I was deep into the service when I gave a slight involuntary jerk. The woman beside me turned.

"Sorry," I muttered. Her eyes widened. I broke free from her stare and stepped back. What was wrong with me? She was the woman I had seen through the store window. The hatchet face, the piggy eyes. But it wasn't Mrs. Skagit. Of course, it wasn't Mrs. Skagit. What was wrong with me?

Then it happened again, only this time I knew it was the leather pouch under my dress. It had pulsed. I tried to still it with my hand.

The woman gave me a brief calculating glance.

Vasilii's father came from the altar through the central door.

I took in a long deep breath. The carving had settled down.

The service was about to end. The priest offered prayers for the Czar, the royal family, and the president of the United States.

And who is *the president?* I let my mind wander. *Lincoln's dead. Maybe Grant?*

Then he swung the chain holding his incense burner out across the congregation. When it arced in my direction, I jumped as though I had been struck.

The woman clamped her hand over my arm. Father Shaiash-nikoff intoned his blessing and the service ended. I jerked my arm away and hurried over to Booker. We joined the congregation as it flowed like a dark river into the night air.

THREE
TO THE BEGINNING
OF THE WORLD

10. Booker

I've been letting Anna tell this story. Well, a lot of it is her story. More than mine. I was along accidentally because of the bookmark, which had found it's way back to me from the book of poetry. But now, thanks to Anna, it was torn and not working. But this next part, well, it happened to me as much as to her.

After we left the church, we returned to the hotel. I was starved but neither of us wanted to face running into the buttoned-up woman again or anybody else, for that matter. We found Ivan and he showed us into the kitchen where we helped ourselves to several thick slices of bread, some cheese, and a couple of apples.

"You looked like you almost knew that old man," I said after we had returned to our room. I was sitting on my bed. The apple was a bit mushy, but it tasted good.

"Peter Rostokovich," Anna said. "A real old guy with that name used to visit my gram."

"You think it's the same guy?"

"It couldn't be, but maybe they're related. My gram used to invite him for tea. But he was drunk so much of the time I just didn't like to be around him. She said he had had an unlucky life. His whole family was unlucky. She felt sorry for him."

"What about that boy?"

I jumped as a blunt thud burst against the wall and sprayed the windows with rain pellets. The air closed on itself like a fist. *Wind*, I said to myself as everything was suspended in an eerie stillness. Then the pressure in the room exhaled.

"That boy?" Anna didn't seem to notice the storm. "Peter was pretty certain the fox belonged to him, wasn't he? I don't know. Everything is weird."

I was wired, but Anna curled up and fell asleep almost immediately. My brain slipped from Vasilii disappearing into the fog and then reappearing to berry picking with no bears. His mother had recognized the writing on the bookmark being about a raven, a real raven. *And what's an unreal raven?* I drew the comforter over my head. The old man had been scared to death of the carved fox. I hadn't shown him the bookmark. In all of this I was just pushed along, shoved here and there, like it hadn't been me who had found the fox, like it hadn't been me who had made it possible for us to travel here.

I must have fallen asleep because the next thing I knew it was light.

"I'm going to church," Anna said. "Do you want to go with me?"

She was standing at the window.

"We went last night," I said and tried to burrow further under the covers.

"I'd like to see it again."

"Do you mind if I don't?"

"You can do me a favor," she said and nudged my shoulder. I uncovered my head as she removed the cord with the leather pouch from her neck. "Maybe church isn't the right place for this."

"Sure," I said.

The pouch was on the stand beside my bed when I woke up again. A wind half-heartedly bumped against the window, but the rain had stopped. *Time to find something to eat,* I said to myself as I stepped into the hallway. A door on the opposite side of the hall was so close to the outside wall that it was unlikely to be a guest room.

Just a quick look.

Steep stairs rose toward the roof once I had squeezed past a bucket and a mop. I avoided the tag ends of rafters that narrowed as the stairs climbed into the attic. A window at each end let in enough light to show that boards had been laid across the timbers down the center of the floor. There was a trough on each side. I could almost stand up as I made my way to the far end, past a couple of wooden crates, and crouched down. Right below me the roof of the store tilted away. The church was in the distance. Service must still be going on. I started back and stopped to snoop in a crate stenciled *Gift of the Woman's Home Missionary Society*. It was stuffed with jackets, pants, dresses, and gloves. Right on top was an old-fashioned, small-billed baseball cap. It fit perfectly.

In the dining room I filled a plate with cold scrambled eggs, added a roll and a piece of crispy bacon, and returned to the room. I had just finished eating when Anna walked in.

"Better pack your things," she said. "Vasilii's father has agreed to take us to Nikolski."

"And what if I don't want to go?"

Anna gave me a sideways glance and said, "His dad has been planning to go there on church business for some time. Vasilii suggested we follow up on Old Man Rostokovich's idea that I talk with his sister."

I just sat there.

"Look," she said. "I need your help."

That was a first. I handed her back the pouch.

"Vasilii's going to come with us."

"We need to think of a way to get back where we came from."

"Aren't you a little bit curious about the ivory fox?" she asked. "Anyway, we've been gone so long, that we've probably got our mugs on milk cartons."

I explained how time just sort of stops when the bookmark is used.

"That doesn't make any sense," she said. "But if you're telling the truth—"

"I am."

"Then it doesn't matter if we're gone a bit longer."

I hated to admit that she had a point. She gave her right hand a good rubbing.

"Man, this itches."

"Let me see it."

She held it out. A dark rash with irregular edges covered her palm. She rubbed it again, drawing the surface blood away from the marks that stood out clearly.

"This might sound goofy," I said.

"Like what doesn't, Booker?" she asked.

Instead of answering, I took out the bookmark and laid the torn edge across her palm. The letters there met the stain almost perfectly, like they had once lined up with each other.

"It's like the ink from those letters ran into your hand," I said. "Is that cool or what?"

"It's creepy, that's what it is!" She tried to cram her hand into the virtually nonexistent pocket on her dress. That's when I remembered the crate in the attic. I swear she counted every pocket as she made her selections. In the end, with her wool shirt, wool pants, and well-buttoned jacket, she looked like a Klondike prospector.

That afternoon we visited the cemetery. None of the crosses had names on them, but that didn't seem to surprise Anna, who went from one cross to another. Vasilii was able to name a few people who had been buried in the more recent graves.

"Those old-time Aleuts," he said, "like Old Man Rostokovich, you'd be surprised at how superstitious they are."

I glanced at Anna to see if she was about to argue with him, but she was busy inspecting one of the white crosses.

"Even my parents, occasionally," he continued as we climbed the gentle slope above the graveyard in order to get a good view of the bay. "You saw how my mother reacted to that paper you showed her."

"The bookmark," I said. "Do you know anything about that raven she mentioned?"

"Nothing," he said.

"That man who helped out at the creek yesterday," Anna cut in.

"Chris Hansen? He's been around a couple years. Nice guy. He's a fisherman, of course, one of those Norwegians."

"Does he live here?"

"He does odd jobs for the A.C. Company and sells them whatever furs he gets so they let him live in one of their little red cabins. He married one of the daughters of Sergie Borenin."

"Do you think we could go see him?"

Vasilii looked out across the wide bay. A small sailing schooner had its sails filled by the wind.

"That's his boat," he said. "We can visit him when we get back."

The next morning when Vasilii helped me into the front hatch of his two-hatch kayak, I saw that the inside was a web of sticks, narrow ribs, and long poles. Even lashed together it looked pretty fragile. It was covered snugly with a dark skin that had a warm smell to it. *Like I'm crawling into some sort of seal,* I thought. It tilted when I climbed into it, and even after I was tied in with a wide leather apron, it acted like it had a mind of its own—or maybe because I *was* tied in with a wide leather apron. Vasilii sat in the rear hatch. He handed me a double-bladed paddle that balanced perfectly on my palm. He rattled off instructions. I didn't understand half of them and just hoped I wouldn't be screaming and thrashing around in the water too much of the time. Anna had refused to crawl into the interior of the *baidarka* she was assigned to. Vasilii laughed and said that women and children usually traveled tucked among the dried fish, teakettle, and bedrolls. The hunter who owned the *baidarka* wasn't pleased to have a female sit in his forward hatch, but the way she handled the paddle—which was better than I did—soon won him over. Before long he was smiling and kidding and calling her his partner. Father Shaiashnikoff sat in the center of a three-hatch *baidarka*. Our group was completed with eight other men, paired in two-man kayaks.

The first leg of the trip was short. The sun was out, and I was glad I had that baseball hat from the attic. We passed the hillside where we had filled buckets with blueberries before we landed at the end of a long bay and started hiking. Men carried the kayaks, but Vasilii and I handled our own supplies. The trek was less strenuous once we were above the thick entangling grass. Still, it lasted several hours, and I was exhausted by the time we descended from the summit and camped along the shore of an immense bay.

The next morning we were back on the water. I think Anna was relieved when we bypassed the village she said her relatives were from. The priest told us we'd stop on the way back.

"While the weather holds," he said, "we should press on."

The second evening, after kayaking along steep bluffs and across awesome fjords, we arrived at a village called Kashega. We had passed a lot of high mountains, but this village was tucked in among low folded hills. Word must have spread that the priest was arriving, because people started showing up. Soon skin boats lined the grassy rim of the beach. Father Shaiashnikoff had service in a small chapel that I learned was named in honor of the Transfiguration of Christ. The priest had insisted we bring our own provisions so as not to be a burden on local people, but the village insisted on hosting us to tea and a light supper.

"Did you see the icon above the iconostasis?" Vasilii asked.

"The what?" I took another slice of smoked salmon.

"The screen or wall separating the people from the altar," Anna said with her own mouth full of the fragrant fish.

"My godfather sent that icon," the priest said, a note of pride in his voice. "It has his signature on the back."

"Father Veniaminov," Vasilii added. "He also sent the portrait of Czar Alexander that you saw in our home."

"Metropolitan Innocent," his father corrected. "He was the Metropolitan of Moscow. I used to get letters from him—even in Aleut, but he died last year. We had services in his memory for forty days."

"Saint Innocent?" Anna exclaimed. "I've read about him."

"Some people called him a saint," the priest nodded and looked impressed that Anna knew about this guy. "He was famous. He had a terrific laugh. And his eyes—" The priest sat quietly as he remembered. "Such kindness, such intelligence."

"He traveled all over in a *baidarka*," Vasilii said. The conversation turned to scary trips in skin boats. A few older men were looking uncomfortable, and Vasilii whispered, "We're getting close to criticizing the weather, and that's a taboo with these old guys." He added with a wink at Anna, "Just another old wives' tale."

He was good at irritating her.

"I was caught here once for six days," the priest said, gesturing around him. "It was so stormy the roof of the church blew off and my tent was torn into shreds. The people, however, were so kind to us. They gave us shelter and food when ours ran low. Even though they didn't have much, that is what they did."

The third day, our *baidarkas* brought us to a larger village nestled along a bay among low hills. The church was a lot like one of those semi-underground homes. It was dedicated to the Epiphany of Our Lord. *These people must really know their Bible*, I thought on hearing yet another intriguing name for a church. After church services the next morning, we headed away from the island. By now I was pretty confident that the wooden frame of my boat wouldn't disintegrate into floating pick-up-sticks. We arrived off another island and followed the coast. I was enjoying myself thanks to calm seas and a light breeze.

"It won't be long now," Vasilii said as two men rowed out to us in their own kayaks. The closer we got to the village of Nikolski, the more *baidarkas* joined us. As we neared the shallow bay facing the village, the men broke into rhythmic singing.

What a great omen, I said to myself, as voices from the shore joined in.

It was soon clear that the villagers' joy centered on the priest. Vasilii, Anna, and I melted into the crowd and set about exploring while he visited his parishioners and caught up on news. We hiked outside the village where the hills were low and rolling. The jagged peaks that surrounded Unalaska were missing, but I saw a steep mountain in the distance. A stream meandered into the sea from a small lake on the north side of the village. The lake looked very flat, but then I realized *all lakes are flat*. We walked south of the settlement for about a mile.

"Appreciate this spot, Booker," Anna said.

"Why?"

"Look to your left."

I did.

"That's the Pacific Ocean."

There was water as far as I could see.

"Now look right." Anna pointed and said, "The Bering Sea. Two of the world's greatest bodies of water at your fingertips."

I was impressed, I admit. "Where are those Four Mountain islands?"

Vasilii pointed west, but all I made out was a smudge on the horizon.

His arm dipped a bit, and all three of us felt the ground quiver.

"Did you feel that?" he asked.

"An earthquake, Booker," Anna said. "Better get used to them. They happen all the time."

11. Booker

We returned to the village where we learned Anna and I would be staying with the chief's aunt while Vasilii would be with the second chief and his family. We had a couple of hours before he was to assist his father with services. Anna offered to help the chief's aunt get a room ready, so Vasilii and I went looking for somebody who could tell us where Peter's sister lived. In a village the size of Nikolski, that would have been anybody. A woman was removing clothes from a line that stretched from her *barabara* to an upright post. Being careful not to appear like the nosey outsiders we were, we came up to her from the side. Vasilii said quietly, "*Aang, aang.*"

Anna had used those words before. Some kind of *hello*.

The woman frowned over a towel she had started to remove. When he repeated the greeting, she grunted back and tossed it onto the lid of a wooden barrel. We watched her, somewhat embarrassed at being deliberately ignored. She removed the last piece of clothing, gathered the dry laundry into her arms, and turned to enter her home. She saw us still there and demanded, "What you want? What you looking at?"

"Do you know where Fevronia lives?" Vasilii asked. "Her brother is Peter at Unalaska."

"I know who her brother is," she said aggressively, and then she shrugged. "What you want that Old Lady for? She's got no time for you."

"Her brother asked us to say hello," Vasilii said.

"Agh!" The woman snorted in disbelief. "What do you want?"

"Peter said she could tell us about those old-time charms," he said, "and about those Islands of Four Mountains people."

"I can do that," she said. "*Haqada!*" and she ordered us to follow her inside.

I bet she wasn't singing when we came ashore, I thought.

Like Peter's house, this one consisted of a small room that led into the main living area where light came through two small windows. These were far cleaner than in Peter's home. Still, it took a moment for my eyes to adjust to the dimness. I saw that every surface that could be polished was polished and everything that could be cleaned was spotless. I instinctively checked my shoes for dirt. The woman directed us to a table and two wooden chairs whose backs were protected with red-and-white gingham slipcovers. The table was covered with a white oilcloth, crisscrossed with pale-yellow lines. A vase held a bouquet of dark-blue violets. The woman went to a counter where she poured dark tea from a teapot into two china cups. She added hot water from the spout of a fancy brass container with an oval body. A *samovar*, I recalled from somewhere, probably some book I had read. She placed the cups on matching saucers and set one before each of us. She was being surprisingly nice after the grumpy way she had greeted us. She even brought two plates, one with sliced bread and the other with smoked salmon.

"Thank you," I said.

Vasilii crossed himself before he took a sip of tea. Then he began by telling how Peter had relayed the story of the boy who had drowned when his boat capsized. He had barely started when the woman interrupted. "He lost his magic charm," she said. "That's why he died. Why he was killed that way, poor thing. It was that woman who wanted that thing, you know."

"What woman?"

"Volcano Woman. *Chuginadax̂*." She pronounced it something like *Choo-gee-náh-thaxh*. "Old Lady Fevronia can tell you. People say she saw her."

Who saw whom? I wondered.

"She knows a lot of those old-time things, that lady, she does. You don't know where she lives?" And the woman cackled as though this was the funniest thing in the world.

"No," said Vasilii, "we don't," and he drank more of his tea and waited.

He seemed to take the long pauses of silence in stride. I found them uncomfortable. I was getting antsy and almost suggested we leave when a curtain covering a doorframe was pulled back and I was looking at the oldest woman I had ever seen in my life. There were deep lines all over her face, like the ground had dried and left all these cracks. When I looked into her eyes, I instinctively stood up. The Elder Cousin might have remarked that this was simply good manners, but it was more. Vasilii also got to his feet as the tiny hunched woman made her way toward us. She was dressed entirely in black, with a knitted shawl draped across her shoulders. She placed a hand on the back of Vasilii's chair. He turned it slightly and stepped to one side. She looked at him. Her eyes widened.

"Chief," she said with certainty in her voice, "not priest."

Vasilii stared at her. He snapped to as she started to sit down. He pushed the chair in for her.

"Sit down," she said softly, and he brought another chair to the table. I was still gaping a bit when the grouchy woman asked, "Chai, mother?"

Mother? I thought. *She's her mother? What a fake!*

"Aang, aang, Galena."

Galena set a cup of tea in front of her mother. The old woman lifted it and took a sip. She stared at me over the rim. I felt exposed and vulnerable. Then she looked away and put her cup down.

What had she seen? What did she know about me? Time traveler? Mouse? Sparrow? Something else?

The three of us drank tea in silence. Fevronia's daughter never sat down but stationed herself on the opposite side of the room where she tended the hot water and tea. We just sat there drinking tea forever. Finally Galena suggested in a voice that sounded like an order, "Ask her!"

But before either of us could speak, the old woman turned in her seat and took a sack from a nearby shelf. She removed what looked like most of a dead bird and started chewing on it. I jerked and splashed tea on the table. The elderly woman smiled slightly while Galena scolded, "Mother! *Ayaqaa!* Such a show-off!"

While Galena quickly wiped up the spilled tea with a clean cloth, Vasilii explained. "It's a puffin skin. She's softening it with her teeth after it's been cured. It will be used in a bird-skin parka. You don't see many of them anymore. There are very few people who can make them."

Fevronia placed the bird skin on her lap, turned, and took another cloth sack from the shelf. From it she withdrew what looked like the dark feathered skin of an enormous bird. But then I saw arms and cuffs, and a neck opening with a collar. The whole thing shimmered the way feathers do in sunlight.

"Cormorant skins," Vasilii said. "It's a bird skin parka. It's reversible. Feathers inside when it's cold and outside when it's raining."

And when it's both? I wondered. Fevronia carefully folded the bird skin parka and returned it to the shelf in his sack.

"They're wondering about that boy," Galena said to her mother. "The one from Kagamil. Him and his daddy, poor things."

Fevronia didn't say anything. She just looked at Vasilii.

"They called him *Chaknax̂*, that boy," Galena said. "It means "Stink" or "Stinky.""

"Little Wren," Fevronia whispered. "That was his name. He was my grandfather's brother."

"The boy?" I asked.

"His father," Fevronia answered. "He was called Little Wren because he was small."

"You never told me he was your relative!" her daughter said.

Her mother gave a quiet shrug. She looked at me. "If you go there, tell him his brother's granddaughter sends him greetings. I would like that."

"What do you mean?" her daughter protested. "Nobody lives out there anymore. Crazy lady, what are you telling them?"

"How do we get there?" Vasilii asked.

She looked directly into his eyes as though she was measuring his readiness.

"Go to Chuginadak," the Old Woman said finally. "They'll be at Chuginadak picking berries."

"Crazy lady!" her daughter interrupted. "Fox trappers go there sometimes, that Chuginadak, but that volcano is always busy. People don't go there to pick berries. It's too dangerous."

Fevronia rattled her empty teacup on the saucer and Galena took it to the samovar for refilling. With her daughter on the other side of the room, she asked, "Where is she at?"

"Who?" Vasilii asked.

"I heard you were traveling with that girl."

12. Anna

The chief's aunt in whose house Booker and I were to stay was a friendly woman who made me feel right at home. Her husband and son were away on a sea otter hunt and wouldn't be back for a month or more. She said she had everything under control, so I walked down to the beach and looked out over the water. The Islands of Four Mountains were like pale-blue shadows in the distance.

Was it possible, I wondered, *that somewhere among them there was a boy waiting for what I could bring him?*

I remembered the man by the creek at Unalaska, Chris Hansen. Hansen was a common name. Dad owned a very old framed photograph of a thin man leaning against the hull of an upturned skiff and smiling. I wished I had studied it more closely.

Even if I don't know Norwegian, I might be more like him than like any of my Unangax̂ ancestors, I thought. I would talk with him when we got back, see if he was who I thought he might be. See what he said.

Thinking of that photo reminded me of my mother's photograph. It was strange to think of that photo without being in trouble. I had always used it to make myself feel better when I got bawled out at school. I could still see it in my mind's eye, but now that other woman floated in front of it. Maybe she was off to Akutan and her husband. Out of my life. Again. Or maybe she was still there at Gram's, waiting, if what Booker had said about time was true. Had Gram really driven her away? Then why had she come back? Mrs. Skagit had lied, I was sure of that, but I still wondered why she had returned.

I took out the pouch and poured the fox onto my hand. The carving had always been warm but now it was almost hot. Holding it was one thing that felt real. I held it up close and stared into its eyes.

"We'll get you home," I said as a seagull swept overhead and let out a cry like a sharp knife. The fox slipped through my fingers. I caught it in the air and felt it twist toward the Four Mountains.

By midmorning the three of us were back at the church for another service. I didn't need the carved fox acting up, so I had hidden the pouch beside some heavy grass. All the villagers had dressed in their finest clothing. As Vasilii slipped his robe over his head, I realized that everybody involved in the service somehow changed into somebody else. They weren't the same people I saw every day on the street. I thought of our ancestors putting on masks for special occasions. Maybe what they did and what we did in church weren't so different. I kept my eyes on Vasilii, but not once did I get a smile or a wink. Twice, in fact, he seemed to forget where he was and had to be prodded by one of the older robed attendants.

"That old lady was asking for you," he said to me when we stood outside as the last of the parishioners returned home or left to join Vasilii's father and his primary attendants at the chief's home for tea and refreshments. Us "kids" were expected to follow shortly.

"Fevronia?"

"Yes, and she said something else. That boy who drowned, his father was some sort of great uncle to her."

Booker joined us and added, "She was in the front row, dressed all in black. She looked like a raven."

Vasilii smiled. "She made me nervous, like she knew I was about to make a mistake or something. I'll be right back." He walked over to a young man standing by himself.

"When we were at her house," Booker said, "she talked like this uncle was still alive and living out on that island. Weird."

Vasilii gave the young man a friendly slap on his back and returned to us.

"Do you have the fox, Anna?"

I walked to where I had tucked it safely away. I handed the carving to Vasilii. He nodded at the young man who came forward.

"What do you think, Gregorii?"

The man shook his head and smiled and said, "I don't know. Could be." He looked again. "Probably isn't."

"What was that about?" I asked after the guy had left.

"Gregorii's uncle is training him. He's learning all those healing secrets and things, all those really old-time things. He agrees with Old Man Rostokovich. He thinks it's an amulet, a magic charm."

"He didn't say that."

"Maybe you weren't listening."

That afternoon Vasilii returned to church to help prepare for yet another service. Booker and I walked south of the village, crossing low rolling mounds of grass and heather, until we reached a wide sandy beach. From there the sea stretched toward Asia and the south. The Islands of Four Mountains had vanished in a bank of clouds.

"I need to find Peter's sister," I said. "Can you show me where she lives?"

"Sure," he said. "We'll have to get past her daughter. She's a terror. Fevronia is probably busy chewing on birds."

I ignored that last statement. I rubbed my hand. Rubbing it had become almost automatic.

"That mark going away?"

"If anything," I said opening my palm, "it's getting bigger."

After vespers, people crowded into the home of the second chief for a delicious dinner of fish pie—salmon layered with rice and onions, spiced with fresh *petruski*, a kind of wild parsley, all of it inside a flaky brown crust. There were fresh berries and the hot palms of *alaadikax̂*. One of the men remarked that the A.C. Company schooner *Bertha* was expected in three or four days to collect furs from the sea otter hunters.

"Father," Vasilii asked as he glanced toward Booker and me, "would it be possible for us to remain and take the ship home when it arrives?"

"Why would you want to do that?" his father asked. "Yes, thank you, Helena." He held out his plate. "Excellent fish pie."

"We've been talking with an older woman here, Fevronia Rostokovich," Vasilii continued.

"Yes, I know her," his father said. "Her married name is Ermeloff, but everyone still calls her Rostokovich."

"Some families are touchy like that," said the second-chief's wife.

"She wants to meet Anna," Vasilii nodded at me. I hoped his father wouldn't ask why I wanted to meet her. "Besides, it would be a good opportunity for me to practice that long-ago language."

"I suppose it would," the priest agreed. He spoke with the chief, confirmed the *Bertha*'s expected arrival and departure dates, and arranged for Booker and me to stay a bit longer with the chief's aunt and for Vasilii to continue at the second chief's.

"You may stay," he concluded, "but be good! The *Bertha* should get you home in a week. Help out while you're here. Don't just be lazy."

Services the next morning were finished early to give the priest time to go from house to house, blessing them and consulting one final time with his parishioners. Then he and his companions climbed into their sleek *baidarkas*. One of the men who had come in a two-man *baidarka* took Vasilii's boat. Every available Nikolski man would accompany them north along the island's shore until they headed across the pass to Unalaska Island. Vasilii, Booker, and I stood with the women, children, and old men on the beach. We watched them set off. Within minutes, the kayaks were rippling among the waves. The high tips of the double-bladed oars briefly caught the light, but soon all I could see were the waves themselves.

It took a day and a half of navigating around barriers before I finally saw Fevronia without her daughter being present. Vasilii and Booker didn't understand my insistence that Galena not be present when I showed her mother the ivory fox. Finally, the chief's aunt was persuaded to invite Galena for tea, while commenting something about "that old grump."

Fevronia herself came to the door and invited us in. The moment I placed the carving on the table, she snatched it up and carried it to the window where she turned it from side to side. She gauged its weight by bouncing it slightly on her palm. She stared into its minuscule black eyes. She studied the circles on its back and, with unexpected gentleness, she stroked it three times with her forefinger. Not once did she close her hand over it before she brought it back to the table and dropped it unceremoniously, where it landed upright and, I could have sworn, glanced up indignantly.

"You've made up your minds?" she asked while looking at Vasilii.

Made up our minds to do what? I felt like I had been left out of an important part of the conversation.

"Yes," he nodded at me. "She wants to return it."

I did. That was true. But Vasilii and I both knew that nobody lived on the Islands of Four Mountains.

The old woman looked at Booker. "Will you remember me to my relative?"

Now what she was asking?

"Yes, ma'am."

"Will you remember me to my uncle no matter what happens?" she repeated.

He shifted in his seat.

"I promise. Yes," he said.

"Are you saying you can help us get to Kagamil?" I asked. "That there's somebody there I can return the fox to?"

Once again she ignored me. She simply shrugged her shoulders, slipped on a heavy shawl, and walked outside. I rapidly returned the carving to its pouch, strung it around my neck, and rushed to catch up. The old woman hobbled along with surprising speed. We followed her through the village, making sharp corners and staying away from the window where Galena might have been sitting, drinking tea and complaining. Once outside the village, we walked along the beach until a gap in the thick bordering grass opened to the pebbled shoreline. A breeze blew off the land, and when she pointed due west, her outer cape rippled across her shoulders.

"It's thirty miles to Kagamil," she said.

"But I thought you said we should go to Chuginadak," Vasilii said.

"Start with Kagamil," Fevronia insisted. "Kagamil is closer. From there you'll see your way to Chuginadak."

"Thirty miles?" Booker asked. "That's a long ways."

Fevronia ignored him.

"You get what you need," she said. "I'll wait here."

I pumped Vasilii and Booker as we headed back to the village. "So we're going to Kagamil?"

"I know it sounds crazy," Vasilii said. "But it's what you wanted, right?"

It sounded more than crazy, but it was what I wanted. The chief's aunt was laughing when Booker and I walked into her *barabara* to collect our few belongings. She actually seemed to be enjoying Galena's company.

"You seen my old lady?" Fevronia's daughter asked, and we knew we had been caught.

"We did," I admitted.

"Ah, I thought you would," Galena said and turned to the chief's aunt. "They are wanting to go out to those Four Mountain Islands."

"Is that true?" The chief's aunt held her teacup a couple of inches above its saucer.

"We need to try," I said.

She lowered the cup. "You have to be careful."

"That's what I told them," Galena said, proof of what a liar she was.

When we stood at the door with Booker's backpack holding our few things, the chief's aunt said simply, "I'll expect you back."

For three hours we took turns rowing the wooden skiff across the calm water, through the quiet air, and under an overcast sky. Fevronia had led us farther along the beach to where a skiff was tied above high water. It was a simple affair, much like the one Vasilii had taken berry picking. There was ample room, but I could tell Booker was nervous, even after he was firmly seated at the bow. Vasilii manned the oars in the middle, and I was at the stern. I looked back at the old woman, who stood as though it didn't matter whether or not we ever returned. I watched until she and the village and the coastline had blurred away and all I could see were the high slopes of the mountains.

"It's getting hazy," Booker said. That was an understatement. All the greens and blues and whites were now shades of gray. We never got any closer to Kagamil.

"We're getting there," Vasilii said. I had to look again. "You can pick out more details along the shore."

I could see a rough volcanic shoulder and burnt cliffs that dropped directly into the sea, but nothing else. This was not the first time Vasilii had been able to discern objects in the distance long before we had made them out. I had read where old-time Unangax̂ attributed their good eyesight to a moderate use of salt. So much for pretzels and popcorn.

Booker leaned forward and rested his chin on his crossed arms at the bow. I closed my eyes and listened as the skiff sliced through the mild waves with a steady rhythm. *But we never get any closer*, I complained again to myself as a soft clatter of wings erupted. I opened my eyes to a flock of small birds peppering the air like tiny electric fans. They struck the water, and half of them disappeared beneath the surface after food.

The haze thickened into a heavy mist. Vasilii rested the oars, but the skiff drifted steadily on. The water around us was as flat as a map. We passed through sheets of mist, like pale walls completely obscuring Kagamil. When I looked toward the bow, Booker was little more than a shadow. I took in a long breath and let it out. The fog drew back from the skiff, the way circles radiate from a stone dropped into calm water. Then it rose over us like a soft gray shell. For a moment it was like being inside a tent on a sunny afternoon. And then it broke apart and fell gently into the water. Dampness tickled the back of my neck. I saw Booker's hands grip the top edge of the skiff as it bumped against something solid that angled us in a different direction. Vasilii was about to lower the oars when the boat coasted on its own up a gentle swell. It paused, and we passed into a thick bank of clouds.

"Like osmosis," I heard Booker whisper as the air became almost as solid as water.

The skiff stalled at the top of a small wave. It was balanced there. Just for a moment. Like when the tide changes. Then the air relaxed, and we coasted down the other side. The breeze returned and with it more visibility. Vasilii dipped the oars into the water, and Booker gasped.

"Anna!" he shouted. "It's happened again."

He held out his arms. His wool jacket was now opaque gut. My jacket had also changed, as had Vasilii's. All three of us were dressed in *kamleikas*, the gut raincoats of ancient Unangax̂. I had a moment of panic when I thought I was stark naked under what felt like a raincoat made from rows of clouded plastic. But only the outer layer had changed. I gripped the top edge of the skiff. It was rounder and softer. I stared in wonder: the skiff had become a skin-covered craft, as wide as before but built with a frame of lashed and fitted poles.

Baidar was the Russian word, but I have no idea what we used to call it.

Booker started to take off his cap and his fingers touched wood. He removed a plain wooden visor, gawked at it, and placed it back on.

I thought Vasilii would freak out. He was totally amazed. He held out his arms to look at the fine workmanship on his *kamleika*. He caught my eye and shook his head.

"I can explain!" I shouted. Like I could explain anything.

He lowered the oars deep into the water and drew back with all his strength. "Now we're getting someplace!" he laughed.

I looked at the gut raincoat I was wearing. Had we slipped even further into the past?

Strong currents and Vasilii's vigorous rowing carried us away from Kagamil and toward Chuginadak. Before long, the shore was shadowed with cliffs and rocky outcroppings. Above this there were green and gentle hills, rising up like the gentlest of waves.

Vasilii paused the oars and pointed up where a high ragged peak broke across the summit. "I've heard that old-timers call that *The Beginning of the World*," he said.

I saw openings along the shore where we could have landed, but Vasilii kept the skiff running west until a massive symmetrical cone thrust up in front of us.

"Chuginadak Volcano," he said and nodded upward.

I had seen photographs of the volcano, renamed Mount Cleveland after a future U.S. president, but here it was in person.

"There's supposed to be a small bay between the volcano and this end of the island. From there, a pass leads over to the Pacific side."

A line of white ripples hinted at submerged rocks.

"We'll have to be careful going in," he said.

He took us past a protruding point that plunged into the sea like a stone arm. We crossed the dark mouth that I guessed opened into a sea cave. Stone pinnacles, crusted with grass, jutted just off shore. Cascades of reddish-gray rock were frozen in their slow-motion tumble to the beach. The wide headland before us was a single smooth wave of dense heather that continued up into the higher hillsides. I had the odd feeling that this island was something that was, well, if not actually alive, then at least *waiting for us*. Waiting for me.

The surface of the water became clearer the closer we got to shore, but its depths remained clouded. I glimpsed a sheet of light, a blink, as though a pack of cards had fanned out and instantly closed. *Fish*, I thought. Booker and I had traded places, and I was at the bow when Vasilii said, "Lean over and keep an eye out for rocks as we come in."

"Good thing it's calm," I said as I positioned myself.

"Calm?" Booker's voice rose a bit when he saw a necklace of breakers washing onto the distant beach.

As I studied the water, an image of Fevronia flowed into my mind. She had seemed totally indifferent to our journey, but now she started to glow in my mind like a distant lighthouse. I pictured her on Nikolski's shore holding her arms out with her palms turned toward the water. She moved them back and forth, parallel to the sea, slowly stirring the air and sending a gentle breeze that quieted the sea like an expanding ripple. My mind drifted off, and I forgot all about looking for rocks. I felt totally relaxed and safe. She lifted her arms above her head, held them there briefly, and dropped them to her side. A gull cried out. I felt a drum roll of gravel under the skiff as we coasted in to shore.

13. Booker

I would have liked to have had time to think about what was happening, to put things in order. But we had *landed*. Land is always better than water, even under a boat. Anna extended a hand, and I jumped to the beach, skidding on fist-sized gray stones. Vasilii followed, and while Anna and I held the skiff, he located a log jammed among boulders that weren't going anywhere. We pulled the skiff over and Vasilii secured it. The three of us stood and listened to the tug of the sea on gravel while a slight breeze shuffled through the grass that towered on the bank above us. The wide dark-green blades separated out of stalks as thick as fingers. When Anna pulled on one, it stayed put, as though it had grown there for centuries.

Which it probably has, I said to myself.

With Vasilii leading, we pushed through the grass to higher ground. A quick fistful of grass usually kept me upright. I scrambled on my hands and knees up a final expanse of gravel to a patch of shorter grass and stood up. And there was the volcano right in front of me. It was like amazing. I mean it was like a perfect volcano. The bottom third was covered with green grass. The symmetrical slopes then angled upward more steeply as the grass gradually gave way to rock. A few ravines were marked with lacy tatters of snow.

"The Nikolski people," Vasilii said, "tell how a woman used this volcano for breathing."

A plume of smoke feathered from the peak in confirmation. I was getting so I believed everything I was told.

"It's a composite volcano," I said, groping for something that made sense. "Shield volcanoes are flatter." I could tell Anna was about to comment inappropriately when Vasilii resumed walking. We climbed a gravel bar and skidded down the other side, where there was a small creek too swift and deep for us to cross. We followed it back toward the beach, where it spread out across the sand and gravel. Vasilii said, "We can cross here."

"I hate wet feet," Anna volunteered. "And backtracking."

"I wouldn't worry," Vasilii said. And sure enough, our boots were gloriously waterproof. I don't know what they were made from, but they were very comfortable and, despite the wet rocks and the running water, I didn't slip once.

"Sea lion flippers," Vasilii said as he tapped one of his soles.

Oddly shaped pebbles were scattered across a patch of fine sand. I slipped two into a pocket. When Anna caught my eye, I said, "One for me and one for the Elder Cousin. He likes souvenirs."

He must be wondering, I thought, despite what he had said about time, just where I had gone. *And when*, I said to myself, *I might be getting back.*

We followed the creek back to where the beach ended and the heavy grass began. Vasilii stopped and turned to Anna. "Before we go on," he said, "I think you should tell me."

I looked from him to her.

"I suppose so," she said as she dropped a stone she had picked up.

"I can tell that you don't know half the stuff about living here that an ordinary person would know," he said.

"Half?" she said. "I hardly know anything at all."

"It's like almost everything is new to you," he said.

"It's me," I said. "I thought I was going to Ireland."

I started to explain about the bookmark, but Anna interrupted and told about Captain Hennig—not the one Vasilii knew, but the other Hennig—how he had looted things from Kagamil. How one thing had led to another.

All the while, Vasilii just stared at the creek as though he were considering following it back to the beach and back to the skiff and home.

"And you got here, how?" he asked me.

"With this," I said, and took out the bookmark. "It's what I showed your mother."

"How does it work?"

"It doesn't," I said. "Not anymore."

"I thought she kept it."

"I can't get rid of it," I said, not that I really wanted to, not that I could explain.

"And that's how we got here?" he gestured around us. "With that, whatever it is."

"I don't think so. Like I said, I can't get it to work the way it's supposed to. It got torn."

Anna gave me a quick unapologetic glance.

Vasilii looked from me to her. "So, you are each other's *angaayux̂*?"

We gave him a blank stare.

"Partners," Vasilii said.

"I wouldn't go that far." We both spoke at once.

107

Vasilii raised his eyebrows and shrugged. "That still doesn't explain this," and he touched his gut *kamleika*.

"It's probably the fox," Anna said and removed the carving from its pouch. She flattened her hand and set the carving in the middle of her palm so that it faced away from the volcano. It just sat there. Then she pivoted it a quarter of a turn. The carving rotated back to its original position.

"Do that again," Vasilii said.

She did, and again it pivoted back so that it faced down the beach.

"Let's take it where it wants to go," he said and stood up. "*Haqada!*"

Háh-kah-thah I said to myself, trying to pronounce the command to get moving that I had heard time and time again. We headed away from the volcano.

"If the Kagamil people come here for berries," Vasilii said, "they'll probably choose a bay close to Kagamil and away from the volcano. This eastern half of the island," he gestured toward the gradually rising slope, "is our best bet."

Walking wasn't difficult once the grass was shorter, but it was up and down and up and down and up. The "ups" were always longer than the "downs." Eventually, we had a view of the northeastern shoreline.

"I don't see any berry pickers," Anna said.

"I don't see any berries," I added and plopped down.

"You won't find blueberry bushes like at home," Vasilii said, and he bent over to pick a few smooth berries from the thick carpet of creeping evergreen foliage that covered the ground. The round berries were so dark blue they were virtually black. "More like these."

"Moss berries," Anna said to me as Vasilii handed me a half dozen. I tossed them into my mouth. They were full of tiny seeds.

"Raven's berry," Vasilii said.

"Not bad," I said as I squeezed out the juice, leaving a mouthful of pulp and seeds.

"Spit," Anna said.

I did and reached for a few more berries. "Actually, very good."

We now worked our way closer to the shore, staying as much as possible up where the plants were low. Eventually, a wide expanse curved below us, and we began a gradual descent. Everything in front was shadowed by the hills behind us. By the time we arrived at the beach, evening had arrived. I wasn't worried. I knew from experience that it would stay evening for a long time. It would get dark, I knew that too. But it wouldn't stay dark for long.

"I guess we should have thought about where we were going to spend the night," Vasilii said.

Now I was worried.

"You're not suggesting we go back, are you?" Anna asked.

"No," he said. He sat down on a wide driftwood log and removed a folded cloth from his pack.

"Time for some food," he said and uncovered a curved reddish stick.

"Dry salmon," Anna said as she sat down beside him. "I love that."

"I've got something, too." I unwrapped some fragrant rolls the chief's aunt had insisted I take before we left her house.

"*Alaadikax̂!*" Vasilii said. "Excellent."

After we had eaten, Vasilii rewrapped his dried fish and put it away. He stood up and walked to where the beach grass was especially thick. We watched while he flattened a stretch of grass with his feet and then, over this space, he tied together two clumps of long broad grass, one from each side. He threaded a second handful of grass through each side of the first pair and tied those, again using the grass to tie itself. He repeated this until he had what resembled a tubular tent. He crawled inside, turned around, and smiled.

Our knots unraveled almost as soon as we tied them. Vasilii took over and by threading the tips of succeeding clumps through those already secured he had an almost solid surface.

"Good for one night," he said.

"You're amazing," I said.

He might have smiled a bit, I wasn't sure. Anna had gone inside her grass tent to inspect it, and now she crawled out. Vasilii gave her a hand to get up. Before he let it go he said, "Don't tell me what happens. In the future, I mean."

"As if I knew," she said. I could tell she was upset. "Too much has happened. Too many years. Look at me! I hardly know what kind of Aleut I am."

Before I could say Unangax̂ and get walloped, Vasilii spoke softly. "*Listen. Share. Don't be boastful. Do the things you know are right.*"

I gave him a blank look.

"It's what it means to be Unangax̂," he said. "Some things change and some things don't. Those long-ago people used to do stuff we don't do today," he continued. "When they came to a new beach, they would stomp barefooted on sea urchin shells to make the place their own. My feet would bleed like crazy if I tried that. They used to give their kids names that would shame them and make them angry. Now we're named after saints."

"Strange thing to do," I said. "The odd names, not the saints."

"Not if you want your kid to be independent," he said.

"What kind of names?" I was intrigued.

"*Wart, Egg, She-Runs-at-the-Mouth.*"

"Still, it's an odd thing to do," I repeated.

"There were others," Vasilii said. "Lots of them: *Pimple, Big Eyes, Stink.*" Then he leaned over and whispered out of Anna's hearing, "*Wiping His Butt.*"

I think I turned beet-red.

Anna said, "*Tutukux̂.* Periwinkle. That's what my gram is called."

"Do you have one of those names?" I asked her.

She had taken out the ivory fox and didn't answer. Instead she asked, "Do you really think we'll find the Kagamil people?"

"Fevronia said they would be picking berries somewhere on this island," Vasilii said. "We'll go out tomorrow."

"How did they disappear?" I asked. "Anna told me nobody has lived on these Four Mountain Islands for a long time."

Vasilii picked up a stone and threw it out to the darkening sea. "They were said to have been very war-like, those people. They were whalers who had secret rituals. The people on Umnak hated them and when the Russians came along, they thought they had found some convenient allies."

"*With friends like that,*" Anna quoted, "*who needs enemies?*"

"One story is that the Umnak people got the Russians to destroy the villages on one of the Four Mountain Islands, killing the men and forcing the women who survived to move elsewhere. Maybe the same thing happened to the other islands."

"That's awful," I said.

"But there were later Russians who said they had skirmishes with Four Mountain people, so some villages must have survived. Nobody knows for certain. When Captain Hennig got the mummies from Kagamil, my father asked Peter Rostokovich to tell him the story. Like Peter said, he and his sister are descendants of those people."

"Do you think she's a witch?" I asked. I mean, why not?

"See what I have to put up with, Vasilii?" Anna said.

"There are good witches," I said, although I would have been hard-pressed to name one other than what's-her-name in *The Wizard of Oz.*

"If anything, she's a shaman," Anna said.

"I thought shamans were men."

"Not always."

"Anna's right," Vasilii said. "Old women can have unusual powers."

She didn't have to look quite so smug.

"There's a story about two old women who even changed the weather," he continued. "They made it real hot and people died. Men who were fishing came ashore and dropped from exhaustion. Women who were cleaning fish collapsed and died. The whole village died except for the two old women."

"Holy cow," Anna said.

"Then those old ladies went from house to house. They collected all the containers of good seal oil (and left the bad) and took all the good dried fish (and left the bad). They carried it all home, spread out a grass mat, sat down, and had a feast."

Vasilii paused. "This story actually came from Nikolski. Old Man Peter told it. Fevronia could probably add the juicy details."

Like wiping their butts, I wondered?

"While they were eating," Vasilii continued, "several skin boats came ashore. People got out and came up to them and said, 'Raise up our grandfathers and our great-grandfathers! Bring them back! Bring them back!'"

"That's an odd thing to say," I said. "If everybody had died."

Vasilii looked at me. I had to admit that time wasn't behaving in a normal way even now.

"Anyway," he went on, "the old women struggled to their feet. Their bellies were so full they had a hard time standing up. 'We didn't mean to make trouble,' one of them said. Then they hobbled back inside their house and started singing and dancing. They sang and danced until everyone who had died stood up and laughed."

"And that's the end?" I asked when Vasilii didn't continue. "It stops just like that?'

"That's it," he said.

We crawled into our grass tents before it was dark. I awoke once during the night. I heard the sea sweeping along the shore before I snuggled deeper into the warm and fragrant grass.

The next morning after a brief breakfast of the three remaining *alaadikax̂*, we headed east up a gentle ridge of low grass. I knew it was east because of where the sun was. We walked for over an hour crossing several ravines that led down toward the shore. The grass again grew taller the closer we got to the beach. By this time, Anna had pushed to the lead. She clambered down a gully, and I could hear her struggling ahead through a tangle of blades and roots and who knows what.

Then she let out a yell, and I heard her crash to the ground. By the time Vasilii and I caught up, she was on her hands and knees, locked in a petrified crawl. And no wonder. A man stood about three feet away. He wore a raincoat a thousand times more beautiful than what the three of us had on. He was young, but he had gray hair, and more to the point, he was holding a wooden visor in one hand and a club in the other.

I just stood there.

"*Aang, aang.*" Somehow Vasilii still had his voice. "Excuse us for interrupting your work."

The man lowered his club. "Not at all," he said in a voice that showed no surprise. "Welcome. Visitors are rare. Even easterners on all fours."

Anna struggled to her feet, blushing like crazy.

"Fine weather," Vasilii said with a voice that was pretty close to normal.

"Yes," the man said. "And it's going to get better."

Anna just gawked at him.

Vasilii pointed at himself and said his name. Then he indicated Anna and said her name. When it came my turn, I said my own name and put out my hand. The man didn't seem to know what to do with it, and he handed me the wooden visor. It was decorated with colored bands and graceful swirls. Balanced halfway down the bill was a small ivory bird.

"Ash," he said.

Finally a word I could pronounce.

"Hat," I said, giving the English equivalent.

"What a dolt," Anna perked up. "That's his name, Booker. *Ash*."

"We have been searching for you," she said as I returned the visor. He seemed very happy with it.

"For me?"

"You and any other Kagamil people."

The knuckles on the hand that held the visor turned white.

"Filth," he spat with contempt and turned away.

"Wait," Vasilii said. "We didn't mean to offend you."

The man looked from Vasilii to me to Anna. I could tell she was the most confused of all three of us. Fevronia had said we'd find the Kagamil people here. So who was this man? He slipped on his visor and said, "I can show you what they're like."

We followed him back onto the slopes at a pace that forced Anna and me to almost run. He limped, but it didn't slow him down in the slightest. We hiked up several low ridges until we came to the edge of a wide valley that circled a bay. The slope below was peppered with clumps of deep-blue lupine.

"I lived with the Kagamil people a long time ago," he said as he took a seat on the grassy ground. We joined him. "My sister and I were captured in one of the wars out west. And because of this"—he tapped his right leg—"they made me a slave. Well, I would have been a slave in any case, but they gave me the dirtiest jobs. Women's work."

I touched Anna's arm before she could object. What a hothead. Unangax̂ had slaves?

"Packing water. Cleaning up their filth. They starved me and dressed me in rags. But now!" He spread his arms toward the distant bay, "Look at what they have become!"

We saw three heavily patched open skin boats approaching the shore.

"I count about a dozen people," Vasilii said. The boats coasted onto the graveled beach and people climbed out, pulling the boats above the waterline. Even I could tell their clothes were tattered and mended. They glanced nervously around as they walked away from the water.

Ash stood up and circled an arm over his head as though he were stirring the air. The harder he swung, the stronger the breeze became.

"They have lost everything!" he shouted in triumph as he hurled the gust toward them. It swept down the mountainside. "Even courage has deserted them." He smiled as the crowd panicked and rushed back to their boats and pushed away from the shore.

"Maybe they need their magic charm," I said. Anna threw me an angry glance.

"You have one of those?" he asked gently. "That's why you are looking for them?"

We just sat there without answering him. Then he said, "How you treat those charms is how you will be treated."

I remembered almost identical words from Old Man Peter.

Finally Anna said, "It belongs to them."

"I told you," Ash said. "How they made me and my sister slaves."

"Maybe they've changed," Anna said. And then, forgetting we had just seen two boatloads of them, she added, "There's almost nothing left of them now."

It was like she and Ash were talking in and out of time. Ash was talking about a time not too long ago while Anna was talking about the future, where we had come from. Where I wanted to return.

"You saw how they are," he said. "You can't get near them."

"Can you help us?" she asked.

He stared down at the now empty beach.

"Would you help us? I mean, help us return it?"

He looked back toward the volcano.

"No," he said simply.

I thought that was the end of it. Time to go home.

"You could leave it there," he said, gesturing toward the beach. "Maybe they would find it."

"I don't think so," Anna said. I wished she wasn't so stubborn. Of course, we could leave it there.

"You could show it to the Woman of the Volcano," he said.

"Who?"

Vasilii picked a few of the round black moss berries from the carpet before him.

Ash again looked at the towering peak. "She is the guardian of that mountain, the caretaker of its fire."

"Volcano Woman." Vasilii pronounced each syllable softly as though for the first time he believed what he heard himself saying.

"Let me get this straight," Anna said. "You won't, but you think this Volcano Woman might be willing to help us?"

"You can ask," he said.

For the remainder of the morning, Ash led us across the rugged eastern half of the island until we stood at the base of the volcano. The summit always looked like it was a week's walk away. The lower slopes were softened with grass and low-growing bushes. The upper sides were all rock, stiff and fragile surfaces. We zigzagged up a series of switchbacks and crossed ravines of hard snow.

We're walking into trouble, I said to myself.

As the cone narrowed, the trail became steeper. We crossed to the opposite side of the peak. In the distance, a pure volcanic cone rose from the sea. A second island had some low land off to one side of its volcanic peak. Still another volcano loomed in the south.

I had now seen all four of the mountains. The breeze was always at our backs as though it followed us around and around. After we had circled the narrowing cone three more times, we came to a wide expanse that perched on a long escarpment—that's a word I learned in science and thought I'd never use. From here there was a nearly vertical descent to the sea. The ground was surprisingly green with lush vegetation forming a skirt around the muffled dome of one of those partly underground homes. Whoever this woman was, she occupied quite the piece of real estate.

"I will tell her we have arrived," Ash said. It was like the Woman of the Volcano had been expecting us. A notched log protruded from a square framed opening at the top. Ash used it to descend inside. We stood there, admiring the view toward the jagged out-croppings of the eastern half of the island.

"What are you thinking?" I asked Anna.

"I'm thinking we need to be careful."

Vasilii nodded agreement.

FOUR
FED UP
WITH HISTORY

14. Anna

Awe and bewilderment flowed over me when the Woman of the Volcano climbed out of her dwelling and stood before us. I had a vague but impossible sense of recognition, a crazy mixture of foreignness and familiarity. *Her eyes are like Fevronia's,* I thought, *only stronger.* I immediately stood a little straighter.

She wore a ceremonial parka, a reversible, full-length bird-skin gown with the feathers inside. The outside was a masterpiece of decorative appliqué. Both the sleeves and the lower half of the garment had red-and-white horizontal panels separated by narrow rows of intricately arranged squares of brown leather. Ribbons of dark fur-seal fur hung across the surface. The seams were decorated with hundreds of long wisps of white hair that brushed the garment like smoke. I probably resembled a bug-eyed loon, but, holy! as Gram sometimes said, this was amazing.

The bottom hem and the cuffs had semicircular white bands and checkerboards of black-and-red rectangles. These were fringed with dark fur. Ash's parka was wonderful, but I could have stared at Volcano Woman's for hours. Wide bands of appliqué framed the upper front, repeating the patterns from the hem. The collar was soft white hide, but I saw deep-brown fur seal on the inside.

Her long black hair shimmered in the evening light. As she turned her head, heat lightning hovered where it brushed her shoulders. She raised her eyebrows with polite wonder. And when she asked, "Who have we here?" it was as though she already knew. I again heard Fevronia's voice, now layered with the warmth and assurance of centuries. It was disconcerting and comforting at the same time.

All three of us stood like toy soldiers on parade. But even so, I felt strangely alone.

Volcano Woman came no closer.

Ash emerged from the *barabara* carrying a sea otter pelt that he spread like a blanket on the grass, arranging its surface free of folds or wrinkles. She lifted the hem of her garment and seated herself on the pelt. Despite all her magnificence, she seemed indifferent to her surroundings.

At her nod, Ash shook out a large grass mat and indicated that we should sit down. He uncovered a bentwood container and from it filled four wooden bowls with fresh berries. He placed one before the woman and gave one to each of us. Then he backed away and climbed down into the *barabara*. We waited until the woman had straightened her bowl slightly.

"Please," she said softly, "begin."

She smiled at Booker who had, I thought, rather skillfully already sampled one of the berries. As I crushed a moss berry in my mouth, a swift sweetness flowed into my throat and flooded every corner of my body. I had never tasted anything like it. The light in the west had faded, and when the woman dipped her fingers into her bowl, I glimpsed a flickering beneath her translucent fingernails as though her body ran with fire instead of blood. The moment she withdrew her hand, the tiny lights were extinguished.

"You have come a long way," she said.

"Yes, ma'am," Vasilii answered.

"And you are wanting to visit the Kagamil people? They are, you may have surmised, no particular friends of mine."

I glanced down. I thought she was their protector, but maybe not. Maybe each island had its own guardian. Or maybe they had done something to offend her.

"Nevertheless, I may be able to help." As she took a few more berries, the circumference of her bowl glowed. "Once I understand your purpose."

I instinctively knew I had to tell the truth. Bluffing wouldn't work, and lying was out of the question.

"I have a charm that belongs to the Kagamil people," I began.
"May I see it?"

I withdrew the cord from around my neck, opened the flap of
the pouch, tilted out the carved fox, and handed it to her. She refused
to touch it.

"Place it on the otter skin," she instructed. She had tucked her
hands inside her sleeves, and now she inclined her head toward
the carving. "Yes. I am familiar with this. The fox has been their
guardian spirit. This could belong to them. Where did you get it?"

"It has been in her family," Booker began, but I interrupted.

"It was stolen."

"More than once, it seems," the woman murmured.

"I found it among things a thief had on his ship."

I paused. Actually, Booker had found it, but the whole crazy
story was just too complicated to start explaining. If honesty was
demanded here, then why not ask?

"Will you help us return it?"

I did my best to hold the woman's stare.

"I will do more," she said as I surrendered and lowered my eyes.
"I insist you spend the night. Tomorrow, we will go to the Kagamil
people. They are always coming here, sneaking around, looking
for my berries."

I put the charm away.

As if responding to a silent command, Ash returned. "I have
prepared three beds," he said. The woman rose and walked to the
framed entrance. Wisps of steam slipped from under her parka.

"Stay outside awhile," she said. "Enjoy the view and come inside
when you are ready. Ash will get whatever you need." Then she
turned and climbed down the entrance pole. Ash collected the
bowls, rolled up the sea otter skin, and followed her.

I turned to Booker and Vasilii and whispered, "What now?"

"Let me see the carving," Booker said.

I handed over the pouch. He removed the fox, and before I
could object he had slipped it into a pocket on his backpack and
buttoned it securely. He took one of the small irregular stones he
had collected along the creek and slid it into the pouch before

handing it back. I nodded, not entirely convinced that this was a good plan, but willing to go along until something better came to mind. Ash returned just as I hung the cord around my neck.

The four of us sat, admiring the view. Two sparrows flitted around us before one came to rest when Ash held out his palm. The other bird brushed my hand with its wings. I extended my index finger and then, surprising me as much as the others, it courageously landed. I held my hand perfectly still.

15. Booker

Like the knickknacks at the Elder Cousin's, I said to myself as I spied a dozen carved figurines on a high shelf. The walls inside the Volcano Woman's home were like polished obsidian. They probably were obsidian. They magnified the light that came from a few stone lamps. It was super to see one of those things actually in use. Elaborately decorated grass mats suggested passages to other rooms, while shelves held grass baskets and beautiful bentwood containers with ivory handles. I really wanted to hold one of the spears that were arranged on a wall.

Ash served a meal of steamed roots, with more fresh berries and meat that was delicious. It even stayed delicious after I asked, "What is this wonderful stuff?" and was told, "Sea lion heart."

The woman entered the room. "Entered" is maybe the wrong word. She wasn't there and then she was. It seemed perfectly natural until I thought about it. She said we should continue eating. She seated herself on a grass mat. I took another bite of meat, and Anna helped herself to a few more berries. The woman looked a long while at Vasilii before she turned to me. Vasilii caught my eye as though to say, *Just be yourself.* But it was like trying to relax with your feet in the fire. I breathed slower when she focused on Anna who was reaching for a few more berries. She followed Anna's hand from bowl to mouth and back to the bowl. Then she stood and with a single unbroken movement walked over, lifted Anna's right hand, and turned it upward so the palm showed its expanding dark stain.

Anna looked terrified as the woman gripped her wrist and rubbed the stain as though she were striking a match. Sparks flew up from her palm. Anna yelped and snatched her hand away.

The woman's voice was almost guttural.

"*Qalngaax̂!*"

For a moment I thought she was cawing. K̲àl-ng-áwxh!

I looked at Vasilii, who simply mouthed, *Raven.*

16. Anna

After that, I was ready for just about anything. I mean, I suspected the stain was serious business, but when Volcano Woman went crazy over it, I almost freaked out. I controlled myself, but all kinds of horrible possibilities went through my mind. It was pretty clear that she had recognized it as something. I didn't trust her. I felt like I was a target she was aiming at.

When it was time for sleep, she said, "I always sit up late and sew, but you've had a long day. You need to rest."

Ash showed us to three alcoves tucked along one side of the large room and then he left, disappearing behind a grass mat to another part of what was obviously a complex dwelling, part *barabara*, part palace. *With a dungeon of its own*, I suspected. I was too keyed up to sleep, but Booker and Vasilii were immediately out. Even in the dim light, there were just too many things to look at, too many amazing things. The sea otter blanket was comfortably heavy and warm. The thick grass matting under me was fragrant and molded to my body. But I was wired. I turned toward the faint light from the stone lamp across the room, past the entrance pole, where the woman was sewing on a bird-skin garment and humming.

I was surprised the ladder had stayed in place and had not been lowered from the opening. *But then*, I thought, *who would dare to come here uninvited?*

I touched my neck where the pouch had hung a short time ago. The woman had suggested it be placed on a peg jutting from the entrance pole.

Some suggestion. More like a command.

Sitting within the largest alcove, she concentrated on her sewing. I crunched down and pulled the warm sea otter pelt around me.

I hardly need a blanket, I thought, *sleeping inside a volcano*.

I watched her hands move with masterful repetition.

If I were closer and could see her fingers, I thought, *I might be able to learn something. Something I could take home.*

I exhaled a slow, deep breath. *Maybe if I pretend to sleep*, I said to myself, *I'll actually fall asleep*. But one eye invariably sprang open. I scanned the room, concentrating—if such a thing were possible— on one piece of darkness at a time. I heard a faint crying from outside as moonlight slowly framed the rectangular entrance hole high above. *Baby fox*, I thought at first. But the strains were longer and deeper. Then everything was still and empty. I focused where the pole-ladder and the small pouch that hung on it were dimly illumined. When the crying started again, my right hand seized up in a cramp. I clamped my jaw shut to keep from yelping while I crushed the contorted fist with my good hand until the muscles relaxed and the cramp dissipated.

The woman held the garment out for inspection, smiled slightly, apparently satisfied, and then she tucked the bone needle into a fold before rolling it up. She placed it carefully inside a bentwood container, stood up, and went behind a grass curtain. I slipped deeper into the blanket and waited until the wick burning in her lamp had gone out. A faint cloudiness floated where the flame had been extinguished.

The whiff of dissolving smoke above the stone lamp curled and uncurled, more like steam than smoke. It drifted toward me. It forked and branched and swirled. My heart made an awful racket. It was like the shadow of a flame that stalled in front of the pole where the pouch hung. Whatever breeze had propelled it now evaporated. It held in the still air as two ghostly wings unfolded. They wrapped themselves around the pole, muffling most of it from sight. I squeezed my eyes shut to clear them, and when I opened them the smoky opaque wings, like a film running rapidly in reverse, were sucked across the room and back into the stone lamp where a small flame suddenly flickered. The woman stepped from behind the hanging grass mat and seated herself. She reached into the bentwood container and withdrew the bird-skin garment.

I stared at the pole. The pouch was gone.

The woman resumed her sewing. After a few minutes, she refolded the garment and again put it away. She lifted the lamp, stood, parted the hanging mat, and stepped behind it. I followed her shadow until the lamp was extinguished and the rustle and creak of bedding told me she had lain down. Firelight sprinkled the air as she shifted to get comfortable.

I squeezed both hands into careful fists. I didn't need another cramp. Then I relaxed and opened them and stretched my fingers as wide apart as I could. I did this two more times, pausing after each repetition and listening. The woman's breathing became heavy and regular. I folded back the blanket and sat up. I straightened my legs, but my whole body stiffened when a faint light glowed behind the woman's hanging mat, as when dark coals in a fire bed are stirred to life. I waited.

The light slowly went out.

More quietly than I had ever moved in my life, more quietly than I thought possible, I took four steps to Booker's alcove and touched his shoulder.

"What's —?"

"Shh." I placed my hand over his mouth. "She's taken the pouch. We need to get out. Wake Vasilii, but be quiet."

The moon had drifted behind clouds, making the room as black as a cave. I led the way, touching the edges of darkness with my fingertips. I felt the rough notches on the pole and began to climb. I was halfway up when I felt Booker and Vasilii's weight under me and feared the wooden frame would vibrate like a drum. As I clambered out, fresh air blew into my face, and the moon returned. I gave Booker a hand and he helped Vasilii. As we stepped cautiously off the sloping roof, Vasilii tapped down the air with his palms, cautioning us to walk as lightly as possible.

We slid our feet quickly and silently through the grass, lifting a foot only when a branch or a clump of roots stopped it. Moonlight lit up the side of the volcano, and shadows darkened the trail as we descended twice around it. I paused once to catch my breath and saw the moon in the distance stirring a far corner of the sea with a golden spoon. We were soon on the rocky switchbacks where, risking that our clumping footsteps would give us away, we charged straight down the side of the volcano, like boulders in a landslide. Vasilii aimed for the narrow flats separating the volcano from the eastern side of the island.

We sprang and slid and stumbled. We leapt onto an expanse of shale that funneled into a ravine wedged with snow. I took a wide jump, hit the snow feet first, fell back on my rear and took off. Vasilii followed Booker, and in seconds all three of us were swirling downward on the dense snowpack under the bright moon. I dug my hands into the crust as I saw the end approaching. In moments we were back on rock and tumbling forward. At times I could have sworn my feet left the ground and I coasted through the air itself. Three times shoals of soft moss berry plants, like banks of dry summer snow, provided slippery slopes and soft landings where we plopped down, lifted our legs, leaned back, and slid. Eventually, the increasingly tall shaggy leaves of monkshood and lupine signaled we were almost off the volcano. A short distance more and we were inside a river of high thick grass. I felt like a swimmer as I plowed through. Booker tripped, put his hands out to cushion his fall, and received a needle-thin puncture on his right palm.

"Agh!" he shouted as he rubbed one hand with the other.

Vasilii nodded. "It's next year's grass. It grows all wrapped tightly together. It's sharp."

"Like a needle!" he said, although it hadn't drawn blood.

The wide sandy beach spread before us. Booker twirled with his arms held out, but stopped when he caught sight of the volcano. The top third glowed as dawn broke and colored a line of high clouds. I saw Vasilii instinctively raise his hands in greeting. I smiled and he shrugged as though saying, "Not sure why I did that." But I had read that it was something old-time Unangax̂ routinely did. We skirted the expanse of sandy beach until it folded into the boulder-strewn shoreline at the eastern side of the bay. Light filtered down like a melting creek.

Vasilii located the skiff, or rather he found the end of the rope that had once tied it to the log. He and Booker stared at me. Like I was expected to have a plan.

I looked at Booker. "Do you have the carving?"

He unbuttoned the pocket on his backpack and looked in. "Still here."

I nodded at Vasilii who said, "Then let's get it back where it belongs." He pointed toward a grassy expanse flowing up the embankment.

I wasn't about to argue. We headed for higher elevation where the grass was shorter. One ridge followed another. At each false summit, the jagged sides of the mountain were outlined again and again, sharper and sharper.

"Wait," Booker said and collapsed on the grass, out of breath. I looked behind where the pure cone of the volcano glowed with morning light. A sliver of steam rose from its summit. A bank of clouds sat on the horizon like a woolen shawl.

Vasilii pointed east. "We'll try for the cove where Ash did that weird thing with the wind. If we're lucky," he said, "the Kagamil people will be arriving to pick berries."

"And if we're not?" Booker asked, but Vasilii and I were already up and walking.

We climbed until a patch of broken shale curved up to a nearly horizontal plateau. Here the rocks were small, flat flagstones, scattered like a deck of cards. Walking here was easy. Soon Vasilii stepped off and began a slight descent. A scramble down and up another ravine brought us to a new ledge of mountain, providing a partial view of a narrow bay. The breeze that had been at our backs had increased to a steady shove of wind, and the sky had grown darker. I felt the collar of my gut *kamleika* and wondered if I would need to raise the hood. I looked back. The top of the volcano was obscured under a cloud-heavy sky.

We climbed further out until the shoreline curved below us. We saw people securing their kayaks and *baidars* above the high water line. Booker wanted to shout, but Vasilii cautioned us to be quiet. Everything was in the open: the mountain slope, the two opposite cusps that formed the valley, the bay and shoreline, and the people preparing for a day of berry picking despite the ominous weather. There were only so many days when the berries would be at their best.

The contours of the mountain again hid us as we descended. We slid on our rear ends into a gully and grabbed at anything growing to keep from landing in the shallow creek at the bottom. Booker scooped a handful of ice water. I think he wanted to follow the creek as it tumbled down the mountain, but Vasilii was already climbing out of the ravine. Booker and I shrugged at each other, and we clutched at the nearest grass to pull ourselves up, hand over hand.

I passed Vasilii and reached the top first. Of course, the top was never really *the* top, but at last we were able to see the Kagamil people clearly. I started to wave when my feet slipped and I stumbled. Or I thought I had stumbled. My feet hadn't moved. The hill had shifted. A clamor from under the earth shook us, and a cliff on our right collapsed in a waterfall of stone and dust.

"She knows!" I shouted. "Run!"

And we were off, yelling at the people below. But the Kagamil people had felt the earthquake. They had abandoned their grass baskets and wooden containers and whatever else they had brought ashore as they swarmed into their boats. There seemed to be an unusual number of foxes suddenly dashing in and out among them. None of the people noticed us catapulting down the mountainside. The weather had thickened and passing sheets of rain washed over us as the rumbling increased.

I glanced behind and caught a running silhouette disappear as a hot geyser erupted from the ground. A crooked line of steam escaped from just under the surface as something rippled down the mountain. A series of abrupt jolts sent our legs dancing. Booker jerked as though he had run into himself. He toppled over and skidded away. My feet were kicked off the ground. I struggled onto my hands and knees as Vasilii was thrown backward.

Damp sand peppered the air. I curled my arms over my head as a gust of fine stone pellets swept past. A rock that must have been the size of an apple shattered as it hit the ground. Booker struggled up the embankment, his legs never quite coming down where he expected them to land. He looked like he was under water or caught in a wild carnival ride. Vasilii rolled onto his stomach and struggled to his hands and knees. I extended a hand just as his eyes widened and he stiffened in panic. Booker was now beside me, and we threw our combined weight onto his convulsing body. My hands sank into his wet raincoat as though it were filled with air. His chest and shoulders shifted as the spasms increased. Unfamiliar bones and muscles protruded under my hands. The mountain gave a terrific jolt. Booker sailed beyond a clump of grass that might have saved him. My fingers slipped as though Vasilii's jacket had turned into a feathered parka. I was thrown into the air.

A cool, damp wind struck my face. I opened one eye. And then the other. The world had turned to water. All I saw was gray water slashed with white fissures. My eyes closed, and I disappeared into myself. If time passed, and it must have passed, I was unaware of it. If time compressed, if I drifted in and out of time, I didn't realize it.

The air became heavy with salt.

My arms and feet dangled like a puppet's cut from their strings. My jacket pressed against my chest.

I straightened my legs and tried to lock my knees.

My body began to carry weight. I opened my eyes.

I was gliding across a world of water. Endless and gray. I closed my eyes again and felt myself drifting outside myself. I heard the steady pulsing of wings. The world tilted. The air became warmer. I was gaining speed, faster and faster, until my feet folded beneath me, and I tumbled onto a carpet of soft heather. All five of my senses collided loosely inside my body, buffeting each other and rearranging themselves into working order.

When I was able to focus, I saw Booker sitting beside me, rubbing his eyes, while Vasilii stood looking down at both of us.

"What happened?" Booker asked.

"We're back," Vasilii said.

"But what happened?" he repeated as he started to stand up. His jacket had two sets of identical tears on the back, three above and one below.

Vasilii only gestured around. We were on a narrow grassy upland high on the slopes of a mountain. Far below I recognized a familiar cluster of wooden buildings and *barabaras*. Unalaska's stately church anchored the far end of the curved shore.

"How did this happen?" Booker began again. His backpack was hanging from a single strap across one of his shoulders. He removed the carved ivory fox and handed it to me. I took it, but he frowned at how dark my palm had become. He was again dressed in his overly buttoned wool pants and shirt. His cap had apparently blown away. A few brown feathers clung to his pants. They vanished the moment he swept them into the air. I saw Vasilii's face and shook my head.

"It doesn't matter how it happened," I said. "It just did." But it did matter, and I think I knew what had happened. Peter Rostokovich had said the Unalaska people could turn themselves into eagles. Vasilii hadn't believed it. I hadn't believed it. But that or something like it must have happened.

I looked at Vasilii and then at Booker, who was frowning as he still tried to piece together what I knew were a series of disjointed memories.

"Sorry if that was a rough trip," Vasilii said. "It was the first time." He shook his head in bewilderment. "And hopefully the last."

"What do you mean?" Panic started to work its way up Booker's throat. I was, like, beyond panicking.

"Storm's coming," Vasilii said. "I guess we should get down to the village."

In the west a churning bank of clouds was drawing closer.

"We call this Mount Newhall," I said as we started walking. *Now*

I'm blathering like Booker, I said to myself as I continued. "It was named after some missionaries."

"Never heard of them," Vasilii said.

"You will." I smiled. "What do you call it?"

Vasilii spoke in *Unangam tunuu.*

"Which means what?" Booker asked.

"'It's a mountain,'" he said and laughed.

Below several folds of the treeless slopes, a line of people had come into view, walking the trail that hugged the shore. A man in front carried a tall, dark wooden cross. Two wide bands of black cloth were tied to it and curled in the wind. Behind him six men carried what was obviously a coffin. Their uneven steps gave the wooden box the appearance of floating on water.

"They're headed to the cemetery," Vasilii said and increased his pace. I made out three figures in dark robes. *The priest and his helpers,* I thought.

We half-ran, half-sailed down the smooth, grassy slopes. For a short time we were tucked behind a ridge, and when we emerged we saw a varied assortment of people about to enter the cemetery. Members of the Orthodox community and men from the A.C. Company were following the coffin single file up the narrow trail through a cluster of graves. Vasilii caught up with Huang Zhen, and asked, "Hey, Ivan, what's this about?"

The young Chinaman crossed himself and said, "Chris Hansen drowned."

A blunt wind sucked away the world. I didn't really know if he was a relative. But I had wanted to know him. I had wanted to talk with him. He might have been my grandfather. He might have helped me understand better who I was.

Vasilii and Booker followed Huang Zhen at the end of the line of mourners, but I stumbled away toward the beach where a wide swath of grass protected the shoreline. I scrambled down the bank. Rows of incoming waves fell on each other while cries of seagulls drowned out the continuity of the service that had begun. Fragments of Father Shaiashnikoff's strong tenor crosscut the rhythmic echoes of the choir. I steeled myself against an unfamiliar grief that rose from my gut until it broke into pieces. I crouched down in a protective cover of grass. The blades wrestled against the wind and struck me like dull knives. I had lost any chance of returning the ivory fox to where it belonged. Now I had lost another chance of figuring out who I was.

I felt the carved fox inside my pocket. I took it out and held it in my open palm.

I'm done with it, I thought. I tightened my fist around it. *It's only brought me trouble. All I want is to get back home. All I want is for things to be the way they were.* And then, as a long sob rose from somewhere deep inside me, I hurled it into the sea.

I joined Booker in the arc of people around the coffin, a simple wooden box resting on three planks above a damp hole. He extended his hand. A mound of dark earth rose from the lush green foliage like the back of a whale. I looked out over the great bay stretching in front of us with its pulsing uneven edges. Clouds had darkened the water. The service drew to its conclusion. The coffin was lowered into the grave with two wide bands of cloth. The rain began as the coffin came to rest on two pieces of wood. The cloth bands were pulled up, leaving the coffin by itself forever. It was raining hard now, and the wind masked Father Shaiashnikoff's voice as he intoned the benediction. He accepted a shovel from the church warden and scattered earth onto the casket three times. He handed the shovel to the person beside him. I waited my turn, which I knew would come after all the men and after the adult women.

Booker, Vasilii, and I pushed against rain and a headwind as we left the cemetery. I asked about using the bookmark to go back in time a few days, a week at most, so I could warn Chris Hansen. Or talk with him. Or something. But Booker had said we couldn't, or at least that he didn't have any idea how to do that even if the bookmark worked. Which it probably didn't. Then I had broken away from them and hurried ahead. I waited among the half-dozen cannons in front of the A.C. Company store until they caught up, and we went into the hotel where the company was hosting a reception.

The damp crowd milled around, standing in small groups or sitting on the chairs placed against the wall. Here and there brief eruptions of laughter accompanied stories about Chris Hansen's escapades and how he'd picked the worst day in weeks to get buried. Five or six Unangax̂ women, all in black, circled a young woman who was seated and holding a child. Vasilii left three young men and made his way to where Booker and I were sitting near the door.

"What's the plan?" he asked. And then he looked at me. "How are you doing?"

"I'm fine," I said. "Why shouldn't I be?"

"You still have something to do," he said.

"I'm done," I replied and turned to Booker. "We're going home." I shoved a cookie into my mouth to keep it shut.

Booker looked surprised.

"Those people on Kagamil," I said, eventually forced to swallow, "are still without their so-called magic charm." Crumbs stopped partway down my throat, and I coughed until I recovered enough to add, "They're probably all dead by now anyway. Nobody's luck has changed. Ash got the revenge he wanted. And this—" I was having a hard time keeping my voice steady. "This—" I gestured around—"it must mean we should leave things the way they are."

Vasilii didn't disagree.

As though to confirm my conclusions about the future of those long-ago people, Peter Rostokovich stumbled across the threshold accompanied by a gust of alcoholic fumes. He lurched forward and latched onto the first upright thing within reach. It happened to be Mrs. Otis. She had not attended the funeral but had heaped her plate to overflowing at the reception. She shrieked and sent cookies and a wedge of cake flying. I wanted to laugh, but it was all so sad.

Poor drunk Peter, the last of the Four Mountain people.

The old man stared furiously at Mrs. Otis as two men moved to restrain him, but he ducked sideways long enough to stretch out his hand and drop a soiled cloth onto my lap.

"It's yours," he said as he was pulled backward and pivoted toward the door. "You lost it," he shouted over his shoulder as he was propelled out into the fresh air.

I unwrapped the cloth. Booker and Vasilii looked down at the small, carved fox and then at me.

"What do you want?" I shouted as I stood and made for the door, cramming the fox into my pocket. "What do you expect me to do?"

How had Peter found the fox? How had he known where to find me? There were a dozen questions I couldn't answer. If he was a Four Mountain person, why hadn't he kept it for himself? Hadn't I made more than an honest attempt to return it? I couldn't have done anything more. It just wasn't to be.

In the end, Booker and Vasilii agreed. The storm had subsided. We had gone out to the cannons. I remembered about the bookmark's small torn fragment tucked between the pages of Dall's book on Aleutian mummies. If Vasilii would bring the book to us, Booker could attempt to unite the two pieces and activate the bookmark. It might work. It was worth a try.

"We were on Hennig's ship when we got here," Booker said. "That's our best bet for getting back."

"Here," I extended a hand to Vasilii.

He saw the ivory fox in my palm and shook his head.

I held the carved fox out to Booker. He just looked at it.

"Please," I said. "If Vasilii won't take it, we can give it to the museum at home."

He slipped it into his backpack. Rain had started to sprinkle, so we went back inside. The reception was over. The crowd had dispersed. Hennig and a few of the A.C. Company men had moved to a smaller room where periodic laughter interrupted their card playing.

"It shouldn't be hard for you to get aboard his ship," Vasilii said.

It felt like an ending. It felt like we were saying goodbye.

"Thanks for everything, Vasilii," I said. "I mean it."

He reached into his pocket and took out two small white objects. "Here," he said. "These are for you."

He handed over two finely carved ivory cleats that he said had been used to secure hunting spears to the outside of a *baidarka*.

Each was shaped like an eagle at rest. One hole allowed it to be fastened to the vessel while another threaded the cord that held the sea otter spears.

"I've had them a long time," he said as Booker examined his. "They came off a real old-time *baidarka* frame that somebody was taking apart for the wood."

We stepped back outside. "I'll be back as soon as I can," Vasilii said and headed to his house to get the book with the small fragment of the bookmark in it.

Chief, not priest, I thought.

"Well, let's get to the boat," I said as I gave Booker a slight tug on his jacket and added, "*Angaayux̂.*"

"After you, partner," he said and started toward the *Eider*. I had taken only a couple of steps when I turned and sprinted back to where the Russian cannons clustered around the flagpole. I ran my hands along the back of the largest one, the one I knew would never be returned once they were shipped away.

"Stay safe," I said to it and gave it a hard slap before I bolted back to where Booker waited. We made our way to the wharf as the rain returned.

17. Booker

The *Eider* was dark under the rain and mist. I was reminded of the day we arrived. We had not known where we were or what would happen. Now I knew where I was. But as to what would happen next, all I knew was that I did not want to get soaked. I convinced Anna we should find the room where we had arrived. It was a closet-sized cabin tucked below the back of the ship. The two narrow bunks built against the hull suggested it had once been used by the crew. Now it was mostly a storeroom, crowded with odd pieces of equipment, wooden crates, and two wooden barrels. I cleared off a bunk and sat down. With only a single porthole, it was pretty dark, but I made out the words *Remington's Horseradish* on one of the crates.

No, thank you, I said to myself.

I leaned back against the wall and yawned.

"I'm going up on deck to wait for him," Anna said.

"Do what you want," I answered. "It's raining hard. He'll find us. He's been here before."

She left. Normally, a storm would have kept me awake. But it didn't. Even worry about whether or not I would be able to reunite the bookmark and get it to work, didn't keep me awake. What did make my pulse race a bit faster was the memory of Fevronia sitting across the table and asking, "Will you remember me to my relative?" and me answering, "Yes," as though I knew what I was saying. That was a long time ago. A long time ago and several islands away. And then I fell asleep.

18. Anna

I waited on deck in the long evening light that was dimmed further by clouds and rain and mist. There was no sign of anybody along the curved stretch of beach. Something had delayed Vasilii, but I was confident that he'd show up. Booker was right: he would know where we were.

I went below deck and found myself a blanket. I removed two crates from the other bunk, burrowed under the blanket, and tried not to think.

Somewhere in the lost space of the night, the ship bumped against the dock. I rolled over and dreamed while waves and wind surrounded me. They lifted me up. I floated above crevices of water, coasted in air currents that angled over the sea. I stretched my arms and banked full-bodied into the wind. Up and across, down and over, higher and wider, I glided in swelling currents until the air thinned, the ship buckled, and the floor toppled away. I scrambled to my feet fully awake, only to be tossed backward as I struggled against gravity to Booker. I shook his shoulders and shouted with as much energy as I could inject into a whisper, "Booker! We're at sea. Wake up!"

With one smooth motion, he hurled himself to the porthole above his bunk and wiped away the condensation. Dawn was breaking, and the gray sea was studded with whitecaps.

"What do we do?"

"We ride it out," I said. "What else can we do?"

"Did Vasilii show up?"

I shook my head. I joined him on his bunk, and we sat with our backs against the bulkhead as the tumult roared a few inches away.

"We need some pilot bread," I said. "It's good for this kind of sea."

"Why did she let us escape?"

"That Volcano Woman?"

"She could have stopped us, you know."

"Maybe she didn't care much one way or another."

"And Ash?" Booker teetered over to a crate. He had a nose for food.

"What about him?" I asked.

He removed the lid on a tin box and handed me a cracker.

"Would he have helped us?"

"Seems unlikely," I said.

He finished off a cracker. He was a tad bit wired.

"Take out the fox," I said. "Let me see it."

He removed a rolled-up sock from his pack.

"You kept it in a dirty sock? Disgusting."

He handed it over.

"Poor thing," I said and blew on it.

Then I brought it closer to my eyes.

"Is this the same one?"

"What do you mean? Of course it is."

"I don't remember the opening here." I pointed where the two front legs crossed. "I need a piece of string."

I made it to a wooden barrel filled with pants and shirts, oilskin rain jackets, hats and gloves. I rummaged around until I found a leather boot. I unlaced it and, using a moment when the ship wasn't bouncing, threaded the leather shoestring between the crossed front paws.

"There," I said as I tied the cord together and handed it to Booker who opened the sock.

"Wait!"

I returned to the barrel, dug around again, and carried back a red plaid handkerchief.

"Try this. At least it's clean."

With the carving safely folded within, he buttoned the handkerchief inside his pack and yawned.

I watched him fall asleep. I have to admit I was getting used to having him around. My own eyes grew heavy, and I must have drifted off. I was awakened by the cranking of an anchor being lowered. The light coming through the porthole was brighter. I saw we were behind the gray protective bulk of an island. I nudged Booker, who yawned and stretched and was about to speak when short rocking spurts and creaks scraped the deck above us. He reached the porthole as something large plummeted past. He jumped aside as I clamped my face to the window.

"They've lowered a skiff," I said. I went to the barrel and handed him a rain jacket before putting one on myself. Both of them were too large, but we rolled up the sleeves and did what we could. I cracked open the door and made sure nobody was around. The brief respite from the storm dissolved into another onslaught as we emerged from the cabin and hugged the outside wall. Three men stood at the stern. One of them pointed toward the island. We slipped around the corner as they stepped into the wheelhouse.

I slid along the wall until I crouched under a small window.

Booker inched down beside me and mouthed, *Where are we?*

"We'll stay anchored," a familiar deep voice said before it was drowned out by wind.

It belonged to Captain Hennig. The second Captain Hennig, maybe the good one. I inched closer to the windowsill and heard him say, "Old Kagamil will give us a little protection. The burial caves—" and rain slammed into the cabin. I crouched down and heard another voice say, "'meantime, break out the cards, 'Ardy."

We backed away. When the rain took a breather and the wind relaxed, the slopes of Kagamil seemed a little greener and a little closer. Maybe because I had held the fox again or maybe because it was almost home, but for whatever reason, I found myself estimating the distance to the nearest shore.

"In this weather?" Booker held his arms out. "You're crazy."

"It won't take long," I insisted. "The wind will practically push us there. I know we won't find any Kagamil people, but I can bury the ivory fox someplace where Hennig One or Hennig Two—or any other pirate in this century or the next—will never find it and then—"

"What?"

"Then we wait until the ship returns to Unalaska, get the book from Vasilii, and go home."

"Or try to," he said.

I could tell he was tempted.

"Look, what's the worst that can happen? We get caught. They'll just think we're a couple of crazy kids."

"We need Vasilii if we're going to try something like that."

But he saw I had made up my mind, and he half-growled, "I know. *Haqada! Haqada!*"

I hoped the card game was exciting enough to keep the men playing as the rain began to diminish to a drizzle. I pulled the line tethering the small wooden skiff until it was directly below us. And then I jumped—although my fall, like when I had escaped from the volcano, seemed closer to floating than falling. Booker adjusted his pack, climbed over the railing, and was about to let go when I shouted, "Untie it first!"

I think he was surprised at how easily the knot came loose. He pulled in the rope, gathered it taut to keep the skiff beside the ship. Then he shut his eyes and clattered down beside me as I positioned the oars and rowed. When I stretched the oars out, I saw that the backs of both my hands were slightly darker, as though a shadow had covered them. But I had never felt stronger as I sent us away from the ship and toward Kagamil Island, closer and closer, aided by a steady breeze. It wasn't long before mist had almost entirely erased the *Eider*.

Rowing became harder as we drew closer to the shore. The water thickened, or so it felt because I had to double my effort to keep momentum. Booker saw me straining against the oars.

"What's happening?" His voice was edged with panic.

"Grab an oar!" and I made room beside me. We pulled together and the skiff broke free from whatever had held it. But now it had a mind of its own. It rebuffed all our attempts to reach the shore. The bow turned away from the island, and we headed back toward the *Eider*.

On deck, a man stared at us, or, rather, through us, past us, over our heads, almost as though we were obscured by a cloudbank. We were within twenty feet of the schooner when he turned and walked into the cabin.

"Awesome," Booker said. "Is it the same one?"

"Same one what?"

He held up an arm. "This!"

I looked at my own gut raincoat. "Unbelievable."

We were carried beyond the protection of Kagamil Island and toward the northeast coast of Chuginadak. I looked back at a bank of fog, dense blue and semitransparent, hovering on the water where the *Eider* rode. Our skiff was now a slightly smaller version of the skin-covered *baidar* we had been in earlier. The volcano stood far to the west, tall and solitary and menacing as we headed straight into the shore. Booker jumped out like a pro and pulled the skiff firmly onto the gravel.

"Where do you think we are?" he asked.

"I don't know, but it's not where the Kagamil people were berry picking. We must be closer to the volcano. I think we need to head east." I smiled a little. "Maybe we'll be lucky."

"I thought you were just going to bury it and leave."

"Well, I was, when we were going to land on Kagamil. But maybe here we can find somebody to give it to. And if we can't, then I'll bury it and we can go back."

"I think you need to make up your mind," he said.

I touched my gut sleeve. "It's pretty clear that somebody or something wants us here."

We lifted the skiff above the high water line—it was surprisingly light—and secured it in a depression of thick grass. Heavy surf pushed and pulled the gravel below us as waves hit the beach and receded.

The last time I had hiked on the island, the day had been dry. Now the deep grass along the shore was heavy with recent rain, although the day was clearing up. Shoals of the wide blades of wild rye were bent double under the weight of water. Each blade funneled a stream onto me as I ploughed through. Even when we reached higher elevations, the ground cover was wet and the grass was as slippery as a carpet of kelp. Struggling uphill, we wrapped the wet blades between our fingers to gain traction. Gliding downhill, we pumped our arms and hands into the grass to slow down and to keep from tumbling headfirst. My fingers were chilled. Cold, wet, and exhausted, we hiked on until Booker plonked down.

"You'll get your butt wet," I said.

He widened his eyes at the absurdity.

I stared at the distant shoreline and again wished I had Vasilii's ability to see things in the distance.

We set off, now angling slightly down toward what I hoped was the bay where Ash had first shown us the Kagamil people. He was a strange guy. He'd refused to help me return the carving, and then he'd taken us to the Volcano Woman who had been less than helpful. A stretch of hillside protruded in front of us like the rounded bill on a baseball cap. *Still*, I thought as I passed Booker who was adjusting the strap on his pack, *he hadn't been out and out hostile.*
"I think we're going to make it," I said and pointed toward a distant cove where two large open boats had pulled ashore. "I'm surprised that they're here. They must really like these berries!"

"I wouldn't have come," he said, forgetting he just had.

"Berries won't be at their best for very long," I said. "They need to get them before—"

A shadow darted across a high ridge.

"Booker!"

He looked straight back.

"Not there. Higher."

I caught another thin, swift flash.

"Not again!" he groaned and gave me a look that said he understood we were in danger of being discovered.

We ricocheted from side to side as we launched ourselves down the hill. For a moment, the shoreline came back into sight and then it disappeared beneath the crest of another hill. We crawled out of a ravine of dense ferns and stunted lupine and hurried across a bare exposure, leaping from stone to stone. We sidestepped down a grassy incline. Twice he slid into my feet and sent me flying. My legs ached. Every muscle in my body felt stretched to its limit. After what must have been at least a quarter mile, we stumbled onto a narrow ridge directly over the bay where people had come ashore.

"They're below us, Anna. I see a couple of them."

We had reached a rocky saddle that extended like the peak of a grass-covered roof. The view was amazing, but more importantly we could now see the whole bay below. People had climbed into the lower hills looking for berries. We got down on our stomachs, despite the dampness, so our presence wouldn't alarm them.

"Look," Booker whispered. A boy in a tattered gut raincoat was climbing toward us.

"He's not picking many berries," I whispered. The boy paused and looked back down toward his companions.

"Say something," Booker whispered.

"Like what?"

"I don't know. Something friendly. Something in Aleut."

"Jeez," I said as I got to my knees and took a deep breath.

"*Aang! Aang!*" I said, and racking my brain I remembered a phrase from Old Man Bill Tcheripanoff.

"*Slachxisaadax̂!*" Fine weather!

The boy froze.

Then he unfroze, or rather the whole side of the mountain unfroze as an earthquake shook the landscape. A jolt whipped the ground under us and brought us to our hands and knees. I leapt to a grassy oasis, but Booker slipped and in seconds he was surrounded by sliding rocks. He grabbed at anything—grass, rocks, twigs—but nothing held. He careened sideways as more rocks scraped his ribs and a stream of gravel carried him away. He dug his elbows in and arched his back. His raincoat was crushed up and under his armpits. His pack was torn off his shoulders. I saw him brace his legs to cut his acceleration, but the sudden jamming launched him headfirst. He sailed over a cascade of small boulders. A fine dust hovered in the air, and then the rumble of the landslide diminished.

I raced to where he had tumbled, sprawled cattywampus and groaning. When I touched his side, he struggled to sit up but immediately collapsed back. His right leg had slid into a trough over which a boulder the size of a truck tire had rolled. I leaned my shoulder against it, and shoved. I shoved again. If it moved, it didn't move enough.

"My leg's okay," he said. "It's just caught." His palms had been scraped raw, but he grabbed his leg below the knee and tried to wrestle it free.

The acrid stench of a red fox washed toward us as the animal scampered over loose rocks toward the backpack. I shouted. It stopped at my voice, tilted its head as though expecting me to say something intelligible, and then it snapped the pack between its teeth, shook it, and in a moment had dropped it at my elbow.

"Give it to him!" Booker shouted as he tore at his pants.

"Give what?"

Then I was on my knees flinging open the leather pack. I reached in and removed the folded handkerchief. I opened it and held out the ivory fox strung on its leather cord. I held it at arm's length toward the fox. My hands shook. The fox inched closer. My fingers twitched. It wrinkled its nose.

"Don't you dare bite," I said.

But the fox dipped its neck and leaned in closer. I slipped it over its head. It shook the way an animal does to remove a pesky fly, and the cord settled at the base of its shoulders.

"Go!" I shouted and clapped my hands. "Go!"

Booker was pulling on his leg. But nothing gave.

"Find something, Anna!" he shouted. "A stick, a branch! Something!"

141

Fat chance of finding a branch high on a treeless island. I picked up a flat stone and wedged it under the boulder and pushed, hoping to leverage it loose.

"Try a larger rock!"

But I hurled the flat stone away and began digging around the base at the front, flinging stones every which way. Then I stood over Booker and pushed downhill, pushed with every inch of strength I had. It tilted, only a fraction of an inch, but just enough.

Far below, a skin boat had pulled away from the shore.

As Booker rolled to his feet, I glimpsed a boy and then a young fox where the boy had been. I again clapped my hands, and in an instant the fox and the charm were gone.

"Pee-yuu!" Booker said. "Did you smell that?"

"Fox," I answered.

"Stinky!" he said, just as the ground vibrated and a geyser of hot air tore from the rocks. I screamed and grabbed his arm as a voice that crackled like fire began to laugh.

FIVE
MARK OF
THE RAVEN

19. Booker

The bookmark was jolted out of my pocket and into the air where it stayed just long enough for Volcano Woman to spit a sliver of fire at it. The words glowed for an instant, and then it burst into flames. Anna gasped, but I felt something slip into my shirt pocket. Torn and now probably burnt to a crisp.

We were balanced on a loose crust of earth. It tilted as the woman walked around us, inspecting us and trying to decide what to do with us. Wisps of smoke seeped out from the bottom of her grown that seemed filled with fire, and the feathers along the seams gave off sparks when they touched each other.

"I saw what you did, girl." She had stopped in front of Anna. "The charm will do them little good."

"They may surprise you," Anna said.

"Just shut up," I whispered.

"You're a brave thing."

"I did what I had to do."

Actually, I was feeling a bit defiant myself. Probably left over from carrying the ivory fox so long. It would pass. Hopefully.

"Ash will be happy to relieve them of it again," the woman said. "They will be happy to surrender it. Courage comes with obligations."

With that, she signaled for us to start walking on a trail that materialized when she waved in the general direction of the volcano. I stumbled after Anna, feeling a warm presence close behind me. The breeze was in front, pushing against us, as we climbed a narrow path bordered with soft heather, a trail now here, now there, now suddenly gone. Whatever dampness remained in my clothes soon evaporated. When I leaned into the wind, it acted like a full-body walking stick, giving me a wedge of support. I focused my eyes on the ground for stones, flat and loose and ready to slide, and for creeping stems of shrubs, bare and brown and more like roots than branches, that rose just high enough to trip me.

We stepped onto an expanse of flaked shale and made our way across the inward curve of a high valley. After another upward stretch, I saw the great volcano brooding off in the distance, all by itself. Its green skirt rose to a crown of rocks cut with deep crevices packed with years and years of snow and ice. Time had no passage there. Not the minutes and hours and weeks and months that I knew. Not even the years. It was like I had stepped out of time. I was so hypnotized by the beauty of the mountain that I crashed into Anna.

"Booker!" she snapped as she regained her balance.

The woman arched an eyebrow at me when I checked to make sure our collision hadn't knocked the bookmark out of my pocket. We began a descent to the base of the volcano. She pointed toward a boulder the size of a house. Anna again went first. I pressed my left shoulder against the huge stone and turned my eyes away from the embankment on the right. My feet released a slight dusting of pebbles that started a brief cascade of rocks.

Great, I said to myself. *Another avalanche.*

On the far side of the boulder, the trail sloped down until we crossed a narrow valley between the eastern side of the island and the great volcano to the west. After a moderate climb, we approached the ragged mouth of a cave. Sharp stones littered the ground like broken teeth. Ribbons of steam curled out from the two lowest corners. I shuddered at the thought of climbing through those hungry jaws. As though she understood my fear but didn't care, the woman ordered me to take the lead. Rocks cluttered the cave's protruding lip as I stepped into a smooth tunnel that led downhill.

Exactly like inside a throat, I said to myself as I reached out and touched a cool stone wall.

The sound of the wind brushing the entrance to the cave diminished. It had swept the opening like somebody blowing across the mouth of a bottle, but now it whispered and before long it fizzled away. I expected the cavern to be dark, damp, and cold, but the long passage was dry and filled with dim light. And wide. Not so much a tunnel as a series of rooms connected by narrow corridors and bridges. At times I held my arms out, balancing the way I once crossed imaginary chasms on two-by-fours. Back when I was just a kid. Back when everything was normal.

If I could see myself now, I thought, *what would I think?*

The path meandered back and forth, and then we descended a dozen wide stone steps to a landing. Massive stalactites glowed like lamps. My parents had visited Carlsbad Caverns and had hiked along cliffs in western Washington where there were cavities like small caves. Inside one of them they had found light-blue agates and used them in *Death and the Cavity of Fear*.

Mrs. Bainbridge had snorted, "Sounds like an unpleasant trip to the dentist."

This had to be a hundred times more amazing. And scarier. The path that led out from this landing was carpeted with a wide grass mat. Several minutes later, the passage divided into three equally wide corridors. I hesitated.

"Stay on the matting," Volcano Woman instructed.

I did, and from then on whenever an alternative trail branched off, I followed the matted way.

"It's a maze," I said to myself. I wondered if the people in one mythology knew those in another. I was about to ask if she had ever met somebody named Daedalus who had made a famous maze when I became aware of a sweet sulfuric odor, like garlic when Mrs. Bainbridge cooked an Italian meal. The thought of food drove mythology from my head. We passed through a vaulted room where delicate lava straws quivered on the ceiling like jittery fingers. The walls held clumps of white gypsum flowers and what looked like tangles of stone seaweed. We entered a cool chamber. I looked where I heard water trickling and saw rivulets winging across dark polished slabs and sliding into a stone bowl the size of a backyard swimming pool. Judging from the hefty stream that tilted out the far side of the chamber, I guessed the pool was also fed by underground springs.

Well, I guess everything here is underground, I said to myself as the path now followed the stream deeper into the mountain. A few hundred feet on, this stream met another beneath a stone bridge that vibrated slightly as the combined streams tumbled over a waterfall below it.

The trail narrowed and angled upward. The roar of water diminished until the only sound was my own panting and my muffled footsteps on the grass matting as the path changed into steps, dozens and then hundreds, climbing higher and higher. The corridor grew warmer. Any dampness in the air evaporated. The steps widened into a series of ascending ledges until they formed a single gentle slope of smooth stone that terminated at a broad landing. Stone benches lined the walls, and a circular grass mat of astonishing workmanship covered the floor. Anna stood hypnotized by the carpet, but I sank onto a bench.

"Up!" the woman ordered. We went to a door of black polished stone.

"I know," Anna said under her breath, "Obsidian."

She was right.

The immense door swung out at the woman's touch, and sweet air swept in. We stepped onto a wide landing. Before us, a stone bridge arced over a dark chasm. I followed Anna across. I would have closed my eyes if there had been guardrails, but there weren't, so I didn't. I stayed to the center and held my breath as warm air rushed up from both sides. It seemed ages before we stepped off and under a stone archway into a narrow hall. The Volcano Woman parted a hanging mat and there was Ash, standing at a bench and polishing a long black spear.

"So, they are back again?"

"But without their good luck charm or that young chief," the Volcano Woman said.

Anna caught my eye, and I knew she missed Vasilii as much as I did. He might have been as mystified by Volcano Woman and her surroundings as we were, but he had possessed a bit more knowledge and, probably, a lot more courage.

I saw thin stone blades clearly as sharp as razors on Ash's workbench. Lashed wooden handles held other blades in a variety of styles. All of them made me nervous.

"Good to see you," he said and laughed.

"Yeah, right," Anna replied as we followed the woman down a passage lit by glowing stalactites. We came to the large room from which we had escaped. The notched pole was still up. Soft light hovered at the high entrance and told me it wasn't yet night. The woman ushered us behind a grass mat and down another passage that curved to the right before it broadened slightly. She paused before a door fashioned from a huge slab of whalebone with a small square opening near the top. It pivoted open on obsidian hinges.

I started to follow Anna in, but the woman stopped me and pulled the door shut.

I was taken to the next cell. Before she left, she held out her hand.

I knew what she wanted.

She flexed her fingers impatiently. I took out the bookmark.

To my relief, she refused to take it.

"I thought I had destroyed it," she said.

"It's—" I started to explain as I showed her both sides.

"I know what it is."

Then she pulled the door shut and left me by myself. A coarse grass mat carpeted the floor. There was a bedframe of lashed and pegged driftwood, with a mattress and a soft fur blanket folded at one end. In a corner of the room, a stone sink was continuously refreshed by a trickle that fell from a narrow spout. I studied the walls and saw that the whole room had been hollowed out of pumice. Irregular pores speckled the rock. I flattened my palms against the rough stone and fingered a few of the openings. Selecting the largest pore within reach, I placed my mouth near it and whistled through the honeycomb of stone.

"Booker?" Anna answered.

"Are you okay?"

"Considering," she said. "How's it over there?"

"Comfortable. Surprisingly nice. What about you?"

"Wait," she said. I heard her door open. I looked around again.

It's like sitting inside a petrified sponge, I thought. I heard her door close and saw mine open.

Ash set a plate of fish and some kind of rice at the end of the bed. "Thank you," I said. "So what do you think will happen to us?"

"At first I thought you were done for. She looked furious when she brought you in. Now, I don't know," he smiled briefly. "She's been chuckling to herself."

20. Anna

I sat down on the cot and devoured the meal of salmon and rice from the Kamchatka lily that Ash had brought. What a treat! But my enthusiasm over the food was overpowered by irritation when I realized where I was.

I returned the fox, I thought, more than a little peeved, *and ended up a prisoner.* We had escaped once; we could do it again. While I ate, I mentally backtracked the route we had taken up through the volcano, trying to recall every passage in detail so I could lead the way once we figured out the *how* and the *when.*

From deep inside the mountain's core, a gentle rumbling wrapped itself around me.

It's like an idling motor, I thought. While I listened, a thin, melodic line wove through it like a metallic thread.

How had Booker known the young fox was a person? I should have known that. And was it the right fox? Old Man Peter had said a boy needed the carving, a boy named *Chaknax̂* according to Fevronia and her daughter. A boy who would drown without it. *Chaknax̂?* I smiled at the thought of anybody stuck with a name that meant "Stink."

The melody continued, strong, sharp, and keening. It was sad, but strangely comforting. I curled up in the luxurious sea otter blanket. I closed my eyes and fell asleep.

One thing soon became clear: this was a jail like no other. The first morning after I awoke, I went to the door and found it was unlocked. Booker was already out in the hall, and together we started exploring. It wasn't long before we found the workshop where Ash was busy shaping what he said was a sea otter spear. We sat down and watched. That afternoon Ash took us outside for fresh air and exercise. Well, I guess it was only for air. There wasn't enough flat land to do much more than walk around a bit. The food at lunch was fresh and fragrant salmon, steamed roots and rice. Real Unangax̂ food.

After lunch, Ash took me to the main room, the room from which we had once escaped.

"Look around, if you want," he said before leaving me alone. "I don't think you'll be going anywhere. You'd get awfully wet if you did. There's a storm coming."

The room was like a museum. The baskets were phenomenal. Some of them were woven in a way I had never seen before, but others were like the open fish baskets at the museum back home. I examined one that resembled the one the girl on the beach at Unalaska had used. I returned it to the shelf and picked up an oval bentwood bowl.

Even though the islands have no trees, I thought, *my people must have known a lot about wood.*

I turned it over to examine the bottom.

"It was carved and then steamed," Volcano Woman said as she stepped from behind a hanging mat.

I pressed my hands into it to keep it from slipping away.

"Your people had great skills," she said. "Skills shared by no other people."

I knew that. I didn't need to be told.

"I admire your courage," she said and actually smiled a bit.

I don't know if it was courage or craziness, but I looked right at her and asked, "How long are you going to keep us here?"

Instead of answering, she said, "Things disappear. One variation follows another. Ash knows more than his grandfather did about some things. About other things, he knows less."

I knew that. I didn't need to be told that.

"Of course not," she said.

Yikes, I thought, *she's also a mind reader.*

"When I saw the way you were looking at things, I assumed you were interested in the ways of your ancestors."

"I was," I said. "I mean, I am."

If I could master even one Unangax̂ skill and bring it back home, how terrific would that be! As though to confirm my thought, she asked, "What would you most like to learn?"

I had actually thought about that quite a bit, so it didn't take me long to answer.

"I'd like to weave a basket."

"A good place to start," she said.

"Like one of these," I said as I put the bentwood bowl down and picked up a fish basket.

She held out her hands, and I gave it to her. As I did so, she looked at my palms. The stains had darkened and spread to my wrists. The jagged lines like writing had almost disappeared under a general blur. Once more she whispered that strange word, "Qalngaax̂," and then she looked at me as though there was something I should understand.

I turned my hands away.

"And after basketry?" she asked. "Gut-sewing and appliqué? Perhaps. You may not have the patience for bending and painting wood or for carving ivory."

"Those all sound great," I said.

"And fighting," she added. "Fighting above all."

She started to hand the basket back, but the quiver in my hands had erupted into shaking.

"Fighting?"

"Do you know what has happened?" she asked as she put the basket down. "What *is* happening?"

"What hasn't happened?" I tried to quiet my hands. She smiled briefly.

"You are fated to do something remarkable," she said.

"Fated?"

"Destined, perhaps," she said. I knew what *fated* meant. "Fated may be too strong a word. It may be that you will need to make a decision."

She was talking in riddles.

"And decisions have consequences."

She wasn't making sense.

"Because of this?" and I thrust out my darkening palms.

"Little Raven," she said. "Partial raven. You need to be careful."

21. Booker

Even though I'm good at math, it was hard keeping track of the days inside the volcano. I'd wake up and think it was morning, but it wasn't. It was only when we were taken outside and I could see the sun that I had any sense of the time of day. Of course, that didn't help with knowing what day it was. Yesterday had been stormy and today was just as bad. I had gone to Ash's workshop where he was concentrating on a bentwood visor. Anna was kung-fuing the air and letting out a little grunt with each thrust.

"You look ridiculous, Anna," I said.

"Hah-raah!" she shouted and leveled a kick in my direction. I jumped aside and she knocked over a low shelf of tools.

I helped her pick them up. She quit her martial arts practice and sat down beside a pile of long yellow grass. I picked up a long thin piece of wood, something like a branch. It was going to be a spear. Ash had started shaping it, and then he had given it to me with brief instructions on how to scrape it with a curved stone blade. It was supposed to end up as a gently tapered shaft. He had shown me a finished spear, and it was amazing. I was pretty much at a complete loss as to what to do, but Anna seemed comfortable with the grass she was working on.

"I learned this at Camp Qungaayuх̂, the summer Unangaх̂ culture camp at home, at Humpy Cove," she said. "You separate the stalks into the inner, middle, and outer blades. Those are the ones you use when weaving."

The pile of discarded blades was soon much bigger than the usable ones.

I turned the wood every time I scraped it, the way Ash had demonstrated, in order to keep it round. Even so, I kept leaving little gouges. He came over to inspect.

"This is an odd sort of prison," I said.

"Don't scrape too hard. You want to keep it balanced."

He handed it back. "It's not a prison."

"Might as well be," Anna said.

She was right. This whole island was a prison as far as we were concerned.

"Have you looked around?"

We had. We had explored a number of hallways and rooms.

"A bit," I said.

He nodded for us to follow him. We left his workshop and started down a long set of steps that began just off the stone bridge. We were occasionally separated from the abyss by stone walls; at other times, we were right at the edge where jagged rocky pillars loomed up. The dark chasm was made even darker by jets of steam. We came to a landing that opened onto a hallway along which were a dozen rooms. The first one was filled with whale vertebrae. This was followed by a room with shelves lined with wooden boxes containing feathers, beads, and small pieces of bone or ivory. There were small stone bowls holding dry pigments. The shelves in yet another room were stacked with flattened grass baskets and rolled mats.

"Who made all this stuff?" I asked.

Anna gave a snort in reply.

"The best pieces, she made herself," Ash explained. "And the others, well, they came from Kagamil and elsewhere."

The next room stored gut and bird-skin work. There were raincoats and parkas. Near the door was a shelf with small containers like envelopes made from what Ash said was both seal and sea lion intestine. Some were pretty fancy. I had to pull Anna out of the room. We walked into an elaborate kitchen with its own storage closets and prep spaces. All the heat feeding the open grills and ovens had been channeled from somewhere deep inside the volcano. An assortment of wood and stone tools hung on pegs and rested inside cavities hollowed out of the walls. A muscular woman sat on a stool scraping the skin off a long yellow root.

"The Woman-with-Six-Sea-Lion-Sons," Ash said, introducing her. "She is an amazing cook, as you have already experienced."

He was right. The meals had been delicious.

Her eyes sparkled at the compliment. She gave a slight tilt to her head causing the flesh on her frame to vibrate like custard. She smelled, I thought, like fresh bread.

As we started back, Anna asked him, "Did you hear about the ivory fox?"

"That you gave it away?"

"Without your help," she said. "And now you'll be asked to steal it back. How do you like being a hired thief?"

Good grief. But, he didn't take the bait. He simply said, "There are more important things."

"Like getting home," I said.

"Will you do it?" she asked. Totally obnoxious.

He didn't answer.

Back in his workshop, I picked up my would-be spear. "Can I use this when it's done?"

"First things first," he said. "I'll take you down to the shore where you can stand in the sea. That's a beginning."

Anna's laugh evaporated when Volcano Woman walked in and pointed at her three neat piles of separated grass blades.

"Take those to the kitchen."

And cook them like spaghetti? I wondered.

As Anna gathered up the three piles of grass, the Volcano Woman said, "The Woman-with-Six-Sea-Lion-Sons will show you how to braid them together."

"What do you think, Ash?" she asked after Anna left the room. "Auklet or raven or something else?"

Then she looked at me and asked, still speaking to Ash, "Will he do?"

"He's young," Ash said and nodded a smile at me.

My stomach contracted. *Young as in "tender turkey breast,"* I wondered?

I tried to sit a bit straighter and look a bit tougher.

"Well," she said, "even I was young once upon a time. May I see it again?" She looked at me. This time she didn't hesitate to take the bookmark.

"What does it say?" I asked.

Instead of answering, she said, "Stories become clouded once they are written down. They lose most of their power when confined within sentences."

I asked again, "Can you tell me what it says?"

I felt like I couldn't exhale until she said, "It's incomplete."

She glanced at it again. "It's not Raven's favorite story. It embarrasses him."

I started to breathe.

"Enough," she said. "He doesn't like that story. It foretells his death."

"Real Raven lives out west," Ash said. "A long ways from here."

"But I give the disgusting creature a place to stay when he drops in," the Volcano Woman said. "He does what he wants. I don't bother him."

"The story is," Ash continued, "that a man took the form of a Whiskered Auklet."

"A whiskered what?"

The glare from Volcano Woman suggested I should just keep quiet.

"A small bird, tiny, but fierce. It was his guardian spirit. Taking the form of the auklet, the man was able to escape from Real Raven. Not only escape, but eventually kill him."

She handed the bookmark back to me. I studied it.

"And this says all that?"

"Not exactly," she said. "It tells some of the story. What you have there says, *The man hurried down to the spirits that Raven kept in a cave and they told him how Raven used to live, what Raven used to do. And when he heard this, he got scared.*"

"And what does this have to do with Anna?"

"You've seen that yourself," she said. "Something that was in those words has escaped and entered her. With luck, she will become what she has always wanted to be."

I looked from her to Ash.

"If she survives," he said.

Volcano Woman turned to leave. "Her guardian spirit will eventually make itself known."

"But if the raven is already dead—"

"*Was* dead. *In* the story," she practically spat out the words. "But now he isn't."

It was right then that I started to appreciate the way Ash kept his cool. "The power of the man who killed Raven in that story," he said very calmly, "has started to flow into your friend."

"That is one possibility," Volcano Woman said. "The other is that she is becoming a raven herself."

Ash looked away, like he was considering that possibility.

"Or something close to that," she ended.

"Is she or isn't she?" I asked. "Does she know?"

"Knowing doesn't help," the woman said. "Not in this case. Not now."

"She will need your help," Ash said.

My yelp came out at as a squeak, and Volcano Woman gave me a look that suggested: *Mouse, Sparrow?*

"Is that why I'm making this spear?"

Ash shook his head and laughed. "Let's hope you don't have to use that."

It did look pretty pathetic.

"Eventually enough changes will accumulate," he said, "and she will tilt one way or the other. In either case, sooner or later, she will need your assistance, in one way or another."

"You just need to be ready," the woman said and left the room.

22. Anna

"What do you mean *leave*?"

"We have got to get out of here." Booker put down the spear he had been making. It was looking pretty good. "Now. Or soon. Whenever. But we cannot stay."

We'd been having this argument for several days.

"Why the hurry?"

"The hurry is, that, well," he said, "I told you what was happening."

"And I said you were nuts."

"Anna, just look at your hands."

"I know," I said. The shadows had darkened and passed beyond my wrists. "Weird, isn't it? But they don't hurt or anything. It's a rash. I just need the right ointment."

I got a kick out of watching him get so agitated.

If I were turning into something, I would have felt it. If I were changing into a raven or into an auklet, don't you think I'd have felt it? I mean, that's doing something really weird. Volcano Woman herself had said I was *destined*. I was *fated* to do something important, something significant. I had no idea what. Booker had said I might have to kill a raven. I didn't like that idea. Ravens were neat birds. Anyway, if I was changing into anything, it was into a real Unangax̂. The old lady from the kitchen got me started weaving a basket. The first time she saw the stains on my hands and wrists, she backed away like I was contagious. But now she always treated me real nice. She wasn't a very systematic teacher, but whenever I got stuck I'd go down and she'd redo it for me. Not that she ever said much. I'd just have to watch the way she did it and then try to repeat that. Sometimes it worked. Sometimes it didn't. She seemed pleased with every attempt I made. In any event, I was getting better and my basket bottom was gradually expanding into a perfect circle.

I was learning things, true things, things I needed to know. And I was collecting things. Granted, some of it was junk, like the two broken knives I'd taken from the kitchen. But I also had a role of sinew thread and two flat gut containers with feathers along their seams. Those were treasures. It seems like every room I went into had something I wanted. And then there was Ash.

He had been totally unwilling to help us return the fox to the Kagamil people. I didn't blame him. Nobody wants to be a slave. But the Kagamil people weren't all bad. He needed to learn to forgive a little. Like us. I mean, he didn't seem to have a grudge against us for having escaped. If he had been upset, well, he had gotten over it. He should get over his hatred for the Kagamil people.

"Okay," I said. "I'll think about it."

"Good."

"We'll have to make a plan," I said, even though I had no intention of leaving until I had mastered a few more skills.

"I've been working on one," he said, but he didn't look very pleased with it.

"Let's do a little more exploring," I suggested. "Maybe we'll turn up a secret exit. This time I get to lead."

"You always lead, Anna," he said. But I could tell he was happy.

We had the Volcano Woman's main room to ourselves. I checked all the cubbyholes and recesses, but she must have gone out. The log pole was in place; the hatch was open. We had been here before, of course. Almost every day. I had studied the grass fish baskets and the bentwood containers. I had examined the grass mats, trying to figure out which end the weavers had started at. I positioned a stool made from a whale vertebra and stood on it to examine the small ivory carvings on a high shelf. Booker got his own stool and joined me. Three sea otters had parallel lines across their stomachs. Two seals were diving and another was perched on a smooth rock. There were birds with wings tucked at their sides and with wings outspread. Some of the carvings had been stained with dark-black ink. Two had red feet. None of them were exactly like the ivory fox. Speaking of which, I had finally figured something out. We were here because I had returned the carving and been rewarded, chosen to do something grand and given the opportunity to learn all these old-time things.

"Don't," Booker said when I reached for a long-beaked bird. My hand froze as I saw what had alarmed him. Its eyes were moving ever so slightly.

I stepped down and walked over to where a group of masks were arranged on a wall. As far as I could tell, they were just masks. None of their eye sockets had eyes. They looked like they had been modeled after people I wouldn't want to meet in the dark. They had protruding eyebrows and gigantic noses with mouths locked in snarls and grotesque grins. Two masks had wings flapping out behind their ears. One was devouring a rat. They had all been carved with immense skill, but, *Ayaqaa!*

I removed one of the lesser horrors. It looked a bit like a bird.

"Hey, Booker," I said, "trick-or-treat!" I raised it toward my face. Then I tossed it to him. He lunged and, of course, missed. It flew a few feet before crashing into a log. I swear it gave out a weak groan as a crack spread from its crown to its chin and it split into two pieces.

"Crap!" I said. "Let's get out of here."

I slipped behind a grass mat. He followed me down the hall. After we passed under a wide archway, the floor sloped steadily down. Eventually, the passage branched, and I went right, where the walls were carved out of rougher stone. The hallway narrowed until we had to go single-file. A sharp turn took us down three steps into a room lined with stone benches. Booker walked over to examine the walls, and I headed toward a closed door on the opposite side.

"Hey, Anna," he shouted, "the walls aren't rock. They're—" but I had opened the door, and a tide of wailing sent me stumbling against the nearest wall.

"Chalk," I said from where I had landed, "or feathers."

I pushed away from the weird walls and stepped through the door with Booker right behind me. The wailing had diminished to a pathetic crying.

"I don't like this," Booker said as the hall narrowed and darkened until it was little more than a tunnel. At the far end of it, a pinprick of light illumined an opening to the outside world. The light tugged at me. I think Booker felt the same pull because we drifted down the passage like branches that had fallen into a river.

"This could be our way out," I said. Even if I wasn't planning on leaving right away, it was good to know that escape was possible.

We passed a shallow alcove where I could almost touch both sides with my outstretched arms. I stepped down through an arched opening into a wide foyer. I made out iron bars separating us from a deep cave.

"It's like a grotto," Booker said. The kid had some vocabulary.

Body-by-body and beak-by-beak, a crowd of skeletal birds emerged from the darkness beyond the bars. They perched on stone blocks and stood huddled on the floor. Their heads and shoulders were covered with open sores. Scabbed bellies were puffed with air. Every eye focused on us. The birds were consumed with hunger. They were dying of starvation and thirst.

Booker unscrewed the lid of his leather canteen and stepped up to a stone depression just inside the bars. The instant the water hit the shallow trough, there was a cry like the opening of a wound as the birds lunged. The larger ones clawed and crushed their way across the smaller ones. Booker stumbled backward into me, and we scrambled out of the alcove on our hands and knees. I struggled to my feet as a flicker of light quivered at the far end of the tunnel, a shadow shifted, and something swept inside. The birds shrank back in a single breath.

My heart beat in my ears. Every artery in my body pulsed. And then the pulsing shifted to outside my body and began to vibrate the floor. I heard pitiful mewing and turned to see three badly mauled creatures dragging themselves toward the back of the cave where a row of large birds were clicking their sharp beaks. The vibrations in the floor grew louder and heavier, closer and closer. I grabbed Booker's hand and we ran. We ran as we had never run before. I slammed the door as we dove into the room with the chalky, feathery walls. And then we were out of there and past the kitchen and beyond the storage rooms and up the steps and safe.

And I was ready to leave. Honest to God. I was ready to leave.

23. Anna

If I was so ready to leave twenty-four hours ago, why was I still here?

It's because the next afternoon I was told to return to the Volcano Woman's main room.

So I went.

It was packed with birds, foxes, mice, and even a seal or two. I elbowed my way through until I found a whalebone stool and sat down. Booker stayed at the back, near a door. He looked miserable and uncomfortable, what with all those animals and birds giving him odd and slightly hungry glances. Ash took a seat in the front, facing the crowd. The Woman-with-Six-Sea-Lion-Sons was already seated there. The whispered barks and squawks subsided when Volcano Woman strode in, dressed in another spectacular bird-skin parka. She stepped onto a slightly elevated platform as cheering filled the room—if squawks and chirps, growls and barks, and the occasional whistle constitute cheers. She raised her arms and silence descended.

"It is rare that I interfere in your lives," she began and bent her head to the crowd's appreciative murmurs. "But once in a while I am moved to step in and make—" she paused, "adjustments."

Like at Pompeii, I thought, as a nervous rustle swept through the room.

She's talking to a room full of animals, I said to myself. Apart from Booker, Ash, and the woman from the kitchen, there wasn't a human in sight except for myself. Things were about to get odder.

"Everything will be explained in time, but for now," and her voice rose above the murmuring, "I am here to make an announcement."

It took a minute or two for the cheers to subside. She resumed speaking and I managed to catch a few words over the approving squawks and growls before a tumultuous roar drowned her out and she swung an arm toward the crowd. I turned to see who had been announced. The shockwave of wings and fins shaking the room blocked my view. I stood up a little, but the shouting and stamping only grew louder, so I stood on the vertebra stool. I stood on my tiptoes. And suddenly the crowd sank back into their seats, and there I was, like a plastic figure on a wedding cake. Me and Booker. I mean, Booker was the only other person or thing standing. Then he sank down.

"This girl," the woman said as I struggled to hold on to the air—two wings and a paw pushed against my butt and kept me upright—"this young woman, has been chosen."

I stood a little straighter. Of course I had been.

I caught Booker's eye. He had never understood.

"By theft and deception, she has confirmed her transformation."

Into a true Unangax̂, I said to myself.

But what theft? I remembered the odds and ends I was collecting. *Hardly theft.*

Deception? I glanced at Booker. *So what if I had deceived him?* Maybe now he'd realize how important this was. How important I was.

"She will become," and here the Woman of the Volcano spread both her arms out wide, "one of the Dark Bird's companion spirits."

The dark bird's what?

The clamor in the room grew to a crescendo so that even the floor vibrated. The noise from the crowd subsided as the vibration took on a regular beat. The tread from which Booker and I had fled in the dark tunnel had returned. Pain seized both my arms, so intense and sustained that I crumpled onto the stool. It held me like a net as I bent my head to my knees and held my sides. The aching robbed me of every sense except hearing. Louder and closer and heavier, whatever it was had entered the room. Volcano Woman's whisper cut through the hushed parting of the crowd, "Give welcome, all, to the Real Raven!"

"The Boss! The Boss!" squeaked a tiny voice. "Make way! Make way!"

I struggled to sit up. I opened my eyes as a mouse ran full speed into the legs of startled ptarmigan, bounced back, and took off again, his voice a little slurred, "Shmake way! Shmake way!" although there was no one even close to being in the way of the astonishing bird that had entered the room. His broad chest was thrown out. His vicious beak angled upward. He sucked the color out of everything he passed. Here was a sharp chunk of the original night, darkness as old as time itself. I stared transfixed by the great bird's eyes, cavernous orbs from which nothing escaped, in which each pupil hovered like the earth in space.

Creator.

Destroyer.

Raven shook, and his feathers glistened like knives. The air swirled violently, and the mouse let out a terrified squeal.

I shrank into myself as he passed. His breath was like rancid meat. He reached the front of the room. Ash held his ground, only lowering his head ever so slightly. Raven bowed to Volcano Woman with what, I felt certain, was less respect than calculation.

The roaring in the room became thunderous cheering as the Raven turned in my direction.

"Soon," the woman said and held up her hand, "but not today."

I looked toward Ash, hoping for something, but he had walked to a curtained doorway.

I felt myself falling. I fell into a single memory from ages ago. That first night on the island with Booker when Vasilii had said, "*Listen. Share. Don't be boastful. Do the things you know are right. It's what it means to be Unangax̂.*"

I rubbed my palms together.

Get a grip on yourself, I whispered as I drifted back into my senses. I was seated on the stool and terrified. At the center of my right hand was a blackness I had never seen before.

Vasilii's voice was like a rope, but it was slipping through my hands.

"*Listen. Share. Don't be boastful.*"

My palms were as slippery as feathers.

The Volcano Woman's smile was like ice or like fire. Like both. She had betrayed me. This isn't what she had promised.

"The day is approaching when we will gather for the final transformation."

She looked toward the doorway where Ash held open a hanging grass mat. "No one is more efficient at organizing events than Summer-Face-Woman."

A tall stately woman entered the room. Her face was perfectly proportioned, with its delicate mouth and high cheekbones, but her eyes gleamed with gristle and spite. She scanned the audience. Part-hawk, part-viper, she was a thousand times nastier than Mrs. Skagit ever thought of being.

"Summer-Face-Woman is a master at organization," Volcano Woman continued. "She will see that the rooms are prepared. She will arrange accommodations and invite the guests. Have no fear, you will all be included!" Cheering prevented me from hearing what she said next, but it must have had something to do with me because the woman stared directly at me.

Mrs. Skagit's eyes had been piggy and greedy, but these eyes were like the Real Raven's. Hollow and dark. Greed had been entirely eaten away by hatred.

"And myself, my dear, my dear?" A second woman held out both arms as she wobbled through the doorway and curtseyed to everything in sight.

"The Sister-of-the-Moon," announced Volcano Woman. "She will help with your clothing," she said and looked in my direction. "Her sewing is even finer than mine."

"Too kind! Too kind!" The Sister-of-the-Moon again bowed deeply to everything and everybody and floated a little further into the room, her feet scarcely touching the floor.

I saw Volcano Woman whisper something to Summer-Face-Woman and then she left. It was a moment before the crowd realized the gathering was over. A terrorized scream from the mouse brought their shuffling to a halt. The crowd parted and Real Raven exited with arrogant indifference while the mouse skittered from side to side to avoid being trampled. Then the winged crowd rose in a body and flew out the entrance hole. The mice and fox scampered up the notched ladder and the seals just disappeared down a dark passage.

Ash stood speaking with the two strange women.

I sat, petrified, my fingers curled into my palms like talons.

SIX
SYLLABLES
OF MEMORY

24. Booker

I went to Ash's workroom where Anna sometimes showed up, but she stayed in her cell for the rest of the afternoon. Ash was making what he told me was a throwing board for sea otter spears. It looked finished to me. It looked beautiful, but he kept making slight adjustments with a sharp knife.

"What kind of wood is that?" I asked.

"*Lalux̂*," he said, "Yellow cedar."

"It smells sweet," I said. I don't think either of us wanted to talk about what had just happened.

From one side he removed a sliver of wood like a small breath.

"I don't understand," I finally said. "A few days ago the Volcano Woman said Anna was coming into her own. She said her guardian spirit would make itself known."

"I was there," Ash said. "I heard it." He took a wide and slightly curved piece of wood down from a shelf. "I hear you've been breaking masks."

"It wasn't me," I said.

He just shook his head a bit and handed me a stone chisel. "See if you can shape a face out of that."

I turned the wood from side to side.

"Like this," he said, and he used the chisel to remove small flakes along one side.

"So why did she change her mind and say that Anna will serve the Raven and not kill him? That she'd be his companion?"

"I don't know, Booker," he said as he returned the mask and chisel to me. "She understands things. She knows things we can't possibly know."

There was no way Anna could fight that colossal bird. Just the memory of him gave me the heebie-jeebies.

"He was pretty impressive, wasn't he? He can take different shapes, different sizes. He wanted to make an entrance we'd remember."

I put down the mask and took out the bookmark. One side was totally blank. The other still had those strange words. I wondered what would happen if I tore it again. Would the ink from the letters run into me? Would I start changing? Maybe it wasn't the bookmark itself; maybe it was Anna.

"Isn't there something you can do?"

"Not even if I wanted to," he said. "I think she's determined that Anna should fulfill the promise in that story." He nodded toward the bookmark

"It sure didn't sound that way."

I put it away as the woman from the kitchen came into the room with a steaming bowl of something that smelled delicious. She placed it on the workbench while that fluttery woman who had been introduced as the Moon's Sister set a couple of plates beside it.

Ash thanked them as they left.

"The Moon's Sister has some great stories," he said, "if you can get her to tell them."

I started to fill my plate.

"I understand why she is here," he said. "Nobody can sew clothing as beautifully as she does."

I handed him the ladle. "Whatever you do," he continued, "stay away from Summer-Face-Woman."

"She's creepy," I said.

"It's been a long time since she's been here. When I was a boy, the elders would tell us stories about her to get us to behave."

The food, some sort of stew, was so delicious and so nourishing and I was so starved that I hardly paid attention to what he was saying until I heard the words, "And they were all dead."

"What?" I looked up.

"I said that she's had many husbands," Ash repeated, "but every last one of them was dead the morning after she married them."

"All of them?"

"Every single one."

"Wow!" I said.

"She wanted me as a husband," he said with a slight smile, "but I said no." Then his eyes twinkled a little. "At least not yet."

"I will definitely stay out of her way," I said.

"She has a bundle of feathers from the rosy finch tied with a special grass for her magic. It's what she travels with."

"What do you mean?"

"If she needs to get somewhere fast, the rosy finch feathers will take her."

Like my bookmark, I wondered?

"She's brutal," he said. "Well, she would be if she's related to the Raven, which she is."

I thought it was strange to be getting such friendly advice from somebody who was, well, he was like a prison guard, although he had said this wasn't a prison.

"How long will it take for whatever is happening to Anna to happen?"

Any answer he might have given was cut off when Volcano Woman stepped into the room. Now she seemed like an ordinary person. Well, as ordinary as your average volcanic goddess can ever be, but even so I felt nervous. I slipped the bookmark into my pocket and tried to shrink into invisibility. Not possible, of course.

"What is it you want to know, young man?"

"I was wondering how long this will take? How long whatever is happening to Anna will take to materialize?"

"Are you planning to go somewhere?"

Of course I was, but I think she was making a joke.

"I have things under control," she said.

Of course she did.

Of course she did.

25. Booker

Ash had warned me to stay away from Summer-Face-Woman, but that was exactly what I could not do. The next morning, I was sent to the room where the announcement had been made.

"It's not like it was in the old days," a woman said as I paused at the doorway, "before there were numbers or crows."

"Of course not, Sister."

"How long will it take to complete her transformation?"

"Two weeks, maybe more. Two weeks might be pushing it," the second woman said. "That girl is tough."

So it hasn't happened, I thought, *or not all of it.*

I felt like I was standing in the rain and getting drenched, without a raincoat or an umbrella, with no shelter in sight, the sky darkening, and a growl of thunder rolling in over a ridge.

I stumbled in. The Sister-of-the-Moon was fluffing up a feathered parka, and beside her stood the woman with the terrifyingly beautiful face.

"Ah!" she exclaimed when she saw me. She raised an eyebrow at my ability to trip on thin air. She stretched out a hand, but not to balance me as I thought. Instead she pinched my forearm and frowned. "You're a puny thing, but you'll do. There are things that need to be prepared."

"Prepared?" I thought of Hansel and Gretel and the oven.

"For the day of transformation."

"Wonderful day! Spectacular day!" chortled the Sister-of-the-Moon. "There is so much to be done!" And she drifted out of the room.

I was taken to a large room crammed with sealskins, stones, and driftwood, all of it waiting to be turned into something usable. A massive stone fireplace filled most of one side of the room that, once emptied, was to be converted into a reception hall for the expected guests. Summer-Face-Woman left after giving me instructions. I had made two trips carrying sealskins to a storage area further down the hall when a voice at my feet said, "Nobody needs a fireplace inside a volcano."

I studied the ball of fur at my feet. At first I thought it was that hyper mouse who had rushed into the room before the raven, squeaking in a panic and shouting, "Make way!" My surprise then at hearing an animal talk had been wiped out immediately by the entrance of the raven himself. But now I was surprised.

"Hello, mouse," I said, looking nervously down at the rodent.

The creature froze and the hair from its head to its furry toes prickled outward.

"Not a mouse?"

It shook a rather luxurious gray coat back into place and pivoted around.

"You don't have a tail," I realized. "Or not much of a tail."

"It's not all I don't have," he huffed proudly. "But I have what I need."

He may have raised an eyebrow.

And you are a—" I hesitated.

"A lemming, of course," he said. "And you," he asked as he stepped back to get all of me in view.

"Booker John," I said.

"Where are you from?"

"I hardly know," I said.

"In that case, what's your crime?"

"My crime?"

"Why are you here? Mine is not having a tail and being small and liking grass inordinately and . . ."

"Those aren't crimes."

"Of course they are. You're practically bald, by the way," he said. "That may be your crime."

"There are two of us," I said, trying a new subject. "Only she seems to be changing into a raven."

The lemming tightened and shuddered. "I know. I was here for the announcement. I hate the Raven. Hate him! Hate him! Hate him!"

"She's not becoming *the* Raven," I tried to sooth his agitation. "She's become *a* raven, a raven companion. Or something like it. Maybe an auklet. Or nothing at all."

"Where is she now?"

"I don't know. I think she's tired."

"Sleeping is not a crime."

"Of course it isn't."

"But pride and long division almost certainly are."

Where had *that* come from?

"He eats my cousins."

I had to think twice about that.

"Mice," he said. "He raises them and eats them. I hate him."

"I don't wonder," I said.

"So what are you going to do about it?"

"What can I do?"

I felt the need to talk. The lemming scampered up onto my knee, and I told him about our first trip to the island, about Vasilii and the carved ivory fox. How Anna wanted to return it and how at the beginning of our second trip she had. About the boy who was sometimes a boy and sometimes a fox. Remembering him, a talking animal didn't seem that odd.

"Well, it's too bad," the lemming said. "Too bad I can't swim over to Kagamil and tell the boy. Maybe he could help. But I can't. Even a little water is too much for me. In fact—"and here he leaned in closer and whispered—"I'm on this island quite accidentally."

"Accidentally?" I asked.

"Drifted here," the lemming said in an absent-minded sort of way. Before he could explain further, a shadow crossed the doorway. Summer-Face-Woman glanced at the empty spot on the floor and said simply, "Quit wasting time."

I had cleared almost everything from the room when it was time for dinner.

"I think you'll like this," Ash said as he carried a plate into my cell. He was right. The Woman-with-Six-Sea-Lion-Sons had prepared salmon mixed with fragrant rice and what might have been eggs. I felt rejuvenated after scraping the last of it off the plate. I needed revitalizing because before long I was back lugging stones and driftwood until the room was empty.

When I finally stumbled back, I was asleep before I knew it. The next morning I scrubbed the floor of the empty room using water from a wooden tub and a brush that was like rough hide. I worked on my hands and knees until lunch, making repeated trips to refresh the water from a cleft in the rock wall. It had felt good talking with the lemming, and I kept hoping he'd return. Instead, Summer-Face-Woman showed up every so often, towered over me, touched my brush with the tip of one of her sharply pointed boots, and wrinkled her nose in disapproval. The floor looked good to me. But, apparently, not good enough because she had me scrub it again. After that I had to haul whale vertebrae in for chairs or stools around the perimeter of the room. No matter where I put them, I had to move them somewhere else.

Late that afternoon, Summer-Face-Woman took me into a much larger room where she said Anna's final transformation would occur before a crowd of guests. This room had a vaulted ceiling with its own hatch at the top. The notched-log ladder, however, was nowhere in sight. At the head of the room there was a raised stage where beautifully carved whale-vertebrae stools had been arranged. There were two high balconies entered from an outside hallway. The room was impressive and, thankfully, practically empty.

"Here is where the scaffold is to be built," she announced as she raised an arm toward the closed hatch at the summit of the ceiling. "All the way to the top."

Yikes, I thought. *Who's going to get hanged?*

But as she talked I realized that what she wanted was a scaffolding with layer on layer reaching to the roof. It was to be constructed from dozens and dozens of driftwood branches stored in yet another room. I had seen them, but assumed they were firewood. I carried the first load of branches into the ceremonial room, sorted them into sizes, and then returned for more. On my third trip, with branches up to my eyes, I rushed along the corridor, made a sharp turn, tripped on a frayed grass mat, and sent the branches catapulting into the air in every direction. A rush of heat swamped the hallway as Volcano Woman brushed a stick from her shoulder, made a slight adjustment to her gown, and stood there. She didn't zap me into ash or anything. She just stood there.

I was too petrified to apologize.

"I'm glad you're making yourself useful," she said as I picked up a branch.

"I look forward to seeing your mask when I return."

I gathered up a few more fallen branches, nodded to her, and continued on to the ceremonial hall.

She was leaving? Maybe escape was possible.

I fell into a troubled dream that night in which the great ceremonial hall was a museum packed with fossils of small lizards and leaves, footprints, and birds. There was a white fossil fish swimming against the current of the rock. It hovered almost completely still while everything around it moved. I tried to stand that still. "Is it real?" I remember asking. "More real than a painting," came the answer. I awoke to what I thought was a thin line of morning creeping into the room. Buried inside the volcano, of course, there was no way to know if morning had actually arrived. I went back to sleep and slept until I heard a voice outside the door.

"It's about time," Anna said as I opened it and she stepped into my cell. "What are we going to do?"

26. Anna

If I had expected to wake up the morning after the announcement in a nest of feathers, I was mistaken. Whatever was happening was taking its time. For two days from under my sea otter blanket I had been gently prodded by the Moon's Sister. I had listened to sharp commands from Summer-Face-Woman to "get up and quit loafing." I had responded by pretending to be delirious which wasn't hard to do whenever I thought about turning into a raven. Finally, I had crawled out of bed.

"You sound like yourself," Booker said as I walked into his room, his cell. His expression suggested he had expected me to be covered with duck down.

"Of course," I said, feeling defensive. "Who else would I be? What are you making?" He was holding an oval piece of wood.

"I'm replacing the mask you broke," he said. Before I could say anything, the Sister-of-the-Moon arrived with her arms full of feathers.

"Ah," she gushed, "you are up. Wonderful! I need you to do a fitting." And she unfurled a beautiful bird-skin parka. "It can be exhausting, these changes," she continued. "What's happening to you. I should know."

I followed her to my cell. She had pretty much taken over the room with containers filled with bird skins, various threads, and pieces of cured and dyed materials of one kind or another. She handed me the parka.

"Do you think it will fit?" I asked as I marveled at the intricate designs along the sleeves.

"I've had you measured," she said.

I didn't like the sound of that one bit.

I slipped it on. It fit perfectly. I couldn't believe it was going to be mine. After she took a few measurements, I removed it, put on my ordinary clothes, and sat down. I picked up my weaving. It was getting better. Who am I kidding? It was phenomenal. The old woman in the kitchen had hinted that I could learn gut sewing next. *This is the new Anna*, I thought, *the real Unangax̂ Anna.*

And the fighting? That afternoon I went for another lesson. I managed to throw my instructor. He was one of the sea lion sons of the cook, but he wasn't a blubbery sea mammal. He was actually a pretty good-looking guy. I might have distracted him a bit when I gave a passable imitation of his mother calling him for dinner, but he was about fourteen times my weight, so what I did was pretty remarkable. I don't think I'll ever be good enough to floor him without tricks, but I had already learned one or two. Summer-Face-Woman was in the hall when I left. She had seen me outfox the instructor.

"You're learning quickly," she said. "Walk with me."

"I probably shouldn't have tricked him," I confessed as she led the way down the hall.

"It's what I like about you," she said as she placed a bony hand on my arm. "You are willing to do the unconventional. You are willing to take risks."

That sounded like me.

"You know what you want," she continued, "and you have the courage to go after it."

She seemed to know me pretty well, until she added, "We are more alike than you might think."

We had reached Ash's workshop. She followed me inside. We had the room to ourselves.

"Be careful around him," she said.

"What do you mean?"

She meant Ash.

"Just that he may tell you one thing and do the other."

He had already done that. He had taken us to the Volcano Woman suggesting she might help, but she had done just the opposite.

"I think he was glad to see us come back," I said a little defensively.

"Of course he was," she said. "Just be careful. That's all I'm saying."

She left me then. I wondered if I hadn't judged her too harshly. If she looked snarly, well, people can't always help how they looked. I mentioned this to Booker the next day.

"She's super dangerous, Anna," he said. "Ash warned me about her."

"What does he know? He's not on our side. He just does whatever the Volcano Woman tells him to do. He hasn't done anything to stop what's happening to me."

"Do you want it to stop? You don't act like it."

"Don't underestimate me, Booker," I said. "I know exactly what I'm doing."

27. Booker

That evening the Sister-of-the-Moon sent word that Anna would be having dinner with her and Summer-Face-Woman. The same happened the next day. After Ash and I had eaten our meal the second evening, we climbed up the entrance pole in the main room and sat down outside. Far below us, the sea moved against the shore. The volcano itself seemed to tilt into the sea. The sky went on forever. The long evening light lingered across the hills. I tried to remember something my mother had said about the angle of the sun at the horizon. Something equal to something. What would she think if she knew where I was?

I looked toward the eastern end of the island. Maybe there were still berries left for the Kagamil people to pick. I imagined myself hiking there and getting their help to escape.

"Would you like some dried fish?"

He laid out a few pieces of red salmon.

We just sat and nibbled a little dried fish and said nothing. Then he asked, "How is the scaffolding coming?"

After I had moved all the branches into the ceremonial room, Summer-Face-Woman had given me instructions on how to lash them together. I began by making a base from the heaviest branches. It had four cells across and three deep. Each cell was large enough for me to stand inside with my arms stretched out. She returned now and then to deliver a good shake and make certain it all held together. Once she was satisfied, I moved up to the second row. By the third day, the grid extended halfway to the ceiling.

"Okay, I guess," I said. I wanted to talk about Anna. She still wasn't growing feathers. Her nose wasn't morphing into a beak. Although, when I thought about it, she was turning her head less and less and now just jerked it from one direction to another. She wasn't building a nest—although she made little caches of odds and ends, flakes of obsidian swiped from Ash's workroom, small coils of sinew lifted from trips to the storage rooms, things like that. Things she didn't need at all. Twice she had told me I was paranoid when I warned her about Summer-Face-Woman.

"Ever since the announcement," I started, "Anna has been more and more like a stranger."

"She's busy," he said. "She's learning all those things that women are supposed to know."

"Her basketry," I said, remembering the last time I saw it, "is actually getting worse."

"Maybe so," he said.

"Whatever is happening to her," I said, "goes deeper than I expected."

"You're both young," he said. Saying that didn't help a bit. "Things are complicated."

Of course they were. That's what I had just said. Then there was another one of those long pauses that happened whenever I talked with Ash.

"She's been saying some pretty horrible things," I said. She had. The last time I talked with her she had almost bitten my head off. "She said to ask you about the Kagamil people."

"What about them?"

Anna had accused Ash of being responsible for just about everything that had caused them to disappear, or at least to dwindle down until there was just one old woman and her drunken brother. She had asked me to ask why he didn't forgive them.

"Nothing," I said. "She just thinks you're being unfair."

I heard him take a deep breath.

"Not me," I quickly added.

"I can never forgive what they did to my sister," he said. "They got what they deserved."

I didn't know what he was talking about exactly, and I didn't want to know. I wasn't about to get in the middle of an argument between him and Anna. Like he said, things were complicated.

"I saw a lemming a couple days ago," I finally said, starting on a new subject, "and it was talking."

"That sometimes happens," he said. "I've known foxes that could speak, and sparrows."

"I was pretty surprised," I said. I had wondered if the talking animals had anything to do with Anna's changing into a raven or whatever.

"Usually animals and birds talk only among themselves. When they have something we need to know, they tell us."

"Maybe he didn't have time to tell me what I needed to hear," I said. "Summer-Face-Woman interrupted us."

"You're staying out of her way?"

"When I can," I said, "which isn't often."

28. Anna

I thought about what Summer-Face-Woman had said. About Ash saying one thing and doing another. And what was he doing? Not much. Like Booker, not much at all. Here I was going through all these changes, and they were like spectators. Both of them could have done a lot more to help. I got attention from the Moon's Sister and Summer-Face-Woman. They appreciated what I was experiencing. They were willing to help.

After eating supper by myself, I went down to the storage room filled with small bags sewed from gut and bird skin. I just wanted to look at them, to feel them, to again be amazed at how fine the stitches were and how the delicate design work just flowed naturally to fit the shape. Maybe add another one to my collection. I was about to leave when I heard the Sister-of-the-Moon out in the hall.

"It's going to be a mad rush, but everything will be perfect," she said.

I waited a few moments after I heard her and whoever she was with walk past. Then I peeked around the edge. The Woman-with-Six-Sea-Lion-Sons held two bundles of tied grass. The Sister-of-the-Moon had an armful of towels. If Summer-Face-Woman carried something, I couldn't see what it was. They passed several rooms before Summer-Face-Woman opened a door and steam escaped as they went inside. I crept down the hall and stood outside that door for a full minute or more. Then I carefully cracked it open. Their naked backsides were just disappearing behind a heavy grass mat and into a cloud of steam.

I slipped inside. Three piles of neatly folded clothes were on a stone bench. There was a wooden box beside them. Inside it was a bundle of rosy-colored feathers tied with a fine piece of braided grass. I left it there, although I really wanted to add it to my collection. I closed the lid and replaced it exactly where it had been. I considered joining them just to see their reaction, but this craving for secrecy took over and I scrunched down behind a tall stack of grass matting to wait. I think even Summer-Face-Woman had relaxed a bit after the steam bath because when she came out she answered the Woman-with-Six Sea-Lion-Sons who wanted to know how things were going with "that girl."

"Not too well," she said. That made me feel real good.

"She's tough," she said.

That made me feel even better. She appreciated me.

"The potion of compliance," she said, "should do the trick."

The what?

"You always were clever with herbs, Sister," said the Moon's Sister.

"But isn't it," interrupted the mother of the sea lion sons, "I mean, doesn't it require her to drink it voluntarily?"

"It does," said Summer-Face-Woman. "At the beginning it does, but once she has, she's mine."

I wasn't about to be hers. I felt the hackles on my neck rise. Her what? No way was I going to be hers. I managed to stay hidden until they left, and then I walked out of the room without a glance around to see if anybody was watching. I could dang well take care of myself. I think that's when I realized that I was on my own. I had to look out for myself. Nobody would help me. Not those three women, not Booker or Ash or my mother.

My mother? She had abandoned me years ago.

Good riddance.

For two days I drank only what I knew was safe. I avoided Summer-Face-Woman whenever I could, and when I couldn't I pretended to be happy to see her even if I felt like a mouse being played with by a cat. She was kept busy bossing Booker around. He was pretty horrified when I told him about the potion of compliance. We were in Ash's workshop where he was working on his mask. It was starting to resemble something like a head. There weren't any eye sockets or nose or mouth, but it was definitely becoming something. Ash didn't react at all to my news.

"Have you seen the potion?" Booker asked.

I hadn't.

Ash removed a fine cord strung with two beads from around his neck. "Why don't you take these," he said. I turned the rough amber beads so they caught a little of the light.

"My uncle carved them," he said. "He was a healer."

I gave them back. "No thanks."

"One is for strength; the other is for endurance."

"No thanks."

I didn't need anything from him.

If I want them, I said to myself, *I can get them on my own.*

The Moon's Sister was in my room early the next morning, adding another row to the intricate design along the bottom hem of the parka. She was really going overboard with preparations. I watched her fingers as she stitched away. Sometimes she used just a single thread and needle. At other times, she wrapped a second thread around the needle and secured it to the material with a stitch. While she worked away, I wove on my basket, and the morning wore away.

"Are you hungry?"

I looked up. Ash had arrived with freshly cooked salmon surrounded by berries and tender green stems of wild *petruski*.

I took a small piece of fish and nibbled at it. Summer-Face-Woman came into the room carrying a leather flask and a crystal goblet. She walked over to the sink. She held the goblet under a small stream of water that flowed continuously until it was almost full. Then she sat down beside me.

"Will you hold this?" she handed me the goblet.

I took it reluctantly even though it held only water. She unscrewed the cap on the flask and poured in a beautiful light-blue liquid.

The Moon's Sister held up the parka. "Almost finished," she said. It really was a splendid garment.

"Excellent work, Sister," Summer-Face-Woman said as she took the goblet back and carried it to the wall where she placed it on a shelf. I saw that Ash kept his eyes on her.

"More fish?" he held the plate out to the Moon's Sister.

"Wonderful," she said and took a large piece.

"Your sewing is unparalleled," he said.

"Too kind! Too kind!" Then she added, "I love the dark iridescence of superior cormorant skins."

Summer-Face-Woman walked over and stroked the parka. The dark feathers shimmered.

"We are all companions of the Dark Bird," she said.

"Speak for yourself," I replied as I helped myself to another piece of salmon.

"In time," she said and lifted her hand from the feathers. "You will be in time, when this parka replaces your skin."

I jerked violently, and a fish bone lodged in my throat. I coughed, but I couldn't get my breath. Ash pounded my back. A cup was thrust in front of me.

"Drink!" somebody ordered.

I swallowed automatically. The bone slid away and my breathing returned to normal.

"That's better," Summer-Face-Woman said as she took back the goblet. She nodded for the Sister-of-the-Moon to hold up the parka again. "What do you think?" she asked.

"It's magnificent," I heard myself say. "Truly magnificent. Is it really mine?"

"But you're still here," Booker said when I went to his room the next morning. I had awakened with a start. But within seconds, it was like everything around me began to diminish. Like I was only half alive, like I could only focus on what was right in front of me. I stumbled into his cell.

"You seem normal enough."

"It's early," I explained what had happened yesterday. "I haven't had anything to eat or drink yet today."

I held my hands out to him.

"But I will."

The dark stains had reached my wrists.

"It's like I'm losing myself, Booker," I said. "It's like I'm disappearing."

29. Booker

Things soon got even worse. Three days later I delivered a packet of needles to the Moon's Sister from the Woman-with-Six-Sea-Lion-Sons. Anna was sitting there trying to weave what looked like little more than a snarl of grass.

"Is that the last you have?" the Sister-of-the-Moon asked as Summer-Face-Woman carried in her leather flask, filled, I suspected, with the potion.

"I can make more."

"If you say so," she replied. She looked at me. "It isn't easy to make. It takes considerable skill and time."

Summer-Face-Woman emptied the flask into the goblet.

The ground trembled slightly. Earthquakes had been growing in frequency. I tried to remember if quakes were a way that volcanoes had of releasing steam, but before I had decided, Summer-Face-Woman held the goblet out and said, "*Haqada!*"

You've got to be kidding, I said to myself. I wasn't about to drink it.

"Give this to your friend."

It's really quite beautiful, I thought as I looked down into the heavy blue liquid with its peaceful silver strands. I swirled it in a slow circle. So this was the last of it? It rose like a gentle wave to the edge. I held the goblet tightly in both hands as I walked over to Anna. I increased the speed of rotation. The liquid circled faster and faster toward the rim, but not a drop fell over the edge.

I know a little about gravity and momentum.

It's now or never, I said to myself as I shoved upward and instantly yanked the goblet down with all my strength. The liquid sprang out and burst into a shower of rain. I felt triumphant. Like oil on water, the droplets skidded over Anna. They slid across her lap and cascaded to the floor, perfectly round crystals with blue and silver light drifting through them. They bounced toward each other and strung themselves together. Anna snapped out of her trance with a smile of delight. She caught the string of beads and slipped it over her head. Her smile became immediately and horribly vacant.

What had just happened?

"That will hurry things along," Summer-Face-Woman said with something even more like triumph. "She will have a constant infusion of the potion."

I looked from the Moon's Sister to Summer-Face-Woman in panic.

"It was necessary for Anna to take the first sip of the potion herself," Summer-Face-woman said. "And it was necessary for someone other than me to create the beads."

Then she turned to Anna and added, "You'll thank him later, won't you, my dear? Won't you?"

But thanking me was just one of many things Anna couldn't do even if she wanted to. She couldn't even think straight. I learned that every morning Summer-Face-Woman removed a bead from the necklace and dissolved it in a pitcher of water to ensure that Anna got a strong dose to start the day. Even when we were by ourselves, I couldn't have a conversation with her. Words just jutted out here and there like random spikes. For several days she had stayed away from Ash and me. Now she started showing up at his workshop at all times. It was like Summer-Face-Woman had her on an invisible leash and could yank her back if she got out of line.

I studied my mask. I had pegged in what would be a nose after I whittled it down a bit.

"I'm trying to remember what she said."

"Who, Anna?"

"The Sister-of-the-Moon is always telling me, 'Try sewing some gut. Try grinding this pigment. Try making thread from this sinew.'"

She did a perfect imitation of the Moon's Sister's voice. I was impressed, but I was also a tad worried: ravens were good at imitating voices.

"My mother said something that I'm trying to remember."

"I'm going down to the kitchen," Ash said. "Can I bring anything back for you, Anna?"

She didn't look at him or answer. She shrugged her shoulders a little.

She jerked her head in the direction he had gone. She whispered, "Gram never wove baskets. Mom never wove baskets."

I didn't know what to say.

"Whenever I got in trouble at school," she said, "I'd stare at the photo of my mother that Gram kept on her dresser. I'd sit on her bed and stare at it."

"Did you get in trouble a lot?" I guessed that getting into trouble had been pretty normal for her. Normal was what this conversation needed.

"There was something about failure that brought me back to her photo," she said. "I got so I carried it inside of me. I could call it up whenever I needed it."

"Is that what you do now?"

"Now it's rings on her fingers and a perm in her hair. Weird, right?" she asked, looking up at me. "I think I'm missing her. I think I've always missed her. I'm trying to remember what she said."

She stopped just like that and started twisting the grass in her hands.

"Old crows in his bones," she said. Her conversation came in jagged spurts. I didn't even try to follow it.

30. Booker

For somebody who never liked heights, I was getting pretty good at climbing the scaffolding. It reminded me of one of those pencil games where you connected dots with lines until you made a completely closed grid. Only this one had three-dimensions and was not particularly regular. I carried a branch up and had just started to secure it when a tremor, broad and deep, shook the room. I grabbed for anything within reach and watched the branch land inches from old hatchet-head. Summer-Face-Woman hurled it back up. I caught it and got to work lashing it into place. I saw her take a small bundle of reddish feathers out of a pocket. In an instant she was sucked away like dust into a vacuum cleaner.

Off to torment somebody else, I thought as she disappeared. I was now over two-thirds of the way to the top. I climbed up with a long pole and pushed against the hatch covering the opening on the roof. It moved enough to tell me that it was heavily overcast outside. *It will be easy to slip away,* I thought. *While it is dark, while it is silent.* I secured a few more branches, but the closer I got to completing the job, the less likely any escape seemed. Like the lemming said later, "Can zombies climb?"

"Anna," I said after I had carried two plates of food into the workshop that evening, "I have a plan."

She was seated and held up her ragged weaving. We were by ourselves.

"Old crows in his bones," she said.

"Anna," I took hold of one of her hands to get her to look at me. "Try to concentrate."

"Gram said there had been no spring at all," she shook her hand loose. "Patches of snow were anchored in everybody's yard. Old Lady Mrs. Melovidov went out one morning and found this boy. He had been sleeping outside and woke up stiff, 'Old crows in his bones,' she said."

I gave up and started to eat. Maybe if she talked herself out, she'd come back to being somewhat normal and could listen. Although with Anna, normal didn't necessarily mean listening.

"Mrs. Melovidov called her sister for tea. Those two women never ever got along, even if they were sisters. They were always bad-mouthing each other. But that's what she did: she called her sister. Mrs. Melovidov gave the boy her husband's sweater and a scarf. Her sister offered a pair of wool pants and a watch cap. They fed him toast and smoked silver salmon, warned him not to overdo it. They were afraid the cops might show up, and so, as my gram said, 'Those old ladies wouldn't bother anybody about him.'"

She finally stopped talking.

"Those magical feathers Summer-Face-Woman travels with," I started to explain, "must be something like the bookmark. With the Volcano Woman gone—"

"That's how she talked," Anna began again. "'Those old ladies wouldn't bother anybody about him.' I'd love to hear Gram say something like that again."

"That's very interesting," I said, even though it wasn't.

"A few days later the boy left. Maybe he got on a fishing boat. The valley up past the lake, where he had slept, unfolded with buttercups and cowslips opened like lanterns. The snow recoiled from Mrs. Melovidov's yard and from her sister's. Seeds sprouted wherever he had walked. People saw those two old ladies walking arm in arm, first time in ages, laughing and laughing."

I waited to see if she was done. Dinner had been delicious as usual. Anna hadn't touched her food.

"Okay," I said. "What I need to do is to get those feathers. You said you saw them in a small box? Right?"

"Booker?" She looked at me like I'd just walked into the room. Now she grabbed my wrist with surprising strength, "I think it will happen all at once."

I didn't try to shake my arm free.

"Summer-Face-Woman told the Moon's Sister that once I reached a certain point it was like gravity would take over and everything would fall into place."

Her thoughts were fragments, real enough, but just bits and pieces, words that didn't make anything like a complete thought.

"Okay," I said. "Okay."

I started to tell her that even if the feathers wouldn't work for us, Summer-Face-Woman would be a lot less dangerous without them, but just then Ash stepped into the room. Had he been listening out in the hall? He just looked at me and then he looked at Anna. Carefully he pried her fingers from my arm.

"You're tired, Anna," he said.

She gave a vacant look in his direction and began moving her fingers as though she were weaving.

"Let me take you to your room," he said and helped her to her feet.

I said I'd take the plates back to the kitchen. I put my mask into my pack, picked up the plates, and was about to leave when Summer-Face-Woman stormed in. Ash gestured for me to continue on my way, and as I stepped into the hall I heard her shouting that he was interfering, that she had been put in charge, that he needed to go back where he came from, and other things that made me blush. If Ash answered, I didn't hear him. But just as I started down the steps to the kitchen, I felt her flash past me, propelled no doubt with her magic feathers.

"You need a distraction," the lemming said when I finally returned to my cell. He crawled out from under a blanket on my bed. What I didn't need was to sleep with a rodent. I'd given up trying to make sense of the world and resigned myself to talking to animals.

"If you're going to steal that woman's feathers," he continued. Apparently, I had mentioned this to him.

I was tired, and I really didn't want to talk to anybody.

"It's become complicated," I said. "The changes are accelerating. Anna's mind is almost totally darkened. Summer-Face-Woman—"

"Horrible creature," he said. "She doesn't just eat mice, she regurgitates them."

"You offered to help," I said.

"I do remember that. I make a lot of promises."

"Maybe you could stand guard."

He wrinkled his button of a nose.

"Just long enough for Anna and me to climb the scaffold and get outside. Then we'll use the magical feathers and—" I swept my hands wide to suggest escape. Or maybe I swept them apart to suggest the whole idea was hopeless.

"Can zombies climb?"

There it was. I didn't answer. I didn't want to think about getting Anna up the scaffolding and through the hatch. He saw the mask I had removed from my pack.

"What's that?"

"It's a mask I'm making. It's a person."

"It looks like a duck."

He was right, of course. The nose was too long and too pointed.

"Just shut up, okay?"

The lemming fluffed up a bit. "Touchy, touchy."

"Sorry," I said. Arguments with lemmings always end badly.

31. Booker

I spent the morning lashing branches together, expecting to finish the scaffolding before the day was done. However, it was like Summer-Face-Woman didn't trust me to finish it without her being present. After lunch she sent me to help the Woman-with-Six-Sea-Lion-Sons in the kitchen. The room was full of delicious scents: sweet and sharp, crisp and fragrant. The cook put me to work at the sink. I shuffled kettles and pans around with thumps and scuds and scrubbing, scrubbing, scrubbing. But I enjoyed working for her. If the results were not always what she expected, she just laughed her wheezy laugh and delivered a scolding that sounded like praise.

About three in the afternoon, she called me over where she was stirring a large pot of some kind of soup.

"Do you know *petruski*? I need *petruski*."

"You want me to get him for you?"

She snorted a good-natured laugh and held up a few wilted leaves. "Like these," she said. "You'll find them down the slopes a bit."

The slopes? With that, she handed me a satchel with a long shoulder strap and went back to adding ingredients to the pot. I wasn't surprised that she trusted me to go out on an errand because, apart from Summer-Face-Woman who treated me like her private slave, I was pretty much invisible to everybody. I didn't mind.

The world outside was shrouded in mist with just the top of a rocky outcropping visible below. She said I'd find the plants on the slopes, so I headed down toward the jagged rock. If I needed to go farther and if the fog got really dense, I figured I could use it as a guidepost for getting back. The mist dissolved as I moved into it, but thickened again just a few feet away. It was like walking into a constantly shifting cave of air. When I arrived at the outcropping, I saw the gray rock was etched with colored lichen and scabs of what looked like stiff black roses. The ground in front was littered with rocks, not a plant in sight except for a few tufts of grass. A gentle breeze swept away the mist and uncovered green plants farther down.

They were green, all right, but mostly just low-growing plants of some kind. Nothing like the leaves I'd been asked to find. I continued down the mountain until the mist disappeared, and I was under a roof of clouds. A vast stretch of the island was visible before me. A few hundred yards farther down, I found a trail.

Perfect, I said. *When Anna and I escape, we'll use this.* I hurried along it as it descended until the plants became leafy and luxuriant. Next to a heavy growth of the long grass that I recognized, I found what I was looking for. The Woman-with-Six-Sea-Lion-Sons hadn't said how much she needed, so I tore loose several clumps and filled the satchel. For the next ten or fifteen minutes, I did a little exploring. It felt so good being away from the viper-eyed woman, from the constant work, and, to be honest, from Anna. Eventually, my conscience got the best of me and I started back. The volcano was under a solid bank of clouds. I knew where I needed to go: up. And up and up. I started to climb into the raggedy clouds just as a gust of wind sprayed a fine mist into my face. Before long, the hard climb became impossible when the wind delivered a full body blow that sent me stumbling back. But I plowed on, step by step, my head lowered and my eyes focused right in front of my feet until the familiar base of the rocky outcropping crept out from under the fog. I crouched down between two large boulders and drew my knees up to my chest to get tucked in and out of the wind.

I sat there just listening as the wind swirled over me. It was like I was on an island. A very small island. Beyond the short distance that held a few rocks and a few stunted plants, there was nothing but cloudy whiteness. I focused my eyes in and out, in and then out, hoping to latch onto something. I let my eyes drift like I was watching waves on an endless sea. A brief black pebble dipped in the distance. I snapped to attention. I concentrated and saw it lift its wings as it glided out of view. Some large bird was riding the wind currents below me. I stood and started up again, keeping my hand on the edge of the rocky outcropping. I turned around for one more view. The eagle angled upward on the air, steeper and steeper before banking as an upward swell of the wind caught it, and it dove into the mist below.

I had once done something like that, came into my mind. *I've pushed against the wind with nothing under me except the wind.*

Nuts, I said to myself. *I'm going nuts.*

The temperature had dropped. I tried to close the cuffs of my raincoat when the wind blew in and filled it like a balloon. I locked my arms in front and continued climbing. The chill in the air became icy as the wind hurled itself at me. I climbed and climbed until I figured I had gone high enough. I turned away from the wind, thankful to have it at my side. Thankful to be able to take a few steps without fighting. I took three steps and the ground opened under me.

"Grab my arm, *lakaayax̂*! Booker, grab my arm!"

I heard the voice and tried to do what it said. But where was the arm? And who was *lakaayax̂*?

"Grab my arm, boy! That's it. That's it."

Then I was being lifted into the air, and then I was looking into Ash's face.

He carried me for quite a distance. I must have really been lost. When we came in sight of the roof to the Volcano Woman's house, he put me down.

"The Woman-with-Six-Sea-Lion-Sons didn't tell me she had sent you out until dinner when she said the fish soup needed *petruski*. You'd been gone a long time by then."

"I got them," I said and showed him the satchel. I was a little wobbly. He just laughed a bit and helped me through the entrance hatch and down the ladder. Inside, I couldn't stop shivering.

I followed him to his workshop where he had me crawl onto a shallow stone bench lined with soft furs. The woman from the kitchen brought me a bowl of soup that was even more delicious after she tore apart a few leaves of *petruski* and sprinkled them on it. I ate, but I was so tired I could hardly swallow.

"I should get back to my cell," I said and started to get up. Ash touched my shoulder.

"It's warmer here," he said. "Just stay here and sleep."

I handed him the empty bowl before I wrapped the sea otter blanket around my shoulders and snuggled down.

"I'll see you in the morning," he said and left.

I saw my mask on the floor near the bench. I had reduced the nose. *Maybe it's part reptile,* I thought. *Prehistoric reptile. Are there reptiles in Alaska?* Then I tried to remember if reptiles had evolved into birds or birds into reptiles. It was the sort of thing I should have known.

Then, without wondering why, I wondered just how old the Volcano Woman was. *Old enough,* I supposed. *Older than eagles, older than crows.*

I must have slept. Slept hard. For how long, I don't know, but when I awoke the temperature in the room had increased.

"Oh," I said, startled. I tried to sit up. "I thought you were somebody else."

Volcano Woman placed a warm hand on my chest, and I relaxed back down.

"I'm almost always myself," she said. "I can't seem to help it."

She looked at me and asked, "Where have you come from?"

What could I say?

Then she answered her question as though she had directed it toward herself.

"I had errands to attend to. Pressure has been building, and so I have been visiting my cousins. Besides, sometimes I miss speaking my own language."

"Your cousins?" I asked.

"Okmok Caldera, a bit of a bully, is nearby, as is Makushin Volcano and that upstart Bogoslof. They have been making some minor disturbances. My younger cousin is on Atka, and more distant relatives are, well, of course, more distant."

"And you talk with them?"

"Of course. Don't you talk with your relatives?"

I nodded. "What language do you use?"

Everything grew silent as stillness dusted the room. The stone bench, every tool and woven basket, the mat on which I had been resting, all were suspended as a chord from somewhere deep inside the volcano washed over me. It was richer and deeper than anything I had ever experienced. I thought of thunder uncoiling in the distance, of a phrase Mrs. Bainbridge was fond of muttering: *God be praised*, only she said it in Latin: *Te Deum laudamus*, and of the pause that had once surprised me at the end of a concert just before the audience burst into applause.

That was her answer.

"And what language is used," the woman asked softly, "when you visit your relatives?"

"English," I said. "Although sometimes the Elder Cousin speaks Norwegian."

"No," she said. "What language do you *use*?"

"I'm sorry, ma'am." I thought it best to be polite. I had already answered her. "I don't understand."

"Among the world's languages there is one that will cure grief," she said. "There is one that can dispel anger. Among the languages that people speak, there is one that diminishes greed. All different usages."

"I think you must be mistaken," I said and immediately the temperature in the room rose.

"Or not," I added quickly. "Probably not. Definitely, not."

She saw the mask beside me. I blushed when she picked it up and turned it back and forth as though trying to figure out what it represented.

"It's supposed to be a bird," I said. "At first it wasn't."

I hoped she wouldn't laugh too loudly.

"Of course it's a bird," she agreed. I might have been mistaken, but it looked like she used her fingers to smooth the nose into a perfect beak. There was no mistake when she turned it over and blew gently on the back, hollowing it out so it would fit my face exactly.

"Are you ready?" she asked. "It is almost time."

SEVEN
GRAVITY

32. Booker

I lashed the last of the branches in place late that afternoon under the hawkish gaze of Summer-Face-Woman. She inspected the grid row by row, and then she let me go.

"Tomorrow," she said.

Tomorrow what? But I knew. The time had arrived. Volcano Woman was back. Anna was bonkers. There was no way she could climb the scaffolding. There was no way she would do anything I said. Totally depressed, I stopped by the workroom. Anna was there, along with Ash. I saw her finger the bluish-silver beads around her neck and say to him, "Soon you'll be hunting sea lions."

"Yes," he answered with a slight smile. "It won't be my first hunt."

"I have something for you," she said. She saw me at the doorway and made a wide arc away. She handed him a tangled knot of grass. And then, as though to explain what it was, she said, "I've been weaving."

He took it and laughed. It looked like a bird's nest. She fingered the pale-blue beads around her neck.

"I'll accept whatever you give me," he said, "and treasure it."

Of course you will, I said to myself, *after she's dead and gone.*

"YOU!" screeched Summer-Face-Woman. I whirled and dropped to the floor to avoid a swift cuffing, but the doorway was empty.

Anna let out a laugh. "Caw-aught yaw!" she crowed.

Ash gave me a hand up.

"Caw-aught yaw! Caw-aught yaw!" she chanted softly as she walked over. She was pointing at me with her nose. She cocked her head and pinned me with her eyes. Then her face relaxed. Her eyes faded. She frowned at her sleeve. She held perfectly still. I noticed dark hairs had started growing on her wrists. Revolting. Then with a jerk of her arm and a snap of her tongue she caught some kind of bug and—yuck!—ate it.

I picked up my mask, selected a small scraper, and went to my room, leaving them together. I sat on my bed and turned the mask in my hands from side to side. It was perfectly symmetrical. Very lightly, I pulled the scraper down one side. The finest amount of wood dust came off under the blade. I blew it away. It disappeared in the air. *Like feathers*, I said to myself, and again I had the oddest sense of flying. I held the mask up to my face. Whatever Volcano Woman had done, it now fit perfectly.

I heard the three women outside in the hall. Putting the mask on the bed, I walked to the door as they went past without noticing me. They were congratulating themselves on how well everything had turned out. The Woman-with-Six-Sea-Lion-Sons asked, "Will you be staying here after tomorrow's ceremony, sister?"

The Sister-of-the-Moon answered, "It's time I took my son to visit his uncle."

I hadn't realized she had a son. They were heading for their evening steam bath. The Woman-with-Six-Sea-Lion-Sons held a bundle of tied grass. The Sister-of-the-Moon had an armful of towels. I crept after them and heard her say that her son had been pestering to visit his uncle for a long time.

"And you?" the cook asked Summer-Face-Woman as they passed the workshop.

"I'll be taking the girl with me," she replied, "until Real Raven calls for her."

I flattened myself against the wall when Ash stepped out. He watched them until they began to descend the steps to the storage rooms, the kitchen, and steam bath. He went back inside, and I hurried past and down the steps. I found the door with steam seeping under it, cracked it open, and listened before stepping inside. The women were laughing behind a grass curtain. On a long bench, beside their folded clothes, just as Anna had described, was a box. *Feathers or box?* I thought. *If I take the box, she'll know immediately that the feathers are gone.*

Just the feathers, then.

I lifted the lid. The rosy-tinted feathers were tied with a beautifully braided grass band. They were lighter than air. I closed the lid and tiptoed to the door. Just as I reached it, a tremor threaded itself across the floor and up the legs of the bench. The bench quivered and the box shimmied to the edge where it paused for a millisecond and then toppled off. I dove and somehow, miraculously, caught it before it hit the floor.

I don't know how, but the feathers had worked!

"I'll check it out!" bellowed the Woman-with-Six-Sea-Lion-Sons. I returned the box and ran into the hallway. I held the feathers out in front as I skidded around the corner and up the stairs at incredible speed.

"YOU!" I heard a screech from the base of the steps. This time it *was* Summer-Face-Woman's voice.

The workshop was empty.

"Anna!" I yelled and sprinted for her room at amazing speed.

Her room was also empty. I glimpsed Summer-Face-Woman at the end of the hallway and heard her shout an order, "Come to me!"

Not a chance, I said to myself, but the feathers quivered in my hand. She was calling them. I tightened my fist and ran.

"Come to me!"

The feathers squirmed until I felt like I was squeezing a small frantic bird.

"Anna!"

I passed the empty reception room and burst into the ceremonial hall just as the feathers twisted from my fingers. The lemming stood at the base of the scaffolding twirling his arms like a windmill.

"This way!" he screamed and scampered onto the lowest branch. I was halfway up the scaffolding before Summer-Face-Woman began shaking it. I looked down. She stood wrapped in a towel like a crab in a furious tangle of seaweed. She held the feathers in one hand and shook with the other. I scrambled up to the next level and grabbed for the top row of branches just as a tremor struck, deeper and longer than anything coming from the woman herself. The scaffolding heaved sideways.

"Earthquake!" I shouted. Summer-Face-Woman, oblivious of the quake, threw herself against the frame with maniacal fury. In a moment I was in the air, upside down and then sideways, tumbling through the web of branches from row to row. *Like a banana in a blender*, I thought, as the room flipped upside down. The next time I was aware of anything, my arms were tied behind my back, my feet were bound at my ankles, and, wherever I was, I was sitting in the dark.

33. Anna

The amber beads were on my wrist. I turned them on their fine leather cord. They were the first things that had registered with me in a long long time. I remembered Ash standing beside me. He had taken my hand and slipped the beads around my wrist. I'd resisted. I didn't want him touching me. But almost immediately I had relaxed as he fastened the cord so securely I couldn't slip it off.

"Keep them," he had whispered as he let my arm go. "Don't remove them."

That had been yesterday. Now, today, I stood dressed in the ceremonial parka under the inspecting eyes of the Moon's Sister.

"Much too plain," the Moon's Sister decided after she saw them. I don't know if she objected to the beads as much as to the simple cord on which they were strung.

"How about this," I said and tucked them under the sleeve of the parka.

She raised an eyebrow but didn't object.

"Turn a bit, my dear," she said as she checked the decorative border along the bottom hem. If I could orbit her like the moon itself maybe I'd disappear. The parka fit beautifully. I wanted to keep it.

"As I feared," she said, "it needs a slight adjusting, just a smudge."

"I think you mean *smidge*."

"*Smidge, smudge.* Tomato, Tomawto."

"But *smidge* and *smudge* are different words," I said.

"Which is why I have the needle," she said as I slipped the

garment off and handed it to her. She frowned a smidge when she saw the darkening blotches on my shoulders before I put on my everyday bird-skin parka.

I studied the fancy parka as she applied needle and thread. The last time I remembered seeing it, it hadn't been this beautiful. There was a gigantic gap in my memory, a space where things had happened. It was like my memory was an old mirror whose cracks and peelings cut the reflections into pieces. I remembered Summer-Face-Woman had said gravity would take over. I was feeling its pull.

Maybe it's a good thing, I thought. *Maybe it's best to just let it happen.*

I fingered the pale-blue beads around my neck. That's what I'm here for. Forget the past. This is what everything has come to.

I heard the Sister-of-the-Moon say, "You must look your very best, Anna. It goes without saying."

But she said it anyway. She said it again and again.

"It goes without saying."

What goes without saying? I asked myself as I turned the beads on my wrist. It was something important that I couldn't remember. I realized that today was the day. Either the last or the first, but in any case I'd never be the same after today.

I took a steam bath as instructed. I put on a plain parka until it was time for the ceremonial one, the garment that would become my skin. I sat on the bed while the Moon's Sister brushed my hair. I hadn't seen Booker since when? I had a vague feeling that he had been avoiding me.

I fingered the beads on my wrist.

A rustle of wings and the clapping of flippers and padded feet in the hallway brought me to the doorway. The Moon's Sister was right beside me.

"The first guests are arriving," she said. Fat and thin, heavy and light; feathers, fur, muscle, and flab, creating a din of twitters and snorts, quacks and barks, cackles and growls.

We tiptoed to an alcove to watch.

The procession began with a flood tide of small birds filling the hall from ceiling to floor, pushing and shoving as they clambered over one another in an almost solid wall of feathers. Song sparrows and wrens flickered among throngs of marbled murrelets and pigeon guillemots. King eiders competed wing-to-wing with rosy finches while a cluster of fat buntings bullied their way through. Behind them, a sextet of black oystercatchers nervously tapped their spindly legs along the stone floor. Their Day-Glo orange beaks cut at the air like clipping shears.

Ducks of all sizes and varieties came next: mallards and teals, eiders and grebes, and five harlequin ducks with their giddy galloping. A dozen emperor geese unfolded like a magnificent black, white, and gray carpet, while behind them cormorants pivoted their long necks in unison.

After the last of the feathered flock had swept by, I heard the loud shuffle of mammals: two white sea otters, a family of fur seals, and a tussle of excited hair seals trailed by a pack of red, silver, and black fox snapping delightedly at the air. At the very end came men who for an instant were sea lions—probably brothers of my wrestling coach—and women and men who, for moments quicker than sparks, were killer whales. This crowd continuously transformed itself as it jerked forward: human, animal, animal, human.

The Moon's Sister touched my arm. "It goes without saying, my dear, this is all for you. All for you."

I followed her back to the room where she seated herself and picked up the ceremonial parka.

I'm not a shy person, but I did not want whatever was about to happen to me taking place in front of that crowd. Not in front of any crowd. *If something is going to happen to me*, I said to myself, *let it happen while I'm alone.*

Or with Booker, I thought.

I felt calmer when I rolled the two beads Ash had put on my wrists between my fingers. I pressed them into the veins of my wrist until I felt my pulse beating under them.

"Do you still have those beads on?" the Sister-of-the-Moon asked as she looked over at me.

I lifted my cuff.

"Too common! Too common!"

"They're nice," I said.

"We'll let Summer-Face-Woman decide," she said as she rearranged the fancy parka to examine the bottom hem.

I walked to the table and picked up the water pitcher. There was no way I'd be allowed to keep something from Ash.

"This is empty," I said to the Moon's Sister. "Would you mind if I filled it with fresh water?"

"I'd be delighted," she said.

I placed the pitcher beneath the small stream that flowed into the stone sink. While the pitcher filled, I removed the necklace of blue pearls, and there I was.

At Gram's. In her kitchen. And my mother was there, and she wasn't saying anything. She was just sitting and looking at Gram. It went without saying. I began to understand. Nobody had said anything. Not my mother, not Gram. There was nothing for me to remember. She hadn't forgiven Gram. She hadn't asked Gram to forgive her. Mrs. Skagit had lied. Forgiveness had passed between them like an unspoken language. Gram hadn't asked for forgiveness.

I needed to get home. I needed to forgive her by being there. *Her* was both of them: my gram and my mother. I needed them to forgive me.

I jerked around. The Sister-of-the-Moon was sewing away. She hadn't even looked up. I returned to the pitcher of water. I untied the knot on the necklace and slid two beads free before retying it and slipping it back on.

"I think a few more stitches will wrap it up," she said.

I poured a cup for myself and then dropped a bead into the pitcher. I swirled the water to speed up the dissolving and carried it over to her.

"You've been working hard," I said as I poured a cup for her.

She held up the dress for my inspection before laying it to one side and taking the cup. "I appreciate this."

"I really am thankful for all you are doing," I said. I meant it.

"Excellent!" The Moon's Sister said after taking a sip. She raised the glass in praise of its contents before downing it completely.

"Very refreshing," I said and drank from my cup.

The Sister-of-the-Moon asked, "Have I ever told you about the journey I took through the sky to visit my brother, the moon?"

She moved her arm in a wide arc over her head as though mapping the Milky Way. "I had been digging lupine roots," she said, "delicious roots when prepared correctly."

I refilled her cup and she drank it down. "Always eat them with seal oil, never by themselves. You'll have a bad reaction without the seal oil. Anyway, when I pulled the root digger out of the ground—"

"Thank you," she said as I filled her cup a third time. "—there was a hole. A cold draft blew up through it, and when I looked down into it, why—" she yawned widely and stopped talking.

"Yes?" I asked. "What did you see?"

The Moon's Sister tried to focus. She seemed to be traveling through the sky.

"Where?"

"In the lupine hole."

"You need to eat lupine roots with seal oil, my dear. Always," she yawned again. "I mean, never, never, never. Never without seal oil."

Her yawns gave way to contented snoring. I laid her down gently and covered her with a mat. The ceremonial parka was just too good to leave. I quickly changed into it before opening the door just as four regal ptarmigan strutted by, ruffling their feathered coats like ermine capes. I was startled by the rolls of sharp mechanical clicking, like pebbles rattling in tin cans, that accompanied the glances they cast from side to side. Clearly they disapproved of just about everything that wasn't ptarmiginean. A particularly large and fierce member of the quartet stared directly at me. Its eyes were like fire.

Once they had gone on their way, I walked into Booker's cell. It was empty. *With or without him,* I decided, *I need to get away. Even just for an hour or two.* Complete escape was out of the question. I knew that. I didn't need to be told that. I needed to get away long enough for whatever change was going to happen to me to happen in private. And then I would or I wouldn't be able to escape. Then I would or I wouldn't want to escape.

A blend of laughter and music in the distance signaled the guests were in the reception room. I walked to the door leading to the hall as a pair of harlequin ducks bobbed past unsteadily.

I see they've discovered the punch, I thought and smiled as one of them waved a wing at me. It knocked the other off balance and sent both of them careening into the wall. They ruffled themselves together with furious indignity and poked their beaks in my direction. Then suddenly they froze.

A faint growl, like the slow tearing of a sheet of paper, crawled out from behind a nearby corner and sent them squawking in the opposite direction.

A pointed snout followed the growl as a young red fox emerged.

"Are you lost?" I realized I was talking to a fox. It had been studying the ducks and, *was it possible?* licking its lips. The fox raised an eyebrow, and I gasped in recognition.

"You!" I said.

"Me," said the boy, no longer in his fox body.

"But don't you know the danger? What are you doing here?"

"My father thought you might need help. He wanted to repay you."

"Your father?"

"For returning this," and he touched the ivory fox that hung around his neck. "We were picking berries yesterday, and a frantic lemming arrived."

I was too surprised to say anything except, "*Txin qaĝaasakuqing, Chaknax̂.*"

I thank you, Stink.

"I've lost my friend," I said and swept my arm into the empty cell.

The boy flipped back into his fox shape and sniffed Booker's bunk from one end to the other. He was about to repeat the circuit when we heard a congested nasal honking.

"I think the tipsy duo is returning."

He nodded in the direction of the door and gave a long sniff.

"With reinforcements."

We slipped from the room and down the hallway. I heard the harlequin ducks arguing as I followed the fox into a passage that curved away.

"Good," the fox said. "Good." And he began nosing his way along the corridor, pausing every so often to inhale a prolonged draft of air. We passed three or four doors before he stopped at the entrance to a narrow hall. He signaled for me to be quiet. I stuck my head around the corner and saw a door with a scruffy mat in front of it, a mat that stirred and got to its wobbly feet. I ducked out of sight.

The two foxes yipped and yapped a bit and then the old fox wobbled past me and down the corridor.

"I told him he should go see the transformation ceremony," Stink said. "I promised to keep an eye on the door."

The room was dark when I pushed it open, but the light from the hallway showed me enough. Booker, with his arms tied behind him, his feet bound, and his mouth gagged, was sitting up against the opposite wall. He did a sort of frantic dance when the light hit him. And when Stink leapt at him, his eyes widened in terror. But instantly in the boy's body, Stink untied his feet while I loosened the rag around his mouth. Stink made rapid work of the knots at his wrists. Booker was too startled to do anything except gawk at the boy.

"His father sent him to help us."

"His father?"

"Little Wren," the boy said. "Chief of Kagamil Island. We were picking berries when father learned you needed help."

"From whom?" Booker asked.

"One of your rodent friends."

"But you're yourself," Booker said to me as he rubbed his wrists. He saw the blue pearl necklace around my neck. "With that on!"

"I have this," I said and showed him the beads on my wrist. "From Ash," I said.

"For strength and endurance," he said.

"How do you know that?"

I didn't wait for his answer. We avoided the regular corridors. Booker led for a time and then I took over, and deliberately or not, we ended up on a high balcony overlooking the ceremonial room. We crouched down and inched our way to the edge, where we looked down over the guests milling around wing-to-wing and shoulder-to-shoulder. A dark shadow stirred directly under us as the sharp blackness of the Real Raven released a faint putrid odor. Ash was seated on an ornately carved stool on the low stage. There was an identical stool that must have been reserved for me. Volcano Woman surveyed the room from a slightly elevated chair while Summer-Face-Woman stood directly behind her. The Woman-with-Six-Sea-Lion-Sons was seated at the edge of the stage. The crowd stood or sat on three sides of a scaffolding that stretched from floor to ceiling on a grid of branches.

"I made that," Booker said.

Was he nuts?

"*Haqada*," I said, determined to get away before we were discovered. I gave a slight tug to Booker's sleeve just as two men dropped through the entrance hole. All three of us froze. The audience gasped as the men fell and gasped again as they latched onto the scaffolding halfway down and reversed directions. They deftly flipped up and across a set of branches before twisting off to opposite sides. The killer-whale people were extraordinary acrobats. Their swift dexterity turned their black-and-white clothing into gray blurs.

I saw the Volcano Woman beckon the Woman-with-Six-Sea-Lion-Sons to her side.

A green-winged teal in the front row honked her approval and applauded as one of the acrobats made a rapid rotating descent from bar to bar. His arms and legs were swept into a pure tapered flow of muscle. He twirled on the bar nearest the teal. Faster and faster. She clapped wildly and hooted her approval. Then she let out a terrified squawk and fainted backward.

A ptarmigan clucked in disapproval as he ruffled his feathers like an angry grouse.

But I had glimpsed what the teal had seen: a row of sharpened teeth beneath the skin.

Ducks flocked to her aid from every roost in the room, fanning her and anyone within range of their wings. The four ptarmigan scattered while the six sea lion sons roared with laughter. In the confusion, we slipped away and down the hall. The same confusion must have delayed the departure of the Woman-with-Six-Sea-Lion-Sons because we had reached the door to my room before I heard her coming. Stink and Booker slipped into his old room. I stood in my doorway and raised my feathered arms to block the view inside where the Moon's Sister was sitting up and rubbing her eyes.

"I have been sent to bring you to the performance and to see that you are ready," announced the Woman-with-Six-Sea-Lion-Sons when she saw me. "Or the other way around," she added, correcting the order of her sentence.

"We are almost ready." I hoped I sounded like I was pleased and excited. "Isn't that so, Sister-of-the-Moon?"

I turned into the room but kept the view inside blocked.

"That's correct," I mimicked an answer. "Just a minute or two more."

"Then be quick about it, Sister," snapped the Woman-with-Six-Sea-Lion-Sons and departed.

I walked inside. I dropped the other bead into the pitcher of water, swirled it around, and poured it into a cup. The Moon's Sister took a long drink. Her head drooped and her body sagged into a heap. I gently scattered grass over her until she had disappeared from sight.

I stepped into Booker's cell where he and Stink were waiting. Booker slipped on his backpack, and we started off for Ash's work-room and the bridge into the volcano. We hadn't gone more than a few steps when Stink gave a faint bark and said, "You gotta see this." He trotted in the opposite direction, back toward the balcony. We reluctantly followed.

The assembled foxes were bowing in unison before the Volcano Woman. They were like knives reflecting fire: red and silver and black. In an instant they tangled into a ball of snarling and convulsing fury that sent the guests scattering in terror. And then, before an astonished crowd, they unfolded into a perfectly symmetrical, perfectly spherical sea anemone: on their backs, their feet slowly swaying like tentacles in the tide, their bushy tails sweeping in a circumference of gentle sea currents. The crowd erupted with cheers.

The pack sprang into another churning ball of fur, out of which a shape began to emerge as fox leapt on fox in gradually decreasing numbers as a perfect pyramid was created. Fur brushed my legs as Stink dashed away. A final pair of foxes scrambled to the top. And then Stink scampered up all the other foxes until he reached the summit. He arched his back and tooted in victory.

I pulled Booker away as the pyramid collapsed on itself and the room erupted in joyful turmoil. We ran through Ash's workroom, under the archway and onto the bridge. We had taken maybe a half-dozen steps toward the great door that I hoped was still open for latecomers when Stink dashed past, not even a little out of breath. He skidded to a stop and turned around as Booker and I slid to a halt. He looked up at us, boy-shaped, with a boastful smile. "What'd you think?" he asked.

"You're late," said Summer-Face-Woman as her bony hand crashed onto Booker's shoulder. He collapsed onto the bridge and rolled toward the edge. Stink was instantly a fox. He snapped his jaw around Booker's ankle and pulled him back. So there we were, like what, three blind mice confronting the cat?

"Your guests are waiting for you." She pointed at me with her bundle of feathers. "Come," she ordered. "Now!"

"She's not—" Booker was wobbling to his feet. "She's not going."

I had to admire him. Basically useless, but admirable.

The woman looked at him with eyes that were as indifferent as death.

"With me," she said.

34. Anna

Booker glanced at me. *Partners?*

I nodded slightly.

"Just the girl," she said as Booker took a step forward.

"Enough," she said. She drew an obsidian knife from inside her clothing. I could hear Booker's breathing. He moved closer. She pointed the knife at him.

"Back away," she ordered.

Ash stepped onto the bridge behind her.

"Lower the knife," he said quietly, like he was trying to calm a wild animal.

She held the blade still.

"Lower it, Summer-Face-Woman," he repeated.

The instant she whirled around, the blade flew from her hand and buried itself in Ash's shoulder. He crumpled to the ground. Booker dove past me and straight into the back of her legs. She threw her arms up to keep her balance and the feathers went flying. At the sight of Ash pulling the obsidian knife from his wound and hurling it away, something broke inside me. I clamped onto her, screaming and shoving and holding on like a limpet to a rock. Booker was sent tumbling onto the bridge. She thrashed and cursed, but I buried my fingers deeper into her clothing. She rolled me onto my back and forced my arms to the floor. I squirmed and bucked, but all that did was to rock us closer to the edge until the sharp corner scraped the back of my head. Booker grabbed one of her legs and Stink latched onto the other. They pulled, but she delivered a furious kick and sent them spinning away. Now she straddled me and pinned my arms with her knees. I saw Booker reach into his pack. He tossed his mask aside and removed a small red folding knife. I heard it clatter onto the stones and glimpsed him scrambling after it. Every muscle in my body buckled as Summer-Face-Woman leaned sideways to recover her obsidian blade. I raised a shoulder and bent a knee for leverage as first my head and then my neck dangled over the void. I felt myself slipping into the cold air rushing up from the chasm. I saw her lift her blade, saw it catch the light. I gave one final agonizing thrust, wrenching my chest and head up, and my eyes met the blank eyes of Booker's mask. I was instantly calm. I went instantly limp. I gave myself over to gravity as she plunged the knife down, and we tumbled over the edge.

The knife dropped from her fingers, and the mask fell. The rush of air muffled her screams as we plummeted down. She flailed her arms as the air distorted her face into ragged contortions and drove the mask onto my face. I shook it away as I held on to her with hands like talons. A shrieking bark erupted from somewhere inside me before I broke free and let her go. The wind pushed against me. It lifted me up, threw me onto my back and spun me around until I wasn't so much falling as hovering. I was swimming through the darkening air as I plummeted deeper and deeper. The air grew warmer as I turned and floated like the bundle of rosy feathers that drifted by. I struck out with a fist, opened my fingers and caught them. I tore the braided grass that held the bundle together and the feathers floated upward in the warm current. I dove into the air as into water. I stretched my arms and banked into the currents. Far below, Summer-Face-Woman twirled downward, smaller and smaller and smaller until she was nothing at all.

Far above me, like the shadow of a dark ribbon, the bridge stretched from side to side. I glided into a sharp turn and began to ascend. My speed increased and the bridge grew larger. I saw Booker and Stink. They were rushing down the steps along the edge of the chasm. *The wrong way*, I thought to myself. In a moment they would turn into the hall that led to the storage rooms and eventually to capture. I focused on a landing just below them. With every ounce of muscle and speed that I could muster, I swept over the edge and landed. I don't know what I looked like, but they both backed away from me like I was about to bite. Stink actually had the nerve to growl. The mask fell from somewhere in the folds of my parka to the ground. I didn't have time to argue or to explain what I couldn't explain. I ran right between them up the steps.

"This way!" I ordered and, believe it or not, they followed. I had taken only a half-dozen steps when I sensed something hideously familiar. Raven's shadow flickered as he stalked onto the bridge. His feathers clattered like metal and glistened with terrible, terrible beauty. His stench streamed behind him. I saw Ash standing. He had wrapped a wide band across his wounded shoulder and tied it in front. He kept his distance as the great bird sniffed the frame around the obsidian door like a wolf. He pulled it open and stepped inside. In a moment he was back at the edge of the bridge. He bent his beak and delicately lifted a strand of something that had been caught on a sharp stone. I did my best to cover Booker and Stink, hoping to camouflage the boy's fox scent and Booker's whatever scent with the fancy parka. We huddled as close to the wall as possible, wrapping whatever darkness we could find around us. After an unbearable silence, I heard a hushed whispering like paper rubbing against paper as Raven crossed the bridge, swept into the passage and back to wherever he had come from.

I didn't wait to see if Ash followed him. By the time we reached the bridge, he was gone. We ran through the open door and into the alcove that angled down into the volcano. Even before my eyes adjusted, Stink let out an angry snarl. Ash was standing on one side and watching us. Booker and I jumped with alarm, and Stink growled, but Ash just stood there. He nodded toward a pile of sealskins folded on a stone bench.

"Perfect!" I said and tossed one to Booker and one to Stink who was now in a boy's body. Booker flung his around his shoulders and tried to close it at his neck for a sort of ill-fitting cloak.

"It's already hot in here," he said.

Ash let out a laugh, but Stink had spread his at the top of the mat-covered stone incline that led out of the chamber. He made a forward jump and landed on the sealskin. He grabbed the sides and slid out of sight. Booker now understood and followed—after I had turned the pelt around so the hairs pointed backward. In seconds, he was gone.

I looked at Ash.

"You'd better be going," he said. Everything I had wanted to be was standing there telling me to leave. The last real Unangax̂ I would ever know.

"I'll have to tell her," he said.

I racked my brain for something to say.

"Qag̱aasakuqing, Ash, " I said. It was a simple thanks. It was completely inadequate.

"*Lalux̂*," he said, "not Ash. *Txin qag̱aasakuqing.*"

Why was he thanking me?

I turned and vanished from the chamber without waiting for an answer. It was smooth sailing until the first set of steps arrived. From then on it must have been like trying to stay aboard a bucking horse.

Deeper and deeper we rode the sealskins down into the volcano, taking several steps in a single swoop. I hadn't remembered all this downward plunging on the way up. Then the path leveled off. We coasted on the sealskins a few yards before another short downhill burst brought us to a landing. We dropped the skins and ran across the stone bridge where two streams joined together.

Stink skidded to a halt just as we reached the other side. He turned around. I heard nothing. Booker heard nothing. Then we saw a small red fox sprint back in the direction we had come from. We saw a red tail flick nervously from the highest step in sight and then in a moment the small creature was back at our feet.

"Somebody's coming," the boy said.

Now all three of us heard the deep gulps of breathing that accompanied what had to be the six sea lion sons trampling each other in their downward tumble.

"That man is leading them," Stink said as he scampered past. We ran, panting as the trail turned uphill hugging a stream. As I raced past, I dipped a hand into the small lake and flicked cold water across my face. I remembered the room of waterfalls as my head brushed against a few low-hanging tangles of stone flowers and sent them clattering to the ground. I followed Stink as he turned down another hall and into a foyer. Here the carpeted path ended and stone steps led uphill. Booker and I had just started to sprint up when the fox let out a snapping growl and nipped at Booker's heals. Booker turned with a frustrated groan.

"No!" the boy said, or rather, snapped in an abbreviated bark, as he disappeared down a different passage. We heard the rumbling and tumbling of immense bodies in the long passage. Ahead of this tumult, I heard Ash calling my name. I grabbed Booker's arm as he was about to plunge after the fox. I quickly removed the necklace of pale-blue beads and thrust it into what passed for a pocket in my parka. Then I tried to remove the cord with the two beads Ash had given me. Booker saw me struggling and used the folding knife from his pack to cut the cord. I placed the beads where Ash would find them on the first step leading up. Booker laid the open knife beside the beads just as an angry yapping drew us into the passage where Stink was disappearing. Booker followed the fox, but I hesitated.

The avalanche of noise grew louder, and then Ash sprang into the foyer. The two amber beads brought him to a sudden stop. He picked them up and saw me. He looked from me to the beads.

"I'll be fine," I said just as the six sea lion sons burst into the clearing and I ducked deeper into the passage. The first sea lion gave a sharp-toothed smile at the sight of the knife in Ash's hand. Ash signaled for them to follow as he sprinted up the stone steps and away.

The corridor plummeted downward until the three of us stepped into a vaulted chamber where a corrugated dome arced overhead and a mammoth stone extrusion sloped away. We had entered a cave within a cave, a sea cave. I heard the pulse of water and saw pools flooded with anemones, sponges, starfish, and barnacles. We stepped carefully to avoid slipping on the damp stone. In the distance, where the roof lowered and a series of twists led to the open sea, light hovered under the water and illumined the shadowed walls. Now Booker followed me and I followed Stink, who seemed to know his way. At times he led us right beside the walls where I fingered the damp rock. Then we veered away and scooted down across an expanse of sheer smooth stone. After a series of gentle switchbacks, we turned a corner to where a small compact man was holding the lines to a pair of kayaks.

"In, Booker, in!" I held the bow of one while the chief seated himself in the rear hatch and Booker slipped into the forward hatch and tightened the spray skirt around his waist as the chief barked instructions. I leapt into a second kayak where Stink sat in the forward hatch. In moments we were out on the water and heading toward the passage that led to the sea. The cave's entrance was framed by a dark half-circle of descending rock, beyond which I saw a gray sky and a gray sea streaked with whitecaps. As we passed under the cave's overhanging mouth, the silence of the underground cavern was consumed by wind. We struck the open water with enough speed to send us skimming into the choppy waves.

Once free of the cave, I glanced over my shoulder at the avalanche of approaching clouds. Boulders of black air rolled in the west as a gut-wrenching fury cascaded in our direction. A dark form rode the air currents down the side of the volcano. Broad wings hacked at the air. The Real Raven's hoarse victorious barks devoured any chance of escape. We were slivers of vulnerability. He broke upward, soaring into the air, and then I saw him circle back, sending a wake of darkness toward us. He somersaulted and crowed with triumph as he announced his find.

Even from a quarter mile away, I heard the eruption at the mouth of the sea cave as the sea lion men torpedoed into the water and surfaced in an explosion of hair and flippers. Their bellowing roars were like thunder, like the slamming of huge doors. I paddled furiously. I occasionally glanced back, but the chief kept his eyes straight ahead. His paddle sliced the water like the wings of a wren cutting the air.

I could see the coast of Kagamil.

The six sea lion sons were not natural killers. They were show-offs, braggarts, overfed by their indulgent mother, and easily distracted. I didn't know how else to explain the fact that we were leaving them behind. It seemed incredible.

Every time I glanced back, Little Wren increased his lead. But I had to look. And that's how I saw the six dorsal fins cutting the water with the rhythm of band saws. The killer-whale people were swimming in increasingly larger circles, alert and hungry, and three or four times faster than any kayak.

The wind swallowed my warning scream as I rowed furiously. Little Wren was heading toward a tongue of rock that extended off the southwest point of Kagamil. He seemed to fasten his entire boat and being on that single point. Off to my right, I glimpsed a huge killer whale as it barreled forward, arched its body, and shot from the sea. Then it dove in our direction.

I saw the rocky expanse directly ahead. One brush against the sharp, unforgiving edge and our eyelid-thin boats would be shredded. Little Wren aimed for a stretch of relatively smooth stone. He held back and directed Stink and me to pass him and make the first landing. We swept ahead with all our strength and coasted in as the sea relaxed. We slipped from our hatches and sprang for the rocks. The sea cascaded around us as we scrambled up. It swept our kayak away.

I turned and saw Little Wren maneuver his boat parallel to the edge and hold it there while Booker frantically loosened his spray skirt. He hoisted himself from the hatch and scrambled off the bow and onto the rock. With a single deft maneuver, Little Wren was behind him, urging him forward as a killer whale leapt from the sea. It landed on the kayak and splintered it into sticks and skin.

I ran toward the grassy upland where the island rose from rock and water. There, if not free from the attack, I would at least not be swept into the sea. I sprinted with a rush of adrenalin and had almost caught up with Stink when I stopped and turned. Booker and Little Wren were scrambling over barnacles and slipping on kelp, while on three sides the sea churned and writhed. I saw the water building behind them. The roar of the wind drowned out my shouts as a wave swept up and in one smooth motion engulfed them.

I saw Booker grab at anything. His fingers slipped through kelp as he was towed backward. He jammed his elbows and knees into the rock, hunting for leverage. Then he was being pulled forward and up as Little Wren gave him a tug, and they bolted forward. The rocky tongue grew larger and larger as though rising out of the water.

"The sea!" I shouted. "The sea!"

Then Booker looked and understood. The water was pulling away from the shoreline, exposing more and more of the rocky expanse. The sea was swelling behind them into one immense consuming wave ready to break.

Stink and I were scaling the grassy bank, hand over hand or paw after paw, scrambling up as high as we could before the wave broke. I looked down and saw Little Wren slow just as he reached the end of the rock. He stepped aside and gestured for Booker to leap for the grassy bluff. Booker latched onto the grass and scurried up. The chief's momentum had ebbed, forcing him to take a few steps back before he ran and hurled himself forward. He landed short and began slipping backward. Booker slid down and stretched out his hands.

"Give me your hand!"

Little Wren reached upward.

The wave began to crown behind them.

Little Wren hoisted himself upright with Booker's help and they began climbing.

Booker looked back over his shoulder and hollered something to the chief.

"Hurry!" I shouted.

But the chief drew Booker to a stop.

"I just remembered!" I heard Booker shout out his words between gulps of air.

I was ready to swear at both of them.

"Move!" I screamed. I saw a small red fox scamper away.

The wind hollowed out an opening into which Booker shouted to the chief, "Your brother's granddaughter said to say hello!"

And the air was struck with sudden calm.

I walked into a cloud as solid as water.

Booker was beside me. The ground inside the cloudbank opened to a descending grassy slope interrupted by outcroppings of rock. The air was calm. The sky was impossibly blue. The sea below was slowly lapping the shore.

I turned around and stuck my head back out of the cloudbank and felt a deafening blast. The storm was obliterating everything from sight with blinding fury: Little Wren, the grassy bank, the tongue of submerged rock, everything except, burning through the dense diagonal rain, the slopes of Chuginidak Volcano flowing with fire.

EIGHT
STRENGTH AND ENDURANCE

35. Anna

I didn't understand how that cloud remained stationary in the face of all the wind that whipped the mountainside, but there wasn't time to investigate. I turned back inside and hit the slope full speed. I was almost halfway down to the shore when Booker did a sealskin slide without the sealskin, on his rear; sometimes feet forward, sometimes head first, and frequently in circles. He almost passed me. As we neared the shore, the heavier grass slowed our sliding and we stumbled upright onto the beach, and there was Vasilii, holding out one hand while he held a rope tied to a skiff with the other.

"*Ayaqaa!*" he said "It's about time. Get in!"

Without waiting to find out how and why he was there, we tumbled over the wooden sides, swirled upright, and sat down. Vasilii climbed in beside me and handed me a paddle. Further out on the water, the *Eider* swayed gently, wrapped by a tattered scarf of fog. Not a soul was in sight. Rowing side by side, we sent the skiff skimming away from the shore. We headed straight for the ship. Booker glanced nervously around, probably expecting a killer whale's dorsal fin or the roar of a sea lion. We cut rowing and coasted to the port side of the ship where a rope ladder hung down. Vasilii steadied the skiff while I grabbed the ladder and started up, with Booker right behind. Vasilii joined us on deck after securing the skiff to the rope ladder.

We stood looking at each other.

"You had left with Captain Hennig," Vasilii said, "by the time I learned what had happened to the book of mummies."

"And what had happened to it?" I asked.

"The captain had come up to our house and borrowed it again," he said. "You were sailing out of the bay by the time Mother came home and told me."

"You mean it was here all along?" I couldn't believe it.

"Come," he finally said. "I have something to show you."

The three of us stepped into the galley. The table was littered with hard-tack, a half-carved block of cheese, playing cards, three coffee mugs, several sheets of paper, and a nautical chart. Booker picked up a piece of hardtack as Vasilii lifted the chart.

There, resting under it, was

On the
Remains of Later Pre-Historic Man
Obtained from
Caves in the Catherina Archipelago, Alaska Territory,
and Especially from the
Caves of the Aleutian Islands
by
W. H. Dall
1878

"At first I thought you might have found it," Vasilii said, "but when he came back and said he'd lost his skiff at Kagamil and you weren't on board, well, I got a little suspicious. He was anxious to get another skiff and return. I asked to go along."

Booker looked like this whole story was crazy. "Did you know we'd be here?"

"No," he said. "I didn't."

"How'd you know we hadn't used the book and gone back to where we came from," I asked.

"The small piece of your torn bookmark is still inside. I checked."

All I could do was stare at him. "It is so good to see you."

He stepped onto the deck and looked across toward Kagamil.

"They'll be almost ready to come back," he said. "What do you want to do?"

Booker was devouring a piece of the hardtack, so I answered. "We need to try to get home."

"That's what I thought," he said. "I've got a place prepared."

He led the way as we hurried below deck. Booker and I walked into the room, but Vasilii lingered at the door.

"I guess this really is goodbye," he said. "You'll find some hard-tack and cheese on the bunk, along with a couple cans of sardines. I need to take the skiff ashore. You'll be fine here."

Booker reached into his pack and removed a folded touring compass and handed it to him. Vasilii studied the clear plastic base with amazement. He rotated the metal compass and smiled.

I gave him a quick hug and, *Guuspudax̂!,* as Old Man Peter said when he first saw the ivory fox, a kiss on his cheek. I don't know if he or Booker was the more surprised and embarrassed. I know it wasn't me. We followed him up on deck and watched while he rowed away from the *Eider.* Then Booker and I returned to the room. We sat on one of the bunks with the volume resting between us on our legs. He took the bookmark from his pocket. I thumbed through the pages until I found the small piece that had torn off. We slid the two pieces together. I really expected them to fuse like magnets.

Nothing happened.

"I'm sorry, Anna," he said. "I'm tired. Let's get a little rest and try later."

I was too exhausted to disagree. I knew Vasilii would keep anybody from coming here. Booker wrapped himself in a blanket, and within seconds he was asleep. I unfolded a blanket on the other bunk just as a commotion on deck signaled that Hennig and his crew were back on board. I inched *On the Remains* away from Booker's head—he was using it as a pillow—and replaced it with a folded blanket. I sat beside him and started turning the pages, one by one, with the two parts of the bookmark in my hand. On the back of the larger piece, the faintest echo of a scene was beginning to form. I turned it over to where the old Unangax̂ letters were written. Those along the torn edge were little more than faint outlines. All the ink had drained away. I knew where it had gone, of course. My palms were as dark as ever. I held the bookmark in my left hand and dragged it across my right palm. A light path appeared on my skin.

I did it again. The path widened. The torn letters on the bookmark were a hint darker. I ran it over my palm again. It was like a small vacuum cleaner sucking up the darkness. I cleared one hand and arm and started on the others. Before long, both hands and arms were almost normal.

"Now or never," I said. I placed the two pieces of the bookmark together and laid them carefully between two pages. I touched Booker's shoulder while I closed the volume.

Nothing happened.

"I've done what I could, Booker," I whispered to him as I returned to the other bunk. *The ivory fox is where it belongs. The Kagamil people have their courage.* I lowered my head and used the book as a pillow.

The wind must have picked up while I slept. I awoke to the ship diving beneath the waves and surfacing, sending us over an acre of sea and into the air. The vessel tumbled sideways, like a paper cup. It careened down a steep watery trough and slammed into the base of an oncoming wave. The wall of water broke over us, smothering any light. I heard a high mechanical grinding as my body sailed off the bunk. I saw Booker spring awake as the ship dropped and he floated into the air. Then the air tilted, and he cartwheeled through the room just in time to knock me over as I struggled up. I rolled onto my knees as the floor pulled away. He braced himself upright but with every step, the floor evaded him. Overhead there was a prolonged splintering and then a deep gnashing as something large swept across the deck.

The single light bulb in the cabin flickered.

Light bulb? I thought. *Light bulb?*

"Booker!" I shouted and pointed.

He saw it and ran toward me. He threw his arms around me and we hugged.

"We're back!"

The ship buckled and bore forward. And then it began to climb, angling so steeply that we were thrown backward and across the floor as though it were a slide. Booker hit the wall and crumpled. He unfolded himself onto his hands and knees. The wall was now under him, and he started crawling up it. And then he was on his back as the ship righted itself.

The tonnage of steel in the vessel echoed with every wallop the sea delivered, but it was music to our ears. We were back in the twenty-first century, even if the ship's sides were about to spring apart. If the rivets exploded from their sockets, the whole vessel would sink like an iron bar.

"On deck!" I shouted. "Get on deck!"

Booker followed me as the ship rammed into another wave. Hand over hand and leg above leg as gravity pulled us in random directions, we careened toward the ladder. I grabbed a rung with one hand while extending the other back to him. He latched on for an instant before we were jerked apart. Then we scrambled up and into a narrow passage. We burst into the galley just as Albert Hennig, *our* Hennig, the bastard, placed an old leather book on the table. He blanched when he saw me.

"How in hell!"

A blunt wave struck the starboard side and sent all three of us ricocheting off the walls and into each other. I sprang through the door onto the deck. Hennig was behind me as I fled toward the stern, holding on to anything within grasp. But Hennig was quicker, and in moments his massive hands circled my waist. I kicked and screamed. I twisted and scratched at his face. He lifted me above his chest as the gale roared around us. I saw Booker charge into the captain's belly, bending him forward. Hennig kicked out, and Booker sailed across the deck.

As I pivoted in the air, the necklace of blue beads slipped from my pocket. They glittered like ice. Hennig grabbed for them, and I tumbled loose, falling backward. The strand caught on my jacket and broke apart. Hennig tore at the air as beads flew in all directions. I hit the rail on an inward tilt of the ship and then, for the second time that day, I slipped over the edge.

Hennig had caught two beads and was lurching for a third when Booker shot past him with his arms stretched out to grab me. The captain aimed a convulsive kick, lost his balance, and slipped on the loose beads under his other foot. There were half a dozen sharp metal corners on the deck, but one was enough. He crumpled, and the beads rolled from his hands into the sea, and the water became map-flat with sudden calm.

Booker gave a hard yank on my arm, and I toppled back over the railing and onto the deck. We stepped over Hennig's unconscious body, collected every bead within sight, and hurried below before Torgey or anyone else discovered us. But there wasn't anyone else, just Torgey, and Torgey was busy in the wheelhouse. The sudden and unworldly stillness of the sea had spooked him. He shouted for Hennig and waited and shouted again.

36. Booker

Anna put a hand into her pocket and took out two clear beads. Streams of familiar blue light filtered through them as they rolled around her palm. She handed them to me.

"Those are yours, Anna," I said. We were sitting on her grand-mother's couch.

"I know. But you should have a couple. I have more. Who knows when you'll need one?"

"Thanks."

I placed them in my jacket's left pocket because the right one bulged with the copy of *Death and the Uphill Gardener* that I had taken from the ship's table so long ago. It had reappeared once we had returned to this century. I tapped it and stood up. "I need to get this back to the boat."

"Gram," Anna said as we walked into the kitchen, "we're going down to the dock for a bit, okay?"

Her grandmother was whipping condensed milk into a bowl of canned pumpkin.

"Be back for supper, Old Lady," she said. "You missed lunch already. And bring Bookey."

"Booker, Gram. Booker," Anna said as we stepped outside and she closed the door.

"Will your mom be there?"

"Maybe. Maybe so."

Then she looked at me and said, "I hope so. We have some catching up to do."

"Did your grandmother just call you an old lady?"

Anna just cocked her head a little and smiled.

"I'm curious, Anna," I said, changing the subject. "If that boy Stink—"

"*Chaknax̂*," she said.

"—yeah, him, if he got his good-luck charm back . . ."

"Yes?"

"Well, then, shouldn't he have been okay? I mean, that sad story Vasilii told us about the boy drowning and the whole family dying, that shouldn't have happened, right?"

"Maybe it didn't."

"But if it was in that old book—"

"Books are sometimes wrong," she said. "You can't trust everything that gets pasted between covers."

"Do you have the book?" I asked. "The last time I saw it, it was flying through the air in Hennig's galley."

"I don't," she said, "but that must be how we got back. He must have been reading it in the wheelhouse."

That made sense, it seemed to me, but I was still puzzled.

"But how did we get away from the killer whales and Raven and the volcano and all the rest of it?"

"I have no idea," she said. "But Ash said something about magic charms. Do you remember? *How you treat them is how you will be treated.*"

"That old man said the same thing," I said.

"We set the carved fox free. We returned it home and *we* returned home," she said.

"And here we are," I said and stepped confidently from the dock onto the familiar deck of the *King Eider*. I was becoming an old hand around ships.

Once inside the cabin, I bent down to the floor, slipped *Death and the Uphill Gardener* out of my pocket, and stood up as though I had just found it. Nicely done, I thought, until Anna gave me a weird look. I placed the book on the counter in the galley as she introduced me to an old man whose name was Sanders. On the way to the dock, she had told me he had been a crewman for Hennig, but that he hadn't had any part in what the captain and his mate had done.

"Thanks!" he said when he saw the paperback. "I wondered where I'd lost it."

He nodded at the old guy sitting beside him. "This is my friend from Nikolski," he said. "I call him Old Man, 'cuz that's what he is, but his name is Sergie." He turned to the man whose face was lined by perpetual smiling. "Old Man," he said, "this is Sophie Hansen. I mean, Anna Hansen. This is Sergie Rostokovich."

"Pleased to meet you," Sergie said.

And then Anna introduced me as her friend visiting from out of town.

Sanders limped over to the counter, opened a wide-mouthed jar and poured out a plateful of raisin and oatmeal cookies.

"Baked these this morning," he said.

"Don't mind if I do," said the elderly man as he reached out his hand and laughed.

"You'll need to go on a diet," Sanders said as he insisted Anna and I help ourselves before he passed the plate to his companion.

"Is this your ship?" I asked. I thought I had better say something.

"No, no," Sanders said. "I'm more of a caretaker. Hennig's the owner. But I tell you, it's strange. He and Torgey were out toward Kagamil in this horrible storm. I was supposed to go with them but I had twisted my ankle and was up at the clinic, so they took off without me. Torgey told me he was in the wheelhouse and Hennig was not and after a while he got concerned. The sea had gone deathly still all of a sudden, and he went aft and there he was, sprawled out cold. Well, Torgey, he's a pretty good seaman, and he brought the ship in."

I glanced at Anna, remembering the confusion at the dock and how we had managed to slip ashore.

"But once he got back into port," Sanders continued, "well, the feds came around, made a search of Hennig's cabin for looted artifacts. You know, oddest thing. They didn't find much except a wooden crate in the captain's stateroom—and I had seen that, once upon a time. Not much in it, if you know what I mean. But, he had a remarkable crystal spear point in his pocket. Remarkable thing. Anyway, after the feds found that spear point, they took Hennig and Torgey into custody and Torgey told them everything. They even arrested Mrs. Skagit, although that took a bit of doing."

"Built like a tank," said Sergie.

"Hennig was medevaced to the hospital in Anchorage," Sanders said. "Gone a bit strange in the head from the sounds of things. I hear the feds might confiscate this ship and put it up for auction."

"If they do," Sergie said and helped himself to another cookie, "you can move to Nikolski."

I could tell Sergie was studying Anna while he chewed. Then he asked, "A Hansen, eh? Any relation to that Bob Hansen?"

"My father."

"So that would make that old lady Margaret Petikoff your gram?"

"She is, but she wouldn't appreciate being called an old lady."

He chuckled and drank a sip of tea.

"Sergie here is the luckiest old guy I ever knew," Sanders said. "His whole family was lucky."

"Off and on, at least," the old man said modestly.

" 'Course, Sergie," Sanders continued, "he's the last of them, last of his family, that is. I've been telling him about you." He looked at Anna.

"Margaret Petikoff's family is from Nikolski," Sergie said. "Long time ago, of course. I think her grandmother and my grandmother were cousins or some such thing. You know, some sort of distant relatives."

He drank a bit more coffee.

I was getting anxious to leave. I touched Anna's arm and we stepped toward the door. She stopped when Old Man Rostokovich raised his voice a little, "You ever see one of these?"

He had placed a small wooden box on the table. The rectangular container had been carved from yellow cedar, but years of handling had polished it to a dark rich brown. The cover slid between two grooved sides.

"It's an old-time snuff box," she said.

"I'm done with it," Sergie said. "It should be kept by a real Unangax̂." And he slid it across the table to her.

She seemed reluctant to touch it.

"For me?"

The old man nodded and laughed. "But I don't want to hear that you started chewing tobacco!"

"Thanks," she said. "Really. Thanks a million!" She picked it up.

Her eyes met mine. I guessed what was inside before she slid the cover open and saw, nestled in soft grass, a small ivory fox with circles on its back. It seemed to be smiling.

Sergie looked at Anna with a serious expression. "I'm afraid a name goes with it that you might not like."

A while later we were sitting at the table in her grandmother's kitchen. Anna had asked me to stay for dinner, but I had insisted I needed to get home.

"If you have the fox," I started. I wasn't sure how to ask this. "Are you, that is, I mean, can I call you—"

"*Chaknax̂?*"

"Yeah, I mean, really?"

"I dare you."

Then I saw a flowering shamrock in the window. It was a fluffy mass of leaves and blossoms. I started giggling.

Both me and the bookmark were back to our normal selves. As normal as I would ever be. After I said goodbye to Anna and ducked away from a hug, I walked back to the dock and waited behind one of the massive metal buildings until I was alone. Then I inverted the bookmark into my pocket and went home. Nothing to it.

The Elder Cousin balanced at the edge of his chair and his eyes widened as I told him where I had been. He murmured under his breath and jotted a few abbreviated notes in a small spiral-bound notebook. I leaned back and waited. He closed the cover, carefully clipped the pen into his shirt pocket and looked at me real hard.

"You seem very happy this evening," Mom remarked as the three of us sat eating dinner. Spike and Tulip hadn't noticed my absence at all. I guessed they were better mystery writers than detectives.

Before I could swallow and reply, Dad put down his fork and said, "As it should be, my dear. As it should be. He lives a very protected life."

I couldn't stop smiling.

After dinner I was back in my bedroom, glad to be around familiar things. The desk with my computer, the basketball that had rolled into a corner, and the worn nylon backpack resting on the floor. I had placed the bookmark on the shelf above the desk, where my paperbacks were arranged by author and my model planes by size. A glass jar held the two bluish beads from Anna. I climbed onto the bed and opened a world atlas. I turned to the page showing the arctic ice cap sitting like a crown at the top of the world. Further down the page I ran my fingers across the Aleutian Chain and wondered what Anna was doing. Out of the corner of my eye, I saw Vasilii's small eagle-shaped ivory cleat sitting where I'd placed it on the desk. Every now and then when I wasn't looking directly at it, and occasionally when I was, it preened its wings.

WORDS IN
UNANGAM TUNUU

Interested readers should consult Anna Berge and Moses Dirks's *Niiĝuĝis Mataliin Tunux̂tazangis = How the Atkans Talk: A Conversational Grammar*, and Knut Bergsland's *Aleut Dictionary: Unangam Tunudgusii*. Both books are from the Alaska Native Language Center, University of Alaska Fairbanks. The following guide is adapted from Berge and Dirks.

1. "g" is pronounced like the "g" in "girl," but the tongue does not stop all the air. (Shown as "g" in the "Approximate Pronunciation" column.)

2. "ĝ" is pronounced like the Unangax̂ "g" but with the tongue farther back in the mouth. (Shown as "gh" in the "Approximate Pronunciation" column.)

3. "k" is pronounced like the "k" in "kite." (Shown as "k" in the "Approximate Pronunciation" column.)

4. "q" is pronounced like "k," but with the tongue farther back in the mouth. (Shown as an underlined "k̲" in the "Approximate Pronunciation" column.)

5. "x" is like the "k" in "kite," but the tongue does not stop all the air. (Shown as "x" in the "Approximate Pronunciation" column.)

6. "x̂" is pronounced like the Unangax̂ "x" but with the tongue farther back in the mouth. (Shown as "xh" in the "Approximate Pronunciation" column.)

7. "ng" is pronounced as in "song." Unlike in English, this sound can be found anywhere in a word (as in *qalngaax̂* = "raven"). (Shown as "ng" in the "Approximate Pronunciation" column.)

WORD MEANINGS
AND PRONUNCIATIONS

WORD	MEANING	APPROXIMATE PRONUNCIATION
aang	yes; also an informal greeting	áw-ng
alaadikax̂	fried bread	áh-láw-di-kaxh
Amirkaanchix̂	American	Àh-mer-khán-chixh
angaayux̂	partner	ang-áh-yooxh
ataqan aalax qaankun siching chaang	the numbers one through five	ah-táck-an áw-lax káwn-kun sée-ching cháwng
ayaqaa	an expression of surprise	ah-yah-káw
baidar	open skin boat (from Russian)	bái-dar
baidarka	kayak (from Russian)	bái-dar-kah
barabara	semi-underground Unangax̂ home (from Russian)	bah-ráh-bah-rah
bidarki	chiton (from Russian)	bí-dar-kee
chai	tea (from Russian)	cháy
chaknax̂	stink or stinky	cháck-naxh

Chuginadax̂	Chuginadak Island; Mount Cleveland Volcano	Choo-gee-náh-thaxh
Guuspudax̂	Lord (from Russian)	Wóo-spuh-dah
Haqada!	Come! (imperative)	háh-ḵah-thah
iqyax̂	skin boat	íḵ-yaxh
kamleika	raincoat, usually made from sea lion intestine (from Russian)	kam-léy-kah
lakaayax̂	young boy	láh-kha-yaxh
lalux̂	yellow cedar	láh-luxh
Ounalashka	Unalaska (name of settlement)	Oo-naw-lásh-ka
petruski	wild parsley (from Russian)	pe-tróo-skee
putchki	wild celery (from Russian)	pútch-kee
qaĝaasakuqing	thanks or thank you (contrasted with the more formal *Txin qaĝaa-sakuqing*, "I thank you.")	ḵàh-gháw-sah-ḵoo-king
qalngaax̂	raven	ḵàl-ng-áwxh
qungaayux̂	a hump, as on a humpback salmon (Camp Qungaayux̂ is the summer culture camp at Unalaska held at Humpy Cove.)	ḵung-áw-yuxh
slachxisaadax̂	fine weather	sláh-chx-saw-thaxh

spasibo	thank you (from Russian)	spah-sée-bah
tiĝlax̂	eagle	tígh-laxh
tutuqux̂	periwinkle	too-tóo-<u>k</u>uxh
Unangam tunuu	Aleut language	Oo-náng-am too-nóo
Unangax̂	people of the Aleutian Islands (the plurals are *Unangan* and *Unangas*, in the eastern and western dialects)	Oo-náng-axh

POSTSCRIPT AND ACKNOWLEDGMENTS

The true story of how the Unalaska people had their good-luck charms stolen by people from the Islands of Four Mountains and how they got them back was told to me by Nick Galaktionoff Sr., a tradition bearer from Unalaska who received it from a long line of elders, including Alex Ermeloff, Andrew Makarin, and Marva Galaktionoff Borenin. For this, Nick's account should be consulted in *Unangam tunuu* or translated into English and read. Other Unangax̂ tales—including those about the Summer-Face-Woman, the Moon's Sister, and the Woman-with-Six-Sea-Lion-Sons are found in the masterful collection made by Waldemar Jochelson, edited and translated by Knut Bergsland and Moses Dirks: *Unangam Ungiikangin kayux Tunusangin / Unangam Uniikangis ama Tunuzangis / Aleut Tales and Narratives* (Alaska Native Language Center, University of Alaska Fairbanks). The bookmark translation is paraphrased from text 81, *Big Raven*, told by Filaret Prokopyev. I want to thank Dr. Lucy Johnson for the opportunity to study basketry fragments from one of the Islands of Four Mountains. Past and present staff at the National Museum of Natural History, Smithsonian Institution, made it possible for me to examine basketry from Kagamil Island. As I write, analysis continues on the findings from multidisciplinary investigations in 2014 and 2015 of five archaeological sites in the Islands of Four Mountains. The results will undoubtedly add much to our understanding of life on these islands.

This novel benefited from readings by many people. Members of David Weinstock's Otter Creek Poetry Workshop and Nancy Means Wright's writing group critiqued portions of the manuscript. Ann Cooper's and Barry Lane's careful readings helped focus the story. John Melanson's Carol's Hungry Mind Café was the perfect refuge for writing. Aquilina D. Lestenkof provided valuable suggestions and assisted with words in *Unangam tunuu*. Elizabeth Laska at the University of Alaska Press enlisted the generous aid of Dr. Anna Berge for advice on the glossary. Dana Henricks was the best proofreader ever and helped me see passages with fresh eyes. Special thanks go to my wife Shelly, AB Rankin of Unalaska, and Jackie Pels with Hardscratch Press, along with Martha Amore, Debra Corbett, and Debby Dahl Edwardson for commenting on earlier drafts. Without the astute, patient, and generous comments I received from James Engelhardt at the University of Alaska Press and novelist Gerri Brightwell, I would have floundered hopelessly in my first venture into fiction. How strange it was to write something without endnotes or a bibliography. Krista West and other staff members at the University of Alaska Press guided me through every stage. Peat Galaktionoff sent messages and photos from Nikolski to remind me of that unique place. Carolyn Reed kindly allowed the use of her unparalleled art for the cover. For all my friends in the islands, always and forever, *Txin qaĝaasakuqing*. For my family at home, this is for Emma, Maiya, and the boys—Ethan, TJ, Noah, Matias, Marcello, Olen, and Axel.

The author about the time he first heard the story of the people of the Islands of Four Mountains and their lucky charms. Drawn in 1987 by the potter Cavan Drake when he was eight.